IN THE BLOOD

KATE WILEY

Storm

This is a work of fiction. Names, characters, businesses, places, events and incidents are either the products of the author's imagination or used in a fictitious manner. Any resemblance to actual persons, living or dead, or actual events is purely coincidental.

Copyright © Ashley MacLennan, 2025

The moral right of the author has been asserted.

All rights reserved. No part of this book may be reproduced or used in any manner without the prior written permission of the copyright owner. This prohibition includes, but is not limited to, any reproduction or use for the purpose of training artificial intelligence technologies or systems.

To request permissions, contact the publisher at rights@stormpublishing.co

Ebook ISBN: 978-1-80508-448-8
Paperback ISBN: 978-1-80508-450-1

Cover design: Lisa Brewster
Cover images: Trevillion, Shutterstock

Published by Storm Publishing.
For further information, visit:
www.stormpublishing.co

ALSO BY KATE WILEY

The Killer's Daughter
Her Father's Secret
The Killer Instinct

As Sierra Dean

The Secret McQueen Series
Something Secret This Way Comes
A Bloody Good Secret
Deep Dark Secret
Keeping Secret
Grave Secret
Secret Unleashed
Cold Hard Secret
A Secret to Die For
Secret Lives
A Wicked Secret
Deadly Little Secret
One Last Secret

The Genie McQueen Series
Bayou Blues
Black Magic Bayou
Black-Hearted Devil

Blood in the Bayou

The Rain Chaser Series

Thunder Road

Driving Rain

Highway to Hail

The Boys of Summer Series

Pitch Perfect

Perfect Catch

High Heat

As Gretchen Rue

The Witches' Brew Mysteries

Steeped to Death

Death by a Thousand Sips

The Grim Steeper

The Lucky Pie Mysteries

A Pie to Die For

To anyone who has ever brought up random serial killer facts at a party, I am very awkwardly one of you.

ONE

Margot Phalen knew all too well what made a perfect victim.

Which was why she was the perfect person to play the part.

She sat on a bar stool in a Tenderloin dive, her denim skirt hiked up to reveal ample pale thigh, her tank top both too low and too cropped, and a pair of cowboy boots crafting an epic blister on the back of her feet.

This was so far outside Margot's comfort zone that she had almost disassociated from herself. She didn't go to bars. She honestly didn't go out in public outside of work unless she absolutely had to.

She hated being here, but it was a necessary evil. As was the outfit.

The boots, she'd told them, were too much.

Major Crimes disagreed.

As a homicide detective, Margot had little cause to go undercover; in her cases there was no need. But for Major Crimes, when it came to busting drug dealers and sex work syndicates, sometimes the line between reality and fiction needed to be blurred.

And since Margot had very recently been in need of their

expertise when it came to finding out about a high-end escort service, they had come calling with some quid pro quo.

Namely: they did not currently have any detectives who would make good bait to bust a sex trafficking operation.

She couldn't really say no.

Well, she had tried several times, but it hadn't worked.

Which was how she had ended up at a place called Glass Half Empty on a Friday night, pretending to slur into her whiskey and ignoring the leering gazes of the mostly male patrons. Unlike the glossy impression given in Hollywood dramas, she didn't have a fancy earpiece in that would let her hear what the rest of the team—parked nearby in a nondescript van—was saying. She had a wire under her clothes that was sticking to the peach fuzz on her stomach and pulling out tiny hairs every time she moved.

They could hear her, she couldn't hear them.

Which meant if things went wrong, she just had to hope they were paying attention.

A man sat down on the stool beside her, pretending not to notice her at first. She openly swept her gaze over him, because she was supposed to be too drunk to care if someone caught her staring.

He looked too clean-cut for the place. He wore jeans and a nice polo shirt, but everything was too perfect, tailored, clean. He didn't fit in at all. He was about forty, handsome in a forgettable way, with a dusting of stubble on his jaw and dark hair that was probably a week or two overdue for a trim.

When he finally did look in her direction there was a smirk on his face that creased a dimple on only one cheek. She bet the girls went wild for that dimple.

"Can I get you a refill?" he asked. Not a whisper of an accent in his voice. He could have worked at a call center.

"Sure, honey, that's really sweet of you." She had recently spit the last of her whiskey into a beer bottle beside her. Periodically she would teeter off to the bathroom and empty most of it down the sink to she didn't draw suspicion.

The bartender gave her a wary look as he poured her another shot, and Margot wondered if he'd say anything. She'd been here for hours, and if he bought her act, he had to believe she was too drunk to be talking to this—or any other—man. But he just took the guy's cash and walked away.

Margot knew how women ended up in dumpsters, or tossed into the bay. She knew it was just a matter of the right people turning a blind eye because saying something would be too complicated. Too messy.

Her fingertips were white from the pressure of her grip on the glass, and she had to remind herself that she wasn't going to end up in a dumpster. She was here so that that didn't happen to anyone else, either.

She smiled at him, her head bobbing slightly, as if she couldn't quite come to terms with gravity. "What's yer name?" she asked, then reeled the boozy flourish back a little, wanting to come across as drunk but not as if she might throw up on his nice shoes at any moment.

The man gave her a quick once-over, then his gaze drifted back out over the bar, and she suspected he was wondering if there were other options available.

First: ouch.

Second: there were not.

The only other woman she'd seen in the bar tonight was in her sixties and made Margot look positively prepubescent by comparison. Margot didn't put much thought into her appearance on a daily basis, she knew her hair was her most striking feature, the coppery red falling almost to her mid-back if she ever let it down from a ponytail, which she had tonight.

She was attractive, she knew that in much the same way someone knows they are left-handed. It didn't shape her identity, but she was aware that having conventional good looks had probably helped her navigate through the world more easily from time to time.

Right now, she was a bit miffed that those same good looks weren't enough to bait the target sitting beside her. She suspected this was less to do with her attractiveness and more to do with her age. Sex traffickers didn't have rigid rules, but younger women were often easier to manipulate and control. They also often had stronger ties to family, which actually helped traffickers manipulate them better through gaslighting and threats.

A late-thirties barfly might be easy to take advantage of, but wouldn't be as easy to control.

Too bad for him there were no college co-eds who felt like living dangerously tonight.

Margot had thought the choice of location was stupid, but Major Crimes—specifically the lead detective, Harvey Farlane—was certain there was someone regularly operating out of the Glass Half Empty.

They just needed Margot to be patient.

The man scoured the bar looking for anyone who might have thought this dive was the ideal place to try out a new fake ID, or girls hoping to be a little reckless for the thrill of it, but after he had done a pass of the bar at least twice, he must have realized what Margot already knew.

She was as good as it was going to get.

She had already turned her attention to the bar, rattling the ice cubes in her drink as condensation beaded on the outside of the glass. It wouldn't do her any good to appear *too* eager, so she would play it cool now that he'd already rebuffed her.

Disassociation was not a difficult thing for Margot to fake, she was all too familiar with affecting a dead-eyed stare. She looked into the middle distance, her fingertip tracing the lip of the glass, and before she knew it the man beside her was doing his damnedest to bring her attention back to him.

"Hey," he said, his voice almost peevish, which told her he'd probably already said it more than once.

"Mmm?" She quirked a lazy brow at him and acted as if this was the first time she'd ever laid eyes on him.

"Can I buy you another drink?"

She stared at her already mostly full glass, the amber color of the liquid having paled as she ignored it, the ice melting it into something almost unrecognizable. Margot didn't especially *like* whiskey, but it was one of those things that people recognized in a glass. Gin had the problematic appearance of being clear, it could have too easily been water. She needed this dipshit to know—or at least to think—she'd been drinking all night.

"Sure," she said finally, after contemplating his question long enough for a crease to form between his brows.

The man waved at the bartender and pointed to Margot's glass. This time the bartender glowered at them. He'd just topped Margot up only a few moments earlier, and he'd been on the cusp of cutting her off before then.

"Nah, she's done for the night, and if she knows what's good for her she'll call a cab and go home. *Alone.*" He stared Margot down, his expression stern.

She was surprised by the forcefulness of his tone. She wasn't sure if it was just general concern for her well-being, or if he knew this man in particular was bad news, but there was an earnestness he was trying to convey to her with his eyes that Margot found touching.

He didn't want anything bad to happen to her.

That worked fine for her purposes, anyway, because she needed to get the man beside her out of the bar if they were going to catch him getting up to no good.

"Y'know," she said, the word starting too solid before she remembered to dull the edges of her speech and thicken the consonants on her tongue. "I think yer right. I'm gonna go."

The bartender nodded, glad he wasn't going to have to put up with a fight, and went back to serving two men at the end of the bar.

"Hey, I didn't catch your name," the man beside her said. His voice was slippery-smooth, the line well-rehearsed.

"Jasmine," she replied, the name quick on her tongue. Major Crimes hadn't given her a cover story, but Margot was used to wielding a fake name like a shield. Margot Phalen wasn't the name she'd been born with any more than Jasmine was.

Both served a purpose.

Jasmine was the name of a girl Margot had been friends with in her youth. Someone she thought about sometimes, though not enough to try to find. Too much had happened to Margot since she was fifteen to try to rekindle old friendships. Jasmine would never be able to look at her the same way, knowing what she did about Margot's life.

No one from her past would. No matter how much good Margot did in the world, there was still no escaping the sins of her father.

As Margot slid off her stool, her bones as stable as Jell-O, she gave the man at her side a long, lingering look and hoped her expression was in the same realm as a come-hither stare.

Margot was a bit rusty when it came to flirting, if she had ever been good at it to begin with.

Hopefully this guy would get the gist of what she was offering and follow after her. If he was smart, he'd wait a few minutes so the bartender wouldn't be immediately suspicious, since he obviously knew this guy's game wasn't a good one.

Margot grabbed her leather jacket and headed to the door.

As she slipped into the damp night, for the first time in her life, she hoped someone was watching.

TWO

Margot didn't need to wait long before the man from the bar came out the front door. She was standing about half a block away, fiddling with her phone as he approached her.

"What was your name again?" he asked, as if she hadn't just told him two minutes earlier.

"Jasmine," she replied, wondering in her own paranoid way if he was testing her.

While Margot had been pretending to play with her phone she'd noticed there was a new text from her brother. She'd gotten a few in recent weeks, and they were increasingly short-tempered and pleading. Justin wanted something from her—nothing new there—but he was refusing to take no for an answer. Margot had begun to ignore the messages. He would have to wait, but a pit of anxiety swelled in her gut to see yet another late-night plea. While Justin—who now went by the name of David—had at least been on the straight and narrow the last few months, he was always just one bad day from a downward spiral.

She hoped he hadn't had that one bad day.

And she hoped she wouldn't be the reason he *had* that bad day.

But he'd need to wait, because this wasn't the time to deal with her own problems. She had something more important to do, and it looked like her fish was on the line.

"Jasmine, that's a pretty name for a pretty girl." He smiled at her, his too-white teeth dazzling. She wondered what his rate of return was on these terrible pickup lines. It had to be pretty good if he kept using them.

"Thank you. Do you have a smoke?" she asked, hoping to keep him on the line a little longer, to show she wasn't ready to cut and run just yet.

He fumbled in his jacket pocket for a pack of Camels and put two in his mouth, lighting them both before passing her one. Margot had never been a smoker, detested the smell, but whatever worked.

She puffed on the cigarette, blowing out the smoke with a practiced air of indifference. As he took a drag of his own she let her gaze rake over him openly, her arms crossed over her chest so she just needed to lift her hand from her elbow to take a drag. She felt more comfortable that way, though she hoped she was communicating casual indifference.

Margot knew how to fake confidence when she needed it.

The man in front of her was a predator, pure and simple. What he was doing, with his big smile and bad compliments, was no different to a big cat hunkered down in the brush of the savanna, waiting for a gazelle that was too old or too complacent to drift from the pack before being slaughtered.

She was the gazelle.

She just had to pretend she didn't see the tail flicking among the tall grasses.

"What's your name?" she asked, like she actually cared.

"Dustin."

Margot was aware that this was not, in fact, his name, any

more than Jasmine was hers. This shithead had a rap sheet as long as her arm, and she knew every one of his misdemeanors and felonies. She also knew his name was Chris Smith, which was almost as generic a name as John Smith. She personally knew three Chris Smiths. Not counting this one.

She nodded. She didn't want to make this too easy for him. "What do you do, Dusty?"

He didn't bat an eye at the nickname, something that would have certainly caused a twitch from a real Dustin.

"I'm in finance."

"Oh yeah?"

"Trading."

Sure. That was one of those lies that was bordering on the truth. He certainly traded *something* for money, though it wasn't stocks and bonds. Margot's gaze drifted up the street, settling on the van she knew housed the officers who were watching her.

She wondered what they were thinking about how this was going; whether they were just hoping she'd get on with it so everyone could get home at a reasonable time.

"That must be good work." Margot was aware she wasn't slurring as much as she had been before, but it didn't seem to matter to Dustin. She suspected he was already so focused on what came next that it didn't matter to him who was in front of him, so long as she followed where he went.

"I do all right for myself. Actually, I have a pretty nice place. Maybe you'd like to come see it?"

Man, subtle as a hammer.

Margot chuckled and stubbed out her cigarette on the ground, already counting down the minutes until she was back in her apartment brushing the taste off her tongue and scrubbing her hands raw with whatever flower-scented soap was sitting on her counter.

She couldn't rush this, but God did she ever want it to be over.

"Well, I don't know. I don't really *know* you." Margot kept her voice from being *too* dismissive, letting him know she wasn't turning him down, just being coy.

"I did buy you a drink. If you want another one, I've got a good bar at my place."

"Oh yeah?" She resisted the urge to look back at the van. Now the most dangerous part of this for her was coming into play. She couldn't just *go* with this guy. There was nothing illegal about picking up women.

What they suspected Chris Smith of doing, based on numerous reports, was either drugging women at the bar and taking them against their will, or forcing them by physical means to come with him. What followed was assault and then threats. He would tell their families. There was video footage he would leak. He would end relationships, jobs, school careers. He'd say anything to keep these young women on the line.

Because the scariest thing about men like Chris Smith was that he didn't need to keep anyone locked in a basement to make them compliant. He didn't need to ship women off to sex slavery in foreign countries. No, sex trafficking was a much more insidious and frightening beast than that. Most of these girls still lived at their own apartments, or even in their parents' homes.

They did what they were told because they didn't know there was any other way out.

They feared for their safety and the safety of their families.

Sometimes all it took to control someone was a really good threat.

Margot wanted to cut that threat off at the knees tonight.

"You know, you seem really sweet and all, and I appreciate you buying me that drink, but I think I'd better get home." She tossed her hair over her shoulder and gave him a smile.

Chris's brow wrinkled, as if the idea she might reject him hadn't even been a consideration, and her yielding was a foregone conclusion.

"Well, let me walk you," he said.

Margot started to walk away, heading toward the van but still on the opposite side of the street. She didn't want to get out of their sight at this stage in the game. The bait was set, now he just needed to step into the trap.

"Nah, baby, I'm OK. But thanks," she called back over her shoulder.

For a moment there was silence behind her, and she wondered if he might have actually taken *no* for an answer, which wouldn't have been this guy's style at all. She didn't dare look back. She might give away the whole thing if he thought she was just messing with him.

Then, in the stillness of the night, over the sound of her own boots clacking on the pavement, she heard the telltale slap of shoes running. Her pulse quickened and something animal completely overrode all her common sense.

He's going to kill you, her brain screamed.

Because that was what she had been conditioned her whole life to believe.

Her father had taught her not to trust strangers, not to open doors for people she didn't know, not to walk alone at night. He had taught her all the ways for little girls to protect themselves.

From people like him.

As the weight of Chris Smith's body slammed into Margot, sending her staggering even though she'd been braced for it, all she could think about was her father.

What would Ed Finch do in this situation?

Because her father was a predator, just like this man.

Only he'd killed at least eighty women.

And being in jail didn't make him any less present in her

mind as cold fingers laced around her neck and started to squeeze.

THREE

Margot's assailant forced her into a tiny alleyway between buildings. The air stank of fetid garbage and piss, and Margot's eyes watered as each breath she struggled for tasted of human filth.

He slammed her up against a wall, his hips keeping her lower body pinned while he tightened his grip on her throat. He was squeezing to hurt, to make a point, but not to kill.

Though it was hard to convince her fight or flight reaction that this wasn't life or death.

"You little cock tease, you think you can just lead a guy on and then fuck off? That's not how this works, girlie, and you should be old enough to know better by now." He rocked her head back against the brick wall and Margot saw stars.

She dug her fingernails into the skin of his wrists, and she saw how angry it made him, though it did nothing to loosen his grip.

Where the fuck is my backup?

For one brief, horrible moment, Margot wondered if they hadn't seen him attack her. What if they were scrambling to figure out where she was? What if they didn't find her in time?

No. No. She couldn't let those thoughts cloud her mind. It would only lead to panic. And if there was one thing that would not serve her here, it was panic.

What might Chris do next?

What would Ed Finch do?

Incapacitate her, take her to a second location where she would have no protection, nothing to keep him from doing whatever he wanted. Normally, Chris probably relied on date rape drugs to keep women compliant, but Margot hadn't drunk any of the drink he'd bought her.

Ed didn't like to attack women in the street like this. He preferred to offer them rides, convince them he was safe, and then make his move when they were alone and there was no hope of rescue.

Honestly, this wasn't so very different.

Margot had specialized training. She had taken Krav Maga, for crying out loud. She knew she was tougher than this guy was making her look, but he had gotten the upper hand, grabbing her from behind.

She couldn't turn her face to bite him, couldn't headbutt him, couldn't knee him in the groin. This man wasn't an amateur. He knew how to keep a woman from fighting back.

That just pissed Margot off.

Her basic self-defense training kicked in and she let her hands drop from his wrists where they weren't doing her any good. Then she moved her right hand between their arms and her straight fingers shot out with all the force she could muster, hitting Chris right in the throat.

It wasn't the hardest hit she could have done under normal circumstances, but it did exactly what she needed it to. He wheezed, his windpipe damaged, and his grip on her neck loosened. She knocked his arm down, grabbing hold of his wrist and twisting it behind his back as she pivoted out of the way, slamming him face-first into the wall.

Before he could get his composure back, four armed plainclothes police officers swarmed her, guns drawn, Miranda rights being spouted off with practiced precision. Margot couldn't hear a word of what they were saying, everything sounded like she was underwater.

One of the cops from the van placed a gentle hand on her shoulder. He was saying something, but she couldn't understand him. He delicately removed her hand from the back of the suspect's neck, and pried her fingers from the man's wrists.

"It's OK, we've got him," she heard, as the fog lifted from her brain and the scene came spiraling back into crystal-clear focus.

Chris was arrested.

Assault, and assault of a police officer, no less. It should give them plenty of time to get him to fess up to a multitude of other sins. He was in Major Crimes' hands now, and out of Margot's.

But Margot's hands were the ones shaking.

As the male officer guided Margot out of the alleyway and back to the main street, she saw Detective Harvey Farlane crossing the street in their direction. The back doors of the van were wide open. She wondered why it had taken them so long to get to her, or if time had just slowed down so much that seconds had felt like minutes.

"Goddamn, Phalen, are you OK?" Harvey asked, jogging up to meet them.

Harvey was in his early fifties, though his hair was prematurely gray, and he was handsome in the way that dads and accountants can be handsome. Unassuming, approachable.

Just seeing him took some of the edge off, because his, at least, was a familiar face in a sea of relative strangers.

"I've had better nights, Harv, I'm not gonna lie."

He shooed off the officer who'd been helping her and stood in front of her to assess the damage. She could tell he wanted to poke and prod, but he also seemed to understand she didn't particularly want to be touched right now. It was a rare gift indeed to understand and respect when someone else didn't want to be touched just based off their vibe.

Or maybe her reputation as an ice queen had extended well out of the homicide department.

Either way, Margot appreciated the hell out of Harvey Farlane in that moment.

"You should go to the hospital," Harvey said after giving her a once-over.

"I'm fine," she rasped, but even those words were sore coming out, and she knew he was right. Chris Smith had gotten a good grip on her, and while his intent may not have been to kill, he hadn't held back on wanting her unconscious. Her throat hurt, and she'd probably be sporting some nasty bruises for a few days.

Margot wasn't much of a fan of turtlenecks, but she might need to dust some off to make it through the work week.

"Look, I'll take you myself. Least I could do after you put your ass on the line for us with this shit-heel." His hand moved, hovering over her shoulder like he was going to pat it, then dropping down again.

Margot sighed, knowing that the real reason Harvey was volunteering to take her was because he didn't believe she would go on her own. He was right to doubt her. Harvey was a smart man, no wonder he made a good detective.

She considered another effort at protesting, but knew there was no point. Harvey wanted to play white knight to her damsel in distress, regardless of the fact that she had probably partially collapsed their suspect's trachea.

You should see the other guy, she imagined saying if anyone commented on her neck.

It made her snort with half-hearted humor.

"All right," she acquiesced at last. "But you don't have to stay with me. I know you want to start grilling this guy."

"He can stew for a bit." Then he said, "I don't think you should be alone, is there someone I can call?"

She thought about the missed messages from her brother, who was several states away and heaven only knew in what condition.

Margot considered the depth of the question, which Harvey probably thought was a simple enough one.

Was there anyone she could call?

Did Margot have anyone?

She gave him a half smile. "I think I know the right guy for the job."

FOUR

Harvey left Margot in the emergency waiting room after an hour. Based on the crowd around her still, the many faces who had been there when she arrived, Margot wasn't going to be seen anytime soon.

If the attack had happened at a more convenient time of day, she'd have just gone to urgent care, but most of the urgent care clinics in San Francisco closed at five.

Which meant Margot was stuck with emergency med. While she could have used the cop card to get seen sooner—Harvey had certainly wanted her to—Margot knew this wasn't life or death, and some of the people ahead of her looked a lot worse for wear than she did.

She'd been waiting about two hours when the emergency room doors sighed open and a familiar form walked through.

Detective Wes Fox, Margot's partner and probably one of her only earthly friends, came in carrying two large to-go coffee cups and she could have cried with relief.

He looked like he was here for a date, rather than to babysit his injured partner. He wore a long peacoat over well-tailored gray pants and a maroon button down. No tie, thank God, or he might have scared some of the other folks here who had obviously gotten up to some illegal activities tonight. As it was, Wes looked cop-like enough that a few side-eyed glances turned his way.

Wes was handsome. The kind of handsome someone could have made a career out of. His sandy blond hair had been recently trimmed and his brown eyes twinkled as they found her. She could tell that while he was concerned he was also just dying to make some kind of joke.

She loved Wes, though she didn't really know what kind of love that was. She just knew she needed him in her life. And Margot didn't like to *need* people.

Wes was also something of a jackass from time to time, so if anyone could keep her humble rather than letting her play the victim, it would be him.

He plunked down beside her, oblivious to the looks he was getting from some of the waiting room's other clientele, and handed her one of the cups he was holding.

"Tea," he explained before she could sip it. "Gotta protect those vocal chords if the Bellas are going to win regionals."

Margot stared at him. Sniffing the tea—it was definitely peppermint—she sipped it and had to admit the soothing warmth was probably better for her throat than a coffee would have been.

"Wes, I can't decide if I'm more offended that you bought me tea, or that you just made a *Pitch Perfect* reference at a time like this."

Wes shrugged.

Margot knew what he was doing. She could read Wes like a book, and his current actions meant that he had read her cover-to-cover a long time ago. He was making sure to play this so cool it felt like another day at the office. He didn't want her to feel weird about calling him to be with her, or to make a big deal out of the fact he'd come.

It was almost two in the morning. Wes probably had better places to be, more compelling—or at least eager—company to keep. But he was here. With her. It was above and beyond being a good partner.

"Thank you," she said finally, though she couldn't bring herself to look at him.

He nudged her with his shoulder, and she didn't pull away from the touch. She felt her body sag toward him, releasing something that had been holding her rigidly upright this whole time.

Now that Wes was here, she could let her guard down just a little. It was also the first time she'd felt ready to look at her phone, to see what Justin had sent her.

Pulling out her cell, she opened up her messages to the unread one waiting for her, the one she'd been ignoring until now, because if it was going to make her fall apart, she didn't want to be alone for that.

But the message wasn't like the others he had sent recently. This was no cry for help, no plea for money. His spelling was all correct, so he had been sober when he wrote it. For a brief second she dared to think that maybe, just maybe, her brother was actually on a path to recovery after so many stumbles along the way.

However, the *contents* of the message were confounding. The words were all correct, but when combined into a sentence, they made no sense to her.

> Been contacted by the producers of a new series about dad. They want to talk to us. The money is good, but they'll only do it if we both talk.

Margot stared at the message, reading it over and over again.

Wes must have noticed how still she'd gotten, how intense her scrutiny had become. "Everything OK?" he asked.

After a long moment, reading the message one more time, Margot put her phone down and stared up at the discolored ceiling tiles above her.

"I'm not sure everything has *ever* been OK, Wes."

FIVE
1993

Desolation Wilderness, California

Ed Finch hated wishy-washy people. He believed in being decisive, in sticking with what you believed, even if what you believed was garbage. That was why he liked people who put up political yard signs, people who had bumper stickers about their religion on the back of their cars.

He didn't give a shit about Jesus, but he liked when people knew themselves.

It was one of the things he hated about his son.

One of many.

Ed glanced over his shoulder, checking on Justin's progress. The kid trailed behind him by a good ten yards, his skinny shoulders slumped, head looking right down at the path.

Ed, as a kid, had known what he did and didn't want. He knew he didn't care to play with other children, knew how to avoid his mother's darkest moods, knew how to skate by largely unnoticed in school. Ed had been aware of himself from a very early age, even if no one else seemed to understand what to do with him.

He'd always had strong feelings about things.

But Justin didn't seem to feel strongly about anything. Some days, Ed wondered if Justin thought about anything at all, because it often seemed like there wasn't a damned thing going on behind those eyes of his.

Kim, Justin's mother, insisted he was just a sensitive kid. Shy. And she scolded Ed for bullying him. But Ed didn't think it was bullying. He just wanted his kid to have a little backbone. To stand up for what he liked, what he believed in.

How did that old saying go? If you stand for nothing then you'll fall for anything?

He didn't want his son to be a fucking pussy.

That's how this foolhardy notion of a father–son camping trip had come about. It had been Kim's idea. She thought it would be good for Ed and Justin to have bonding time together. Ed had agreed, to an extent. Justin tended to hide behind his mother and sister too much. Ed suspected that Justin was keenly aware of how Ed favored Megan, and used her as a buffer to avoid detection. Well, no more.

It was time for Justin to prove himself as a man, no matter how young he was.

Ed had been younger than Justin when he'd had to learn to make it on his own in the world, and if he could do it, then his son would have to learn how to stand up for himself too. The world was cruel and unjust, and Justin wasn't always going to have a skirt to hide behind.

If he did, God help him. What a life.

No, Ed needed to toughen the kid up, teach him to stand up for himself.

While he wouldn't have picked the middle of the woods as a place to do that, it was what they were currently working with, so Ed would need to make the most of it.

He had plenty of other things he'd like to be doing with his weekend, but at least this way Kim wasn't hovering around him like a paranoid vulture. He'd personally have rather had this bonding time with Megan, but she was a good kid already, smart, clever, and particularly aware of herself even as an awkward teen.

She was one of the only people in the house who wasn't afraid to talk back to him, though she seemed to have a preternatural awareness of when it was safe to do so and when to keep her mouth shut.

He liked that about her too.

That awareness would keep her alive, keep her safe. He couldn't always be there to protect her. She needed to know how to protect herself.

He frowned. Justin needed to toughen up, because living in fear was no life at all.

It didn't matter that life was full of things to be afraid of.

As far as Ed was concerned, the best way around that was to become something scarier.

He glanced at Justin again. With his San Francisco Giants cap pulled low over his eyes, Ed couldn't even make out the kid's face. Probably for the best. No doubt he was wearing a sullen pout that would just piss Ed off.

He didn't want to start the trip that way. He wanted to *try* with the kid before deciding his own son was a fucking hopeless case.

He sometimes wondered if Justin was even *his* despite all the obvious signs that he was. He didn't really believe Kim had slept around, though who knew, maybe she was more brazen than he gave her credit for. It was just that he so rarely saw any of himself in the boy beyond his appearance.

Justin had his nose, the same awkward ears, and if you held up a picture of Ed at the same age, they would have looked like brothers. But, looks aside, the boy simply didn't feel like his.

After ten years, shouldn't there have been some sign that Ed's DNA had made a lasting mark on the kid?

Ed sighed and turned back to the trail.

There were plenty of easier places to camp near home, but he wasn't about to pull the family car into a KOA with pampered lots and nice bathrooms and breakfast options. That wouldn't test Justin at all.

No, they had driven almost four hours inland to Desolation Wilderness, a park area that bordered an inlet of Lake Tahoe. The area was, as its name suggested, more desolate than some of the other places he could have chosen. Areas thick with redwoods, or more verdant landscapes. But Ed had specifically picked the rockier terrain and more open surroundings of Desolation Wilderness because he *wanted* this to be rough on the kid.

Justin was going to learn to be a man on this trip, if it was the last thing Ed did.

SIX

As Margot had predicted, she had not endured any substantial injuries from her strangulation.

The most difficult part of the whole ordeal had been convincing her overly protective doctor that Wes was her police partner and not a domestic spouse responsible for doing this to her.

Once the woman was reassured Margot wasn't in immediate danger, Margot had been allowed to check out, but she was pretty sure the doctor had been debating slipping her some pamphlets for women's shelters.

The long-term effects of the strangulation, she was told, would be some soreness speaking and swallowing for a while, some bruising—which had already begun to form—and she'd been warned of possible PTSD.

Hello again, old friend, Margot thought as she tried to keep herself from laughing.

She was no stranger to trauma-based anxiety.

There was no need to explain her psychological damage to an ER doctor, though.

The drive home from the hospital was quiet, and she was

grateful to Wes for leaving her to her own thoughts. She propped her chin on her hand and watched the city lights slide past her. It was always strange to her, how a city could still be awake at this time of day. It was after four by the time Wes pulled up in front of Margot's apartment building.

The lobby glowed warmly, and she was glad to see the familiar figure of Brody sitting at his desk. It was the things that didn't change that kept Margot grounded. The little, silly things that were meaningless to others but created a whole universe of security for her.

Wes parked up and shifted in his seat so he could look at her. "You want me to come up with you?"

From any other person on any other night, Margot would have thought it was a come-on, an invitation. But that wasn't what he was doing. He had been there when the doctor had told her about the possibility of PTSD, and he'd been there in the past when Margot had freaked out about other seemingly inconsequential things. He'd seen first-hand what happened when past trauma came back to bite her.

There were a lot of things that triggered Margot's fight or flight, even after decades of therapy and a lot of expensive drugs.

She suspected Dr. Singh was going to have a field day unpacking why she let herself be put in a situation like she was tonight. But Margot had long ago set a precedent of using her job as an excuse to do things that weren't good for her already fragile mental health.

He wouldn't be surprised by anything she told him at this point.

She turned in her seat and looked at Wes, noticing his expression twisting when he saw her from this angle; a mix of horror and rage crossing his features as his eyes locked on her neck.

The bruises must be getting pretty gnarly by this point. She would wait to see what they looked like in the light of day.

She pulled her jacket close around her throat. "I think I'll be OK."

"I don't mind."

And she knew he didn't. He'd slept on her couch more than once before, when they'd talked late into the night dealing with all her baggage in one way or another, while he shared his own stories with her more than once, telling her about his family and his life before she knew him. Margot knew she had something special in Wes, something that went beyond friendship, beyond partnership, but it was a thing that scared her as much as it comforted her.

She didn't want to keep him at a distance, but she also didn't want to rely on him any more than she already did. Depending on others was dangerous territory.

"You're going to see me in like four hours anyway," she reminded him.

Wes let out a groan, which made Margot smile. "All right, you just want a break from me, that's how it is."

She chuckled, but it hurt. "I need time to wash this whole night off of me if I'm going to be useful to anyone in the morning."

Wes placed a hand on hers, and she didn't recoil. She let the warmth of his skin seep in to hers, appreciating that his hands managed to somehow be both rough and soft at the same time, and right now it slowed her pulse rather than quickened it.

She let out a little breath, a loaded sigh that meant so much more than she was willing to give name to in that moment.

"If you need anything. *Anything*. I'm just a phone call away."

Margot stared at him, trying to figure out what he was thinking, but his brown eyes were just warm, friendly, and familiar.

"I know," she said at last.

And for someone who didn't believe in putting her faith in others, it was an awfully big thing to believe.

SEVEN

The morning came too soon, barely giving Margot the chance to shower and collapse into her bed for a couple of hours. Still, she was grateful for even the scant sleep she managed, because without it, she wouldn't have been able to face the day.

She explored her reflection in her bathroom mirror, the harsh light of day giving her an altogether too honest look at herself. The bruises around her neck were deep purple, and there was no mistaking them for what they were. The shape of Chris Smith's fingers was evident, and there were little half-moon cuts where she hadn't even noticed his nails digging into her.

There were a few barely noticeable scrapes on her face from when he'd pushed her to the wall, but nothing a little artful foundation wouldn't cover. She was grateful he hadn't punched her, that would have been a lot harder to hide.

It was May, not exactly turtleneck weather, but nor was it the height of summer. This was San Francisco after all, and the weather—while sometimes warm enough to call *hot*—typically erred toward the cool and rainy.

Today, she was actually pleased to see the steel-gray clouds overhead.

She quickly donned jeans and an emerald green turtleneck, something she'd bought in a moment of vanity because of how it made her red hair take on a pretty, coppery tone. It did the job of hiding the worst of the evidence from her previous night.

Margot slipped her jacket on over the turtleneck, put on her black leather boots, and was out the door before she could spend too much time bemoaning her appearance.

At least in her line of work she didn't have to look *good*, she just needed to look like she could do her job.

Luck was on her side, because she wasn't even buckled into her car when her phone started to buzz. Her pulse quickened—as it always did these days when her phone rang—but seeing Wes's name on the caller ID calmed her unsteady nerves.

"What's up?" she rasped, feigning a more casual tone than she felt.

"God, you sound awful." He said, starting off with charm. "Looks like you get to bypass the office this morning, champ. We got a call for a suspected homicide over near Golden Gate Park."

Margot didn't even flinch. It wasn't uncommon for them to be called to crime scenes with no body present but enough indicators of foul play to investigate.

Sometimes the mystery was twofold: who did it, and where was their victim?

She put the address Wes gave her into her GPS, then headed to their potential crime scene. The place was almost smack dab in the middle of Golden Gate Park—a narrow strip of green space in the northwest part of the city. She was still a distance from the park when she began to see the smoke, and that gave her a good idea of her destination.

The location Wes had directed her was at the fork of

Middle Drive West and Transverse Drive, precisely in the middle of nowhere as far as the park was concerned.

Margot could see multiple fire trucks, an ambulance, and several black-and-white city squad cars pulled along the side of the road. There was a huge mass of curious bystanders crushed up to a yellow crime scene tape barrier, and beleaguered uniformed officers were doing their best to keep things civil.

Seeing that she wouldn't be able to pull right up to the scene, Margot parked behind a squad car and pulled her badge out, using the chain attachment rather than the clip to keep her identification visible and cut down on wasted time.

She moved through the crowd, gawking faces eager to get a look at someone else's tragedy, and felt a sick pit of unease. For a moment, Justin's text message came to mind, the invitation to participate in some documentary about Ed. As if the world needed any more content about her father.

But, it was only natural, she supposed. After all, new victims had been discovered. She wondered if Special Agent Andrew Rhodes would be questioned. That would lend a certain air of legitimacy to the whole thing. Not that it would compel her to participate.

Her brother might be eager to talk, but the last thing in the world she wanted to do was have any more involvement with Ed.

Too bad he wasn't interested in letting her be free.

Margot shook off thoughts of Ed, and the invitation to discuss him on camera, and added them to the growing pile of things she would have to deal with later. Right now, the acrid stench of burning car tires was filling the air, and she wondered what the minimum safe distance was to be from a burning car in case the gas tank went up.

She ducked under the crime scene tape, holding her badge aloft before any of the uniformed officers had a chance to protest. Their hands were already full as it was.

Margot spotted Wes standing a few yards away from what looked like a burning sedan, but it was hard to know the make or model—hell, even the color wasn't obvious at this point—thanks to the rolling smoke billowing from the windows.

Wes was speaking to a burly man in firefighter gear, who was almost as tall as her partner and twice as broad. Margot had never actively pictured a lumberjack before, but now that she was looking at this man, she had a good idea of what her mental image going forward would be. He had a salt-and-pepper beard, and his cheeks were smeared with ash.

Wes spotted her and jerked his chin in greeting. "Margot, this is Battalion Chief Angus Reid. Chief, this is my partner, Detective Margot Phalen."

Margot had noticed that over the past few months Wes had started to call her by her first name more than her last. It was a subtle change, one that likely no one else had noticed, but she had. It might not mean anything, but it was still something she'd become aware of.

"Chief, pleasure to meet you."

Chief Reid nodded his head tersely. "I was just telling your partner here that we have the fire under control at this point, but it'll still be a pretty chunk of time before you guys can get anywhere near that car. And I hate to be the one to state the obvious, but there's going to be a metric fuck ton of water damage to the contents. Sorry." He did not seem sorry, but Margot didn't blame him.

"Not like there would have been much left to salvage to begin with," she observed, looking at the blackened wreckage.

She was about to ask why they'd been called to the scene, but didn't want to make the battalion chief repeat anything he'd already been over. Angus Reid didn't strike Margot as the kind of man who liked to repeat himself.

"Now, uniforms were the ones that called you in, but I can confirm their suspicions. The car was still running when they arrived, and we did find a few items near the scene that would indicate there was someone in the car at the time it stopped. I don't think that person is still in the car, but it's hard to say. Fire certainly burned hot enough to obliterate most of what was in there."

"You think an accelerant was used?" Wes asked.

Reid nodded. "I don't think a car burns that way unless someone wants it gone. We usually see fires like this when someone is trying to destroy evidence."

Margot was familiar with that type of crime scene. This wasn't her first burning car, but it was probably the worst she'd seen. Even with the fire out, the heat coming from the wreckage was astronomical, and the black clouds billowing up into the sky were dramatic.

"We'll get you a report on the accelerant when we know more. Let you know when this is safe to be moved, too."

And with that, Angus Reid was gone, moving back to his men with a purposeful stride, wasting no time on the niceties of polite conversation. Margot had to admit, she'd kind of liked him.

"He's certainly a charmer," Wes said, turning to face her.

"Not everyone is as naturally gifted with a silver tongue as you are."

His lip ticked up in a smirk, but even Margot had heard how hoarse her voice sounded. She pulled up the neck of her sweater a little higher, though she knew the bruises were covered.

"How you feeling?" Wes asked anyway, the concern evident on his face. "You up for this?"

Margot snorted. "Wesley. Give me a little credit."

"Margot. You were assaulted by piece of shit sex trafficker last night. You're *allowed* to not be OK."

"Every day I'm more and more convinced you're in cahoots

with my therapist. I hope he's giving you some kind of a cut of my fees."

"Well if you're joking about your already tenuous mental health then you're obviously feeling fine," he said, rolling his eyes. She could tell he wasn't totally ready to let this go, but it also wasn't the time or place to be having a heart-to-heart.

She was about to ask him if he had any more details about the crime scene, when a piercing scream rattled her last nerve and made her heart jump into her throat.

Her hand was on her gun, but she didn't pull it out.

More screams followed the first, and Margot tried to get a sense of what was happening. It seemed that a shockwave of horror was passing through the bystanders, and several of them turned to point to a thick copse of trees just behind the smoldering wreckage.

Margot squinted, trying to make out what was causing the commotion, but before she saw it, she heard Angus Reid's baritone say, "Sweet merciful Mary and Jesus."

A breeze shifted the air and the smoke blew away from the car, giving Margot a perfect view of the blackened body *walking* out of the woods toward them.

EIGHT

Margot had seen a lot of horrific things in her career. She'd seen people killed in hundreds of ways, she'd seen the unspeakable things humans could do to one another.

But she had *never* seen anything like the person staggering out of the trees toward them.

"Jesus," Wes breathed, eyes transfixed on the sight.

Then Margot's adrenaline kicked in, seemingly before anyone else's.

"Paramedics!" she screamed, already running before her brain had even thought to do it. "We need paramedics. We need *help*." Her raw throat was in tatters, but she knew her voice would carry.

A few of the frozen officials at the scene seemed to come alive then, and a team of EMTs were hot on her heels, with a handful of the firefighters.

Margot reached the charred person in seconds. It was obvious their victim was a woman—most of her clothing had burned away, revealing a naked chest—but her exposed skin was so blackened it was smoking, and Margot couldn't fathom how this woman was still alive, let alone moving.

Every step appeared to be agony for her.

And the *smell*.

Death and decay had their own distinct scents, familiar to Margot in her line of work. But she had never smelled anything like this before. Margot wanted to retch, but she could do that later.

As the EMTs began their initial assessment, Margot couldn't leave this woman's side, not now, no matter how revolting the smell, or how traumatic the injuries.

Margot could sense, somewhere in the back of her mind, a new nightmare forming. This was just one of those scenes, one of those victims, that she would never be able to shake. This woman was going to loom over her in her sleep at night, because there was just no way to get an image like that out of your mind once you'd seen it.

Some cases did that to her. Others did not.

This one was a haunting waiting to happen.

But for now, this woman was somehow, miraculously alive. *How* was she still alive? Had she been in that car when it went up in flames? That had to have been at least fifteen, twenty minutes ago. It seemed unfathomable that this woman could still be alive and moving, yet here she was. And an alive victim was something they almost never had.

They needed to take advantage of this while they still could.

The EMTs were checking her vitals, and the shared look of alarm that went between the two of them didn't go unnoticed. Things were bad. One of them draped a thin, blue sheet over the woman, giving her protection from the early-morning chill, and a little bit of modesty over her naked chest. Not that the woman was likely worried about that at the moment. The blanket was also sterile, to help ward off any infection, though wandering in the woods couldn't have helped.

The blanket must have felt excruciating against her skin,

but if she noticed the new pain it didn't show in her face, which was already fixed in a rictus of agony as it was.

"Ma'am," Margot asked as the EMTs continued their work, one whispering into a radio so the woman wouldn't overhear him. Margot's inquiry was probably a welcome cover for him. "Ma'am, my name is Detective Phalen and I'm here to help you. What's your name?"

Margot had no idea if the woman could hear her, or if she even had the capacity to speak, but just as Margot was about to try again, the woman's hand came out from between the folds of the blanket.

She took hold of Margot's hand, and her skin was still blistering hot to the touch, like the fire was deep inside her. Margot's instincts were like those of a child touching a hot stove. She wanted to yank herself free, but the woman's strength was shocking.

The woman's eyes were fixed on Margot, bright blue eyes that stared into hers, pleading.

"*ind im*," the woman said, tears forming in her eyes. Her mouth couldn't move quite right, and Margot could see the frustration as the victim began to realize the limitations of her own lips and tongue.

"What's your name?" Margot asked again.

"*gel.*"

Gel, gel, gel? Gel...

"Angel?" Margot asked. The woman's expression shifted in recognition, but she also shook her head almost imperceptibly. Margot was close. "Angela?" she tried again.

The woman nodded gratefully, though it appeared to cost her. Her eyes briefly rolled back in her head and she lolled slightly, making Margot fear they might have lost her. But just as quickly as it happened, she was back, her eyes still locked on Margot as if they'd never moved.

Margot was stunned by how much she could say with just a look.

"Angela, who did this to you?" Margot didn't need to ask *if* someone had done this to her. There was the distinct odor of gasoline. Someone had absolutely done this intentionally, and there might be only a little time left to find out who that person had been. Though Margot had to admit there was a fighter's fierceness to Angela's grip and expression, and against her better judgment, Margot found herself hoping there might be some miraculous way for this poor woman to pull through.

The odds were certainly against it, but Margot got the feeling if any woman was capable of it, it would be the one in front of her.

"Who did this to you?" she asked again. "Did you know them?"

Again, that tiniest of tiny head nods, something that could have been overlooked if Margot hadn't been so focused on looking for it.

"*Was... on.*" The woman grimaced and let out a little noise of pure frustration. "*On,*" she said again, then shook her head like that might make the words more clear, but the motion seemed to make her pain fire anew, and she mewled instead of saying anything else.

There were plenty of names that sounded like *on*, but Margot went right to the first one. "John?" she asked.

Angela didn't seem to hear her. Her eyes had gone glassy and unfocused, and she was staring out but not seeing anything. The paramedics noticed the shift as well, and doubled down on their efforts, getting Angela loaded onto a gurney and beginning to connect more monitors to her as well as an oxygen mask. The interview was over.

Margot could still feel the heat in her hand where Angela's burnt fingers had clutched at her.

She wasn't sure she'd ever stop feeling it.

How had Angela found herself here this morning, and what had led to such unspeakable violence being unleashed on her? Margot knew nothing about the woman besides her name, and even that was just a best guess at this point.

What she *did* know was no one, regardless of what they'd done in their life, deserved what Margot had just witnessed.

She was going to find out who did this, because that was what Angela deserved.

NINE

When the ambulance left, the crowd seemed to lose most of its interest in the tragedy, though a few looky-loos continued to watch the scene through the safe barrier of their phone screens as they filmed it or streamed it to whatever social media platform might eat up this kind of tragedy.

Was it easier to stomach if they didn't look right at it?

Margot's own stomach churned, as the nausea she had tamped down earlier came swelling back, threatening to purge the contents of her already empty stomach. She swallowed the urge down. A few nearby officers and firefighters had not been able to.

Wes, who had been lingering behind her as she questioned Angela, looked shaken, even if he wasn't going to lose his lunch. Margot rarely got to see that from Wes, who was made of some of the sternest stuff on the force. But she saw it in the downturn of his normally grinning mouth, and in the way his eyes searched her, asking the question he didn't dare speak out loud.

"I'm fine," she assured him, even as she looked down at her hand, still coated in charred black that had come from Angela. "Fine," she said again, and this time mostly to assure herself.

She didn't want to wipe her hand on her pants, that felt wrong, and somehow disrespectful.

Wes seemed to realize how transfixed she was on her own hand and jogged away for a moment. When he came back, he was holding a plastic water bottle. Margot had no idea where he'd gotten it. He took her hand in his and poured the water over it, the bits of black vanishing almost instantly. Soon her palm looked completely normal, and Wes wiped the sleeve of his dress shirt over it to dry it off.

Margot stared at him, wondering how something so repellent managed to be almost tender under his supervision.

"Thanks," she muttered, pulling her hand back before she got caught staring at him too long. "How much of that did you catch?" Angela's voice had been low, and Margot's wasn't much better. With the din of the crime scene and the instructions being shouted to the firefighters, Margot wouldn't have been surprised if she'd been the only one to hear what Angela had said.

"I think I got most of it. I'm fucking shocked she was able to speak at all, if I'm being totally honest."

"Me too." They were headed away from the area where Angela had appeared. Uniformed officers were moving through the nearby trees, taking delicate steps as they scoured the ground for any sign of evidence—or anything seemingly innocuous that might prove to be evidence later—and Margot followed Wes back to the car.

The smoke had begun to clear, but there was still an awful lot of heat coming off the body of the vehicle. Reid had been right, it would be a while before they were able to properly scour the wreckage. But Margot needed something to focus on, otherwise she'd get too caught up in the feeling of Angela's hand, which still felt like it was pressed against her own.

Margot waved down the nearest uniformed officer and

instructed him to find more officers to help comb the nearby woods. While the car was the most obvious starting point for the fire, Margot couldn't be sure that the victim hadn't been set alight somewhere else. If there was a secondary crime scene in the woods, they'd want to find it quickly, and the more people they had working on that the better.

She gave her wrist a shake and squatted down near the car, the radiant warmth touching her even at a slight distance. The smell here was different than it had been with Angela, more burning plastic and rubber, and it seemed to help clear her head a little, though it would certainly give her one hell of a headache later.

There were bits and pieces of Angela's life littered over the ground, and while Margot couldn't get anything helpful from the car itself right now, there was a story to be told just looking at what remained.

"I think our most likely option is that someone lit her up while she was still in the car. That or they followed her to the trees, but I think maybe it's too exposed a location for that. Our perp wouldn't want to draw any *extra* attention to himself after the crash and the initial fire. So let's assume it started here unless one of the uniforms finds a point of ignition out there. The victim said she knew the person, or at least that was the implication she gave me from what she could tell me. But none of this makes any sense. She was on the other side of the car. If she got out the driver's side door, she would have headed that way." Margot pointed to her left, the opposite direction from where they'd found Angela.

Wes followed her finger, and she wondered if he was picturing the flight the way it should have happened.

Angela would certainly have been disoriented and in excruciating pain when she got out of the car. It was possible she might have gone the other way because her attacker was still nearby. Maybe he'd chased her and she'd been forced to go the other direction to hide among the trees. It was also possible that she was just so disoriented from the pain she moved in whatever direction she'd been pointed when she stumbled out of the car.

"What if he was the one driving?" Wes asked.

Margot met his gaze, her brow arching uncertainly.

Wes said, "Look at the stuff that's on the ground. It's her purse, her wallet—burnt to shit—things that she wouldn't have been holding if she was the one driving, so it wouldn't make sense for them to fall like this. But if she was in the passenger seat, and he grabbed her bag, maybe thinking there was something in it... maybe there *was* something in it, then douses her in gasoline, lights her up, and makes a break for it, dropping what he doesn't need as he gets out of the car..."

Margot closed her eyes for a moment, picturing the scene as Wes described it. It made sense, at least in part. It didn't explain how the car had veered off the road, but maybe that had happened *before* the fire had started.

Which meant in an area like this, there might have been someone who saw the crash itself, might have noticed how everything had begun.

Margot's head swiveled back to the barricade, wondering if any of the lingering gawkers might actually be witnesses. How long had it been since the car had crashed? Would anyone have hung around that long? She beckoned one of the uniformed officers from the barricade over. His name tag read *Spence*, and he had the look of a lifetime beat cop. Some folks liked that job and just never tried to leave it. Margot wasn't one to judge, most people saw homicide as a stopover necessary for promotion. For Margot, it was a lifetime commitment.

The officer, hair graying at the temples beneath his cap, gave her a nod as he approached. "Detective." His voice was rough, professional, but also friendly. Margot could tell right away this man wasn't the type to treat her differently because she was a woman. She was constantly surprised by how much of an issue that remained for some men on the force.

"Have you been here since the barricade went up?" she asked.

His head bobbed. "Yes, ma'am. I was one of the responding officers to the original 911 call."

Margot couldn't believe her luck. "Was the caller still on site when you arrived?" she asked.

"No, ma'am. I think the original caller was a driver who happened to notice the wreck in passing. Long gone by the time I got here."

Well, so much for good luck.

"Any of the folks here been here since you arrived?" she asked, peering past him at the stragglers who continued to watch the scene. He followed her gaze and looked at the people as if seeing them for the first time.

"No, can't say that any of them have been here long enough to have stuck out. Sorry."

So much for that. "Do you recall anything unusual from when you arrived?"

His professional demeanor slipped for a moment as he turned his attention back to the smoldering car. "More unusual than that?" His chin jerked to the wreckage.

She watched him instead of the car, trying to see if there was any chance he just wasn't telling her everything, but Officer Spence seemed completely earnest.

"Thanks," she said. "If you can remember anything else, maybe anyone lingering by the scene, just let me know. I know this one was a lot to take in, so something might come back to you later."

Rather than dismiss her, he gave her a nod before heading back to the barricade line.

That left them right back at square one. She returned to Wes's side, both assessing the wreckage they couldn't touch. Margot wondered if it might hold the key to their case, or if all potential hopes of finding evidence within had gone up in smoke.

TEN
1993

Desolation Wilderness, California

"Dad?"

Justin's voice was meek, uncertain. Like even the singular syllable had taken some courage for him to utter. Ed sighed, knowing it was audible, but Justin immediately misread his frustration.

Ed wasn't annoyed that Justin had spoken. He was annoyed that Justin needed to muster up the balls for just one word.

"Spit it out, kid. No one is going to speak your mind for you." Ed was unpacking the little pup tent they'd be sharing. Since he had assumed Justin lacked the physical strength to carry his own tent—he'd been correct, even the bag with his sleeping bag and most basic gear had forced Justin to take several breaks—they were stuck sleeping in what Ed had, and what he could carry.

The pup tent was a throwback to his own youth, the years *after* he and his sister had left their childhood home in Oakland. After their mother had died.

As it turned out, their mother had lied to them about a lot of things. Not about their father leaving them and having no interest in raising them. That had turned out to be very true. But she'd lied a lot about her extended family. And as luck would have it, Sarah and Ed had avoided the foster system when their uncle had stepped in and offered to take them.

He was older than their mother by about ten years, so to Sarah and Ed he and his wife had seemed positively ancient. But they'd been kind. Strict—their uncle Stewart was a former military man, and his wife Suzette a middle school teacher—but they were not cruel.

Stewart was an outdoorsy guy, and he had taken Ed on several overnight trips to the mountain, much like this. Ed wasn't grateful for much about his childhood, but the lessons he'd learned from Stewart had stuck with him for a lifetime. He'd learned to survive outdoors. To hunt. Stewart had taught him how to use a gun, how to prepare an animal you had killed, how to move quietly without being heard. Stewart could never have known how Ed would *use* those lessons, but the bonding they'd done in the woods had a lasting impression on the boy.

Ed wanted to impart that to Justin.

Stewart wasn't around anymore, but Ed liked to think he'd be proud if he could see him setting up their old tent for the next generation, though Stewart wouldn't have said it. He was a man of few words. He believed actions spoke louder.

Justin cleared his throat and tried again. "Dad, I'm not..." He paused, already reconsidering what he was going to say. "Are you sure this is a good place to put the tent?"

Ed glanced at the area he'd selected. The landscape lived up to the name *Desolation*. They were on a craggy, exposed area of rocky terrain, where there was a low-lying space with ground soft enough to drive pegs into. Nearby there was a thin span of trees, and if they moved to the edge of the rocky area there was a drop that showed a great view of Tahoe.

Ed couldn't for the life of him think of a better place to put the tent.

His curiosity won out over annoyance. After all, he had told the boy to speak his mind, so he shouldn't scold him for doing so. "I do think it's a good spot, but before I tell you why, I want to know why you don't think it is." Ed intentionally kept his tone light, inviting. This feigned friendliness was something he was especially good at when the need arose.

Ed could convince anyone he was a nice guy.

Even his own son.

Justin appeared cautious. He apparently knew Ed's moods well enough at this point to not inherently trust the tone or the question. Smart kid. Maybe there was a little hope for him yet.

"Well..." He took a deep breath, steadying himself for what he was going to say next. "We're not in the marked campground area?" He phrased it like a question, but Ed didn't answer, just waited to see if there was more. Justin measured the silence, his eyes searching Ed's face like he was trying to read a book, except the book was in a language he didn't know. "And there was that warning at the trailhead that said *No overnight campers on trail*."

Ed scratched the stubble on his chin, nodding slowly, taking in the boy's words.

A follower, then. Someone who insisted on coloring inside the lines. Ed had hoped for a little more from his flesh and blood, but Justin was young. And Ed had to admit that he had impressed on Justin the importance of listening to *him*. He supposed it was only natural that a disposition for listening to all authority might follow.

So he'd need to teach the kid that some rules were meant to be broken, it was just a matter of knowing the difference.

"I'm going to let you in on a little secret," Ed said after a long pause.

Justin nodded slowly, eyes wide and transfixed.

"Sometimes it's OK to do what *you* want."

The boy stared at him, uncomprehending. "But—"

"No, no, just let me explain for a minute. Do you know why that sign is there?" Ed didn't wait for his son to answer, he just plowed ahead. "It's there for the people who *need* it. For the people who would come out here and disrespect the land. The people who would litter the ground with beer cans, play their music loud, scrawl their names on the rocks. People who don't *deserve* to spend the night here. You understand?"

Justin nodded slowly, though Ed wasn't wholly certain if the words had sunk in or not.

"But we're not like that, are we? We know the rules of nature, we know to leave only footprints, right?"

Justin, who had started Cub Scouts that year, nodded a little more eagerly.

"So the rules don't really apply to us, do they?"

Ed watched his son work through this, the idea that rules could apply to only some people, while others were above them. This was something Ed had learned when he was about Justin's age, but Justin wasn't going to be able to learn it exactly like Ed had.

Because Justin wasn't ready for that kind of lesson.

At least not yet.

Finally, a light seemed to go on in Justin's eyes and he smiled and nodded, almost eager all of a sudden to help his father break this particular rule.

Ed wondered what else Justin might be willing to learn.

ELEVEN

Margot and Wes returned to the police station shortly after noon. Wes almost immediately ducked out to grab them lunch, while Margot rotated the whiteboard where they did their brainstorming. The back of the board was covered in work on the Redwood Killer case—a moniker that had unfortunately stuck in the media—and while Margot wanted to believe they were getting close to a breakthrough on the Bay Area's newest serial killer, she had to admit she was also frustratingly stuck.

And had been for months.

On the cleared front of the board, she started jotting down notes.

JANE DOE got written in large capital letters, then Margot drew a line from it with a note that said *Angela?* At this point they didn't have a solid ID on the woman, and the license plate on the car had been too damaged to read, so they couldn't get anything that way.

Margot had several evidence bags from the scene with items from Angela's purse, but unfortunately none of them were a driver's license or anything that might flash a big neon sign telling them who she was. Yet.

Next to her name she wrote *ean or on?* Then added *John, Sean, Don.*

Too many possibilities to give them much to grab hold of.

As Margot stared at the board, the familiar grinding sound of her phone buzzing against the wooden surface of the desk drew her attention. She stared at it from a distance, a lump in her throat.

For months, Margot had been telling herself to change her phone number, but she knew it wouldn't help. For one thing, she had given out her number to so many potential witnesses in cases, to so many other law enforcement adjacent personnel, that changing it just to avoid one caller would have been more trouble than it was worth.

And that was the other thing.

Once she'd reported the call, she'd never gotten another one.

Ed Finch was in San Quentin, a maximum-security prison. How he'd managed to get a cell phone in the first place was a mystery—though there were always ways to get things into prison, no matter what anyone said—but they'd found the phone and confiscated it.

The damage was done, though. While he'd had the phone he'd managed to communicate with his wife, Rhonda—now Toni—and her son. Whether Ed was the one who had told Ewan to kill, or whether he'd just gently guided the boy in a direction he'd already been headed, no one really knew.

Whatever Ed had said to Ewan had been in calls, so there was no text record, and the boy wasn't talking.

Though he was due for trial soon, so chances were good he'd be sharing a cell not far from his hero before long.

But in talking to Ewan and Toni, Ed had gotten the one thing he'd wanted most.

Margot's new name.

Even in the months she'd been visiting him, speaking to

him, getting him to fess up about his unknown crimes, she'd refused to tell him her new name. She didn't think he deserved that piece of her.

But now he had it. And Margot was just waiting for him to find a way to use it against her.

So far, that other shoe hadn't fallen, but each day, each ring of the phone, she wondered if that would be the moment her fragile peace was shattered forever.

That she would once again only be the daughter of a serial killer.

She moved across the room and glanced down at the phone. Unknown number. Her pulse ticked up, but she had to answer it.

"Hello?" she asked cautiously.

"Is this Detective Phalen?" a young woman's voice asked.

"Yes, who's calling?"

"I'm Officer Childress. I accompanied the ambulance from the scene at the Golden State Park this morning. I was asked to stay with the woman?" She said this last part like a question.

"Of course, yes."

"Docs thought you should know she's awake. But they don't know for how long." The unspoken part of this was something Margot had been thinking since the moment Angela stumbled out of the woods.

It wasn't a question of how long she'd be awake.

It was a question of how long she'd be alive.

Margot nodded, then remembered that the woman couldn't see her. "Thanks, Officer. Saint Francis?" she asked.

Saint Francis Memorial had the city's foremost burn unit, it was the most logical place for Angela to have been taken, despite there being an emergency room right beside Golden Gate Park.

"Yes, ma'am."

Margot hung up and texted Wes to head to the hospital and

meet her there. It would be faster than waiting for him to return so they could leave together. She headed out to her car and another call buzzed as she pulled out of her parking spot. The phone was connected to Bluetooth, so she hit the answer button without much thought as she merged into traffic and turned down a side street to head to the hospital.

"Phalen," she said as a gruff greeting.

"Hi Margot." For a moment, the wires in her brain short-circuited and she confused two male voices. Two father figures. She swallowed the lump in her throat and told her heart to stop beating so fast.

It wasn't Ed. Not this time.

It was the man who had caught him.

"Hey, Andrew."

Special Agent Andrew Rhodes of the FBI, the man who had put Ed behind bars after seventy-six women had died. The man who was now trying to find out how many more women they'd missed.

She hadn't heard from him in months. Not since she'd told him and his unit that she was done being Ed's pawn.

This moment had been coming, she just hadn't known exactly when it would arrive. This seemed like as bad a moment as any.

"How've you been?" he asked, his tone casual, but in a way she knew was taking some effort to maintain.

"The horrors persist, but so do I," she answered, stuck at a red light. She could have taken out her personal siren but the distance to the hospital didn't feel long enough to warrant it. The siren rarely sped things up.

Andrew chuckled at her response. "I might need to borrow that one. Feels fitting."

"Have at it."

"I think you probably know why I'm calling," he said finally.

Recalling Justin's texts, Margot had a moment's pause. "I

can actually think of a couple reasons you might be calling, but they are both distinctly Ed Finch-shaped."

A pause. "Oh, you must have heard about that docuseries, then. I wondered if they'd find a way to get to you."

"Not me, my brother," Margot said with a sigh. "My lawyer knows better."

This was hardly the first time there'd been a documentary, a podcast, a book, the makers eager to speak to Ed's family, or anyone remotely connected to the case. Margot's default answer was no. Her lawyer knew not to even mention it to her, which was why she wasn't shocked that everyone *but* her knew about the series.

"Well, that's actually not what I'm calling about, but now that you mention it I should let you know I'm going to participate."

She was both surprised and not surprised by this. Andrew had written *the* book on Ed Finch, an instant bestseller still in circulation now. Come to think of it, they would probably be on his case for an updated edition with all these new victims they'd unearthed. Six new names so far, and counting.

Margot didn't know what had been going on with the case since she'd abandoned ship. She felt immense guilt about doing it, but as Dr. Singh had pointed out, she had finally realized there was a boundary she'd needed to place and she'd done it.

He'd been proud of her.

She just wished she could tell herself it had been the right thing and not merely a selfish thing. She *had* needed to do it. Her visits with Ed were chipping away little pieces of her soul, and it wasn't balanced out by the relief being offered to the families of victims. She just couldn't take it anymore.

But now, with the gift of time—and the realization that she didn't need to be in front of Ed for him to get her all twisted up —she was beginning to reconsider her decision.

Had Andrew sensed her resolve slipping? It would be just like him to know precisely when to dig his claws back in.

And if he wasn't calling about the documentary, what did he want?

Andrew Rhodes didn't call just to check in.

Not anymore.

"You are the expert on Ed," Margot said, finally replying to his comment about the series. "I'm sure they made it worth your while."

There was a pause, like maybe she'd offended him by reducing the whole thing to a paycheck. She felt a little bad for the jab, but she was still angry with Andrew for using her as a pawn to deal with Ed. He'd preyed on her desire to see justice done, and overlooked the damage it had been doing to her along the way. She had always thought Andrew wanted what was best for her. He'd been so caring and genuine to her for a long time. But as soon as she had something he needed, she stopped being a person and became one more thing he could manipulate.

He and Ed weren't all that different in some ways.

"I won't bother trying to tell you it's actually a pretty professional team doing this one and that it might be worth listening to what they have to say." Andrew cleared his throat. "I'm sure your brother will have plenty to tell you about it."

Margot pulled into a parking lot for the hospital. Andrew's time was almost up.

"I'm on the clock right now, Andrew. I don't want to rush you, but I know this wasn't a social call."

"Ed's lawyer got in touch with us this week. It's been a while since your old man has had much to say, but it seems like he's feeling chatty. Rosenthal's exact words, I believe, were, *Has the princess decided to come out of her tower yet?*"

Margot scoffed. "What a prick."

"He didn't leave it there. He told us, through Rosenthal,

that if you come to talk to him again, he'll tell us all about the help he had." Andrew's voice thickened on the word *help* in a way Margot couldn't possibly mistake.

Help.

Ed was implying he hadn't done all his killings alone.

Well, son of a bitch.

That meant there was more at stake. This wasn't simply about resolving open cases and putting names to long-buried skeletons.

If Margot went back, they might be able to put another killer behind bars.

TWELVE

Margot didn't have time to dwell on the curveball Andrew had thrown her. She told him she'd call him back when she was done for the day, but she wasn't saying yes or no just yet.

She wasn't just playing hard to get. She honestly didn't know how to process this new knowledge, or how she felt about it. Would it be smart to be face-to-face with Ed at this point, knowing what he knew about her? It might just motivate him to use her name against her.

Then again, staying away might have the same effect.

Ed was unpredictable.

Margot found Wes waiting for her in the lobby. He smiled when he spotted her and that simple gesture was somehow enough to lift off some of the weight she had carried in with her. She wasn't *healed*, but it would get her through the next hour.

Sometimes that was what life was. Looking for whatever it took to get you through the next hour.

"I'll have you know there are two *very* delicious Italian grinders in the car getting soggy as we speak, but they'll still be tasty when we're done."

"I'm not too good for a soggy sandwich," she replied as they headed toward the main nurse's station. After a quick badge flash the nurse at the desk told them to wait as she paged a Dr. Kaur to meet them.

Margot desperately wanted to tell Wes about her phone call with Andrew, but this wasn't the time or place to get into it.

"Hey Wesley," she said as they waited for the doctor.

"Mmm."

"You want to go grab a bite after work?"

Wes didn't skip a beat. "I knew the soggy sandwiches wouldn't be enough for you."

Margot rolled her eyes. "I got an interesting call. I'd like to pick your brain, maybe over some biang biang noodles."

"Margot, can I ask you a question?" He was leaning up against the wall, looking unbelievably casual.

"Sure."

"Do you really love Asian food this much, or do you love Asian food this much because of how close you live to Chinatown?"

This question was not as absurd as it sounded, given that Wes knew she would never venture out for food on her own, and didn't ever do pickup, she relied entirely on delivery.

"First, don't lump a whole continent of cuisine together. There's a massive difference between, for example, Vietnamese and Cambodian food. Second, I would love Thai with my dying breath even if I wasn't a weirdo shut-in recluse. And third, have you *had* biang biang noodles, sir?"

Wes held his hands up in mock surrender. "I have been rightly called out. And no, I can't say that I have, but I guess that's going to change tonight."

Margot felt a grateful lift in her heart. "Thank you."

"Well don't thank me yet. If you're picking my brain, that means you're paying."

"Deal."

Dr. Kaur chose that moment to arrive. She was a middle-aged woman of East Indian descent, and Margot marveled at how, despite the long hours she must work, her skin looked positively luminous, even under the harsh overhead lights in the hospital.

"Detectives, thanks so much for meeting with me before we go in to speak with her. I understand this case is pressing, and we obviously want to find out what happened to her as much as you do, but I'm going to need to run over some ground rules with you before you go in, OK?"

Margot nodded. Dr. Kaur's voice was calm and warm, but also brooked no opposition. It was clear she was in charge here.

"My patient has been able to indicate, with some difficulty, her name is Angela. While I have not yet been able to properly guess her last name from her limited cues, I believe it starts with Good or Hood. Goodman, Goodhome, something like that seems most likely. I'm hoping that helps. It is out of the question to ask her to write anything. The damage to her tissues is astronomical, she cannot bend her finger and has already lost two on each hand from the burns. I likewise don't believe she'd be able to write on a tablet, but should she continue to improve I will let you know if that becomes an option. I'm telling you all this now so we don't waste time in there with her. She has very brief moments of lucidity, and you have to understand we have her on an extraordinarily high dose of painkillers. She is awake, but she's not... alert, if you will."

"She's high," Wes said.

"And you would hope to be, too, in her condition, Detective."

The doctor started to guide them through the halls, her footsteps quick and purposeful. She spoke the entire time she walked, and though Margot and Wes were both taller than Dr. Kaur they needed to pick up the pace to keep up with her. Margot felt like an intern.

"You mustn't touch her under any circumstances. I know

we often have a compassionate urge to touch someone's hands or arm or leg when we speak to them during difficult times. It's human nature. But Angela's skin is so raw and exposed the slightest touch can risk massive infection. I'm going to ask you to wear gloves, caps, and a gown when you go in, please, for the same reason. It may seem like overkill to you, but we are doing everything we can to keep this woman alive, and the fact that she's breathing and speaking right now is a miracle. And you can imagine that's a phrase I don't use often."

They stopped in front of an unremarkable door where the doctor directed them to several boxes placed on a chair. Margot couldn't help but think of the way the chief medical examiner, Evelyn Yao, set similar boxes of gloves and booties up outside crime scenes to avoid contamination.

Except in this case, their crime scene was a living woman.

Margot and Wes donned the necessary safety gear without a comment, though Margot wanted desperately to take a photo of her partner with his perfect hair covered by a protective cap and his expensive clothes hidden behind a blue hospital gown.

"One last thing," Dr. Kaur said. She hadn't put anything on, which told Margot she was either extremely confident in her own cleanliness, or she wasn't coming in with them. "We need to keep her as calm as possible. The stress placed on her body today is enough to stop most people's hearts permanently. At a certain point, a pain threshold can become so taxed the human body will simply choose to stop the heart rather than bear that pain a moment more. I don't know why her heart didn't stop, but it could give out at any moment. She's far from out of the woods. So please, do not overly stress her, and if you think at any point your questions are pushing her to a heightened stress level, I must ask that you stop immediately."

The doctor stared at them, making sure they understood her. Margot and Wes both nodded. This didn't seem sufficient to Dr. Kaur.

"I understand you're homicide detectives, but let's try to keep this as an *attempted* homicide, shall we?"

"Yes, ma'am. Doctor," Wes said. She obviously made him nervous, much to Margot's delight.

"Good. I'll do my best to keep this woman alive, you do your best to find out who tried to kill her, OK?"

Dr. Kaur didn't wait to hear their response, she was already halfway down the hall, walking with the gait of an unhurried woman on a stroll, but the speed of a marathoner.

"She's terrifying. I should ask her out," Wes marveled, watching her go.

Margot raised an eyebrow. "She's too good for you, Wesley." She'd wanted it to be a joke, but her voice sounded more peevish than she'd intended.

"You're right." He pushed open the door to the room where a curtain surrounded the only bed, not to give her privacy but to provide one more barrier between her and the outside world. Margot hesitated before pulling the curtain back.

The room was filled with the steady beep of machinery, things that were keeping Angela alive. The antiseptic smell was intense. They hadn't been asked to wear masks, but Dr. Kaur had made it abundantly clear they were meant to keep their distance.

Margot pulled the curtain aside just enough for her and Wes to make their way within its confines, standing at the end of her bed.

Angela lay before them both different and the same from the last time they'd seen her. Her skin was still a blackened wreckage, though there was much less if it visible now than before. She'd been covered in bandages, many of which were already red with blood.

Margot had no idea what procedures the woman had already endured, or if she was simply being protected to see if she lived long enough for additional measures to be taken. Here, under the fluorescent bulbs, Margot could see there were a few strands of blond hair on the woman's scalp, peeking out from under a bandage on her head.

Her skin didn't offer many clues to the shade it had been when she was unburnt, and Margot didn't like to make guesses based on hair color, since dye could make anyone blond.

Angela stared at them, her eyes glassy but open, like she was seeing but perhaps not processing.

"Angela, I'm Detective Phalen, I was with you at the scene of the fire."

"*Hiiiii*," Angela rasped.

Margot wasn't sure if this meant that the woman remembered her or if it was just a polite knee-jerk response, but she took the invitation to keep going.

"My partner, Wes, and I want to find out what happened to you. Can we ask you a few questions? We'll try to make them easy. Yes or no."

"*ess.*"

"OK, great. Angela, were you driving the car today?"

"*No.*" The word was so shallow and raspy Margot swallowed almost on instinct to wet her own throat. She shouldn't have, because it was just a reminder of how tender she still was.

How had that attack only been last night? To Margot it was now one of the least traumatic things she could think of from the last twenty-four hours.

"Was it your car?" she asked.

"*No.*"

Angela's gaze drifted and Margot wasn't sure if she was losing focus or perhaps something more serious was happening, but she realized that Angela had just shifted her focus to look at Wes.

"*aaandsome*," she wheezed, then started to chuckle but had to stop when her body racked with coughs.

Margot waited, hoping she would recover, and she did.

"*Damn,*" Angela said, and sighed.

Evidently, she still had a sense of humor, and was a flirt. Being high as a kite probably helped loosen her up some as well.

"You should see him when he's not dressed up like he's about to get a colonoscopy," Margot said, offering Angela a smile.

"*Hit that,*" the woman rasped, and this time it was Margot's turn to bark out a rough laugh.

"I'll take it under advisement."

"Angela, was the person driving a man?" Wes asked, leaning into his theory.

"*Ess.*"

"Did you know him?"

"*Ess.*"

"A boyfriend? Partner?"

"*No.*"

A beeping that had been a steady background noise up until then intensified, and Margot realized it was Angela's heart-rate monitor.

"Wes." She touched his hand.

"I see it."

So this line of questioning might be one they couldn't go down. But it was the only one they desperately needed an answer to. Margot and Wes exchanged a quick glance and seemed to come to the same conclusion.

One more question.

One more question couldn't hurt.

Something then flitted to Margot's mind.

"Angela. You said something at the scene, I thought it was a name. I thought it might be John. But... please don't think you're going to be in trouble if this is right, we just want to find who did this to you. When you said that, did you mean it was a man named John?"

Angela shook her head slightly. Margot could see that the woman's eyes were watering.

"Was he *a* john? A client?"

Angela stared at Margot, her gaze focused and fiery. For a moment, Margot wasn't sure if the woman was going to answer her. Maybe she'd read this all wrong, maybe she'd just offended a victim covered head to toe in third-degree burns.

Instead, a single tear slipped over her charred skin.

"*Ess.*"

THIRTEEN

Margot and Wes left Angela since it was clear their questioning had gone as far as it could without causing her genuine health issues. Still, they came away with much more than Margot could have hoped for at the outset.

"How did you come up with that?" Wes asked as they deposited their used garments in a bin outside the door.

Margot shook her head. "You got me thinking with the theory that she was in the passenger seat. Someone grabbing her stuff from her. It could have been a domestic dispute, but I don't know, something about the whole *John* thing stuck with me. It was a long shot."

"Pretty well-aimed long shot," Wes said. She could feel his gaze on her even when she wasn't looking at him.

"Guess I'm just a good detective." Why did she suddenly feel guilty of something? She hadn't *known* what Angela was going to say, it was only a hunch that happened to hit right.

The problem was, it was going to make their perp that much harder to find. Angela had indicated she knew him, so he must have been a regular in some capacity, someone she wouldn't have been surprised to be in a car with that early in the morning. Had it been a morning call, or an overnight call and he was taking her home afterwards?

That kind of chivalry wasn't exactly the norm in the sex work industry, but if this guy had been someone Angela was familiar with, maybe it was part of their routine.

High-end escort services were a more likely venue for overnight stays.

But, if this guy had been able to afford a high-end service, why would he have needed to steal her purse? Unless he thought she had something of his, something he wanted back.

And to set his own car on fire just to get rid of Angela was a pretty big statement to make.

Wes seemed to practically read her mind as the thoughts whizzed by. "I'd be willing to bet when we get the registration on that car sorted out it will have been reported stolen," he said.

She arched a brow at him, and he continued. "If it had been her car, I'm sure he'd have no issue lighting it up right alongside her. But he's not going to light his own car on fire. No way. He had to be thinking of that car as disposable. Something he could walk away from, no harm no foul."

"No harm no foul," Margot repeated, staring at him.

Wes seemed to catch his error. "No harm to *him*."

She nodded. They were outside now, and clouds had gathered overhead, turning the mid-afternoon into an early evening. He walked her to her car and held the door open as she got in.

"Tell me what you're thinking, Margot."

Margot strummed her fingernails on the steering wheel, staring straight ahead through the window rather than looking at him directly. Her thoughts weren't easy to express, they were bouncing around in her head and none of them managed to form a complete picture.

"I don't know yet. Honestly. I think we get back to the station, look up Angela Good and Angela Hood as options for names. If she's a sex worker there's a chance she might have a criminal record. We're obviously not going to be able to check her fingerprints." An involuntary shudder coursed through her body. "Maybe if we can find her, we can find known associates, talk to them about whether or not she had any regulars. It's as good a place to start as any."

"It's wild to me that we have a living victim and we still don't know who she is." Wes shook his head.

"She's trying," Margot said.

"She's a fighter."

Margot glanced at him and he was looking right at her, but his expression was unreadable. Was there something more to his words, something directed at her? But Wes was never shy about poking and prodding at her when he felt it was needed. That was one of the best and most annoying things about him. He never pitied her.

Maybe that's what she saw there now that felt so familiar, an unflinching concern that mingled with respect.

"Unless you want to hang onto the door the whole way back to the station, you're going to have to let me go," Margot said finally, giving him a soft smile.

Wes, who seemed to have forgotten he was holding the door open, jerked back and then chuckled for a moment before shutting her door and heading back in the direction of his own car.

When Margot had first met Wes, she'd unfairly assumed he was all surface. Handsome, self-assured, and downright cocky at times. But in the years they'd been partners she was constantly learning there were unexpected depths to him. He was a genuinely good man, and that was something she knew was all too rare.

She started the car and navigated back to the station, half expecting her phone to ring at any moment with even more unwelcome news. But after Andrew's call that morning, she was no longer waiting for it to be Ed on the other end of the line.

He'd lost the phone but found another irresistible way to lure her back in.

She realized then, she would go.

Knowing Ed had a potential accomplice who was still free was too much for her to resist, and he had to understand that. She could pretend that Ed himself didn't matter to her, because he was already carrying the maximum penalty he could ever have with a death sentence looming over him. Though, given California's history of executions, she knew he'd probably die of old age before lethal injection.

But to put someone else in there with him, that would be a fight worth weighing in on again. Especially if he could point them to the evidence that would make the trial open-and-shut.

Margot didn't want to rely on Ed for anything, but this was too big a potential reward for her to disregard.

FOURTEEN

1993

Desolation Wilderness, California

Ed knew Justin wasn't sleeping.

He knew the way breath sounded when someone was asleep.

And as a parent, he knew how to tell when his children were faking it.

Justin wasn't sleeping, which was foolish, considering they had several miles to hike the next day and wouldn't be heading home for one more night. It was important to have your wits about you out in the wilderness. His uncle had told Ed that on one of the first trips they took together.

"Ed, son," Stewart had said, his gray brows drawn together in concentration. "We don't give nature her due often enough. We live in our houses, in our cities, and we think nature is parks and backyards and places we can have a picnic. But nature doesn't *care* about us. It doesn't *bend* for us. We are part of nature, but somewhere along the line we thought we could own it, tame it, and that's simply not the case. When you're out here, you need to be sharp, stay focused, because nature isn't going to hold your hand and sing you a lullaby. You understand?"

And Ed *had* understood. At that point in his life he no longer felt like a child, no longer had the simple mind of someone who was innocent. If he'd ever had that. Ed might have understood better than any ten-year-old alive that there were dangerous things lurking in the shadows of the night.

The fact that Stewart's words gave Ed a thrill of anticipation that bordered on fear was something new for him. Exciting.

As Stewart had spoken to him over a fire, a warmed tin of beans their supper that night, Ed imagined things moving just outside the reach of the fire's light.

"You have to be smart, Ed," Stewart cautioned. "It's not just the mountain lions or bears that might hurt you out here. Nature can take you out with a strong wind, loose rocks, a fast-running river. You're never going to outsmart her, son, remember that. Remember to respect her and that's what will keep you alive."

Justin's breath quivered. He was scared.

It was good to be scared, but Ed wanted his son to know fear for the right reasons.

"What's got you spooked, kid?" Ed asked.

Justin gasped sharply, as if he had actually believed he'd managed to fool his father into thinking he was asleep.

"N-nothing."

"Now, none of that. I'm not an idiot. Spit it out."

After a long pause, Justin's reply came out as almost a whisper. "I have to pee."

Ed laughed. He didn't mean to, but the answer took him by such surprise the chuckle was out before he could even stop it. It wasn't malicious, either. He knew he could be hard on the kid sometimes, but he didn't think he was ever unreasonably cruel.

"And you don't want to go out on your own?"

Justin shook his head.

"Well, all right then, you could have just said something." Ed sat up, undoing his sleeping bag zipper. The tent was small, so even if Justin had worked up the courage to go out without saying anything at all, his motions would certainly have roused Ed.

Maybe that's what he'd been worried about.

Ed undid the tent flap and held it open as Justin struggled to free himself from his own sleeping bag and then stumbled outside with all the grace of a newborn deer.

Outside, the night was astonishing in its clarity. Ed was someone who liked the night, he liked to be outside when others weren't. But this wasn't like nighttime in the city, it was something else entirely, and it was a glorious thing to behold.

The sky overhead was black, but the stars were so bright the darkness didn't seem to be complete. You couldn't see a sky like this in the city. Not ever. The Milky Way was a soft smear of light between the constellations, and with no moon to be seen, the stars were somehow enough to illuminate the ground around them.

After Justin did his business in the nearby bushes, he came to stand beside Ed, looking up at the sky with an awestruck wonder that Ed hadn't been certain his son was capable of, he spent so much time staring down at his own shoes.

Ed said nothing, but he put his arm around his son's shoulder and gave it a squeeze.

They stood for a moment, just looking up, breathing it all in, until the sound of laughter startled them both, and put an end to the reverie. It was coming from over the side of the cliff's edge, and while Justin seemed to recoil from it, because it meant they weren't alone out here, Ed was pulled toward it.

That was a woman's laugh.

He peered down over the edge of the cliff, to where there was a stream about forty feet down. While he couldn't see the person who was laughing, it was evident enough that they weren't the only rule-breakers out on the trail.

A small tent was set up beside a hastily made fire, and while he was too far to make out more details, the sound of that laughter stroked its fingers over the inside of his brain.

They weren't alone out here.

But the girls below certainly thought they were.

FIFTEEN

After hours spent scouring police records, Margot and Wes had concluded that either Angela's last name was neither Good nor Hood, or she simply didn't have a criminal record under those names.

Their initial search exhausted, and with nothing more they could do for the day, they left the station. Margot set off with Wes following behind her so she could leave her car back at her apartment, and then they could drive together to her restaurant of choice.

The place was one of those hole-in-the-wall Chinese restaurants called Golden Lion where the menu was primarily in Chinese with English added as an afterthought. The decor was limited, there was a lucky cat sitting on the cash desk with its paw in the air to invite good fortune, and the tables had paper placemats advertising immigration lawyers, real estate agents, and language training centers. Here again, English was an afterthought.

The table had containers of soy sauce and chili crunch at the ready, and as soon as they were seated a waiter brought them red plastic cups and filled them with water.

A few years after her return to San Francisco, on a rare occasion when she'd been to a date's apartment, she'd stumbled across this place as she was heading home. Margot didn't eat out much. Ever. She could get delivery, thank goodness, but the biang biang noodles—wide, chewy, hand-pulled noodles—were so much better when they were fresh.

Conversation drifted over from other tables but all in Mandarin, leaving Margot feeling secure that no one was going to be terribly interested in listening in on their discussion.

They ordered the spicy pork noodles and their waiter disappeared, leaving Margot alone to finally get into what had been nagging at her all day, aside from the complexities of their new case.

She told Wes, in brief, about Justin's text—careful to call him David as she often had to remind herself to do—and then her call with Andrew this morning.

Wes sat back in the booth and took it all in, his fingers laced together over his stomach, his expression inscrutable until she finished. Then he let out a low whistle and gave his head a shake. "Damn, Margot, you really can't have just one normal month of your life, can you?"

She snorted. "What would that look like, exactly?"

"I dunno. Sunshine, rainbows, skipping through fields of flowers or something."

The waiter returned with their bowls, the noodles covered in pork, spicy oil, and bok choi. Wes watched her mix everything together with chopsticks then followed suit.

"Normal sounds boring," Margot said before taking a bite from the long noodles.

"You could probably stand to have a little boredom in your life."

Margot slurped up a noodle, glorying in the texture and the spicy kick of the oil sauce. Her tongue was burning, but she could have eaten this every day if it was reasonably healthy or convenient to do so.

"You're going to go back, aren't you?" Wes asked, taking a little more care with his noodles, since he was wearing a white shirt. Margot watched him struggle before he finally gave up and tucked a napkin into his shirt and went for it.

It was hard to feel frustrated or angry about her situation when she was eating such delicious food with such decent company. She nodded. "I don't think I have much choice. I know he's manipulating me, and I know it's stupid to let him do it, but at the same time, he's dangling something I just can't ignore."

Wes looked thoughtful as he plucked up a piece of bok choi. "What if he's lying?"

"While that's not outside the realm of possibility, I don't think he is. He hasn't lied about anything so far. He wasn't lying about more victims, and if he's implying that someone on the outside helped him, then I believe that's a real possibility. I mean, if you think about it, he killed almost eighty women before he got caught. And while I know Ed would like to believe that's because he's so much smarter than the police and the FBI, the truth is he was just very lucky. And luckier still that he committed his crimes at a time when DNA evidence was a lot less savvy and advanced than it is now. He would never have gotten away with it for so long if he was working today."

Wes lifted one shoulder. "Plenty of them are still getting away with it these days, as much as we hate to admit it."

"Well, hell, Wes, I didn't invite you here to be a Debbie Downer. I already fill that role just fine on my own, thanks."

"Sorry, sorry. And you're right, with the number of crimes he's responsible for and the amount of evidence he left behind, he wouldn't be able to do it now."

What neither of them said but both of them knew was that it wasn't that simple. Ed wouldn't have been able to commit his crimes the same *way*, but any good monster learns how to hunt around their restrictions. They learn. He would have adapted if he'd never been caught.

They ate together in silence for a bit, before Wes asked another question. "Do you have any idea who it might be?"

Margot had been thinking about this since Andrew had spoken to her.

"Ed really didn't have friends, though he did have a buddy for a while when we were younger he hung out with a fair bit. But I have my doubts about it being Jim. Uncle Jimmy."

"Uncle Jimmy?"

"Habit. That was how I knew him when I was a kid. Calling him just *Jim* feels wrong to my brain. But I haven't seen him in decades, I don't even know if he's still alive."

"Why don't you think it's him?"

"I think there's a huge risk to introducing your literal partner in crime to your family. If one of you gets caught, it makes it almost too easy to connect you together. And Ed knew full well that my mom was keeping an eye on him. If he ever got busted for anything, it wouldn't take her long to point a finger at Jim. Plus, the two of them stopped spending time together long before Ed was finished with his killing. I don't know, it just doesn't seem like the likeliest match to me."

"So who else?"

"I don't know. And I think that's the whole point. I think if it was someone I could easily guess, he wouldn't offer it up as such a tantalizing reward, because he knows me well enough to know I could probably figure it out without him."

"Maybe."

The waiter came to clear their dishes and Margot was half-tempted to place a second order to take home, but she resisted the urge.

"Not sure if that *maybe* means you're underestimating me or overestimating him." She gave him a smile to let him know she was just teasing. They paid their bill and headed back outside, but Margot wasn't in an immediate hurry to return home, and Wes seemed to sense it.

"It's been impossible to miss how tense you've been the last few months. I know we talked about him calling you. And now that he knows that hasn't ruined your life he's trying to find a new route to worm his way back in."

"I'm starting to think the only reason he called me in the first place and gave away that he had a phone, was because he wanted me to know I couldn't keep secrets from him. I'd already told him I wasn't coming back, he knew he'd lost the chance to pull the ace out of his sleeve during an interview when it would have the most impact. Dropping it in front of all those other witnesses and all. He needed it to still be flashy, dramatic. And even without an audience, I think he managed that just fine with the way he did it."

Wes nodded. They were in Mission District and it was bustling with life in the evening. Dog-friendly bars had their patios open with dogs curled up under tables while their owners shared a pint in the early night air. Salsa music spilled out of a taqueria. The Golden Lion was a holdover that belonged to another time, and different era. The Mission was decidedly gentrified, with a hipster vibe and plenty of new restaurants popping up every year. But the noodle shop stayed alive because it was exceptionally good, and because it was the only thing like it on the block.

"You want to grab a drink?" Wes said, inclining his head toward a bar they were passing.

Her gut instinct was to say no. To retreat somewhere that she was alone and safe. Because these days, the more time she spent with Wes, the more she realized she was tiptoeing toward something very dangerous, like a bomb she was afraid to set off.

It could blow up her whole goddamn life.

But sometimes Margot wondered if her life might need to be blown up.

"One drink," she said. "I don't have the best luck in bars lately."

Wes paused at the entrance and carefully scanned her face, making sure that wasn't the kind of joke with an element of legitimate trauma in it. Last night, however distant it seemed now, was still as fresh as the bruises on her throat.

She smiled at him to let him know she wasn't any more psychologically damaged than usual, and she was being honest.

While her experience with Chris Smith had shaken her, she wasn't feeling the ghost of it lingering around her anymore. Somehow a lifetime of preparing herself to be attacked by a man who wanted her dead was enough to take the edge off it actually happening.

Who said anxiety never did anyone any good?

This bar was wildly different from the one she'd been at last night anyway. It had a distinctly Mexican theme, with colorful accents and bowls of salsa and free chips dropped off the moment they sat down. The music was modern pop, but that didn't dampen the vibes. The whole place was bustling with life, making her feel miles away from the dive where she'd been playing the victim.

"What'll you have?" Wes asked, getting up to go to the bar.

"I'd normally say a gin and lime, but I feel like I'm going to have to go for a margarita. When in Rome, and all that."

"Spicy?"

"Abso-fucking-lutely."

He grinned and headed off, leaving Margot to people-watch. Without his familiar presence, in a matter of seconds her mood shifted and she felt the lurking fingers of fear tickle the back of her neck. She was out, she was alone, this was when people took advantage.

But no. That was someone else's voice, someone else's warning. A quick look around the room told her everyone here was having fun, people were laughing, a girl at one of the tables was wearing a *Bride* sash, which reminded Margot it was a Saturday.

Weekends tended to have no meaning to her, since her shifts could fall anytime throughout a week. People didn't die on weekdays only, after all. She took a few steadying breaths and focused on the song—which she knew, even if she didn't like it—and the people having a good time around her.

Statistically speaking, the likelihood of anyone in this room knowing who she was, aside from Wes, was slim to none. She didn't frequent the Mission, she was older than almost everyone here, and she didn't socialize.

Dr. Singh's voice pushed its way through the nagging one in her head. "And if no one here knows you?" he would ask.

Then no one here reasonably would want her dead.

Ed would tell her it didn't matter, that a stranger can do as much damage as a known quantity. But Margot now understood that simply wasn't the case. She had been a cop for a long time, and the truth about murder was that it was almost *always* someone the victim knew.

Like Angela.

She knew the man who had done this to her. They might not be a couple, or even friends, but he was someone she knew well enough to be in a car with. She trusted him, as much as someone can trust a john, and look where it had gotten her.

Wes returned just as her mood was properly souring and set a tumbler of green liquid down in front of her. The rim was edged with salt and Tajin and Margot could smell the tequila before she even took a sip.

Tequila wasn't usually her preferred drink of choice, but the marg was good. Strong, but tasty. Wes must have asked for something top shelf, because the tequila was too smooth to be run-of-the-mill Jose Cuervo.

"Thanks," she said after the first sip.

He'd ordered the same thing, which surprised her for some reason. She'd expected him to get a beer, or maybe be a rebel and get a whiskey, but he seemed to be enjoying the margarita as much as she was.

He was constantly full of surprises.

They let their conversation drift from discussions of their caseload, of Ed, of the documentary series, and onto more normal things Margot imagined two people might talk about over margaritas on a Saturday night. Wes shared photos of his nieces and nephews. Margot actually had recent photos of her nephew to show. She hadn't met the baby yet and he was almost two years old, but until Justin and his ex mended some fences Margot thought it was unlikely there would be any big family holiday plans being made anytime soon.

Wes was careful to avoid topics of childhood—he knew it was a minefield for Margot—but he did talk about the dog his sister had just adopted who the whole Fox clan was convinced was a reincarnation of their beloved family Yorkie, Oliver.

Margot opted not to share the story of her only childhood pet, a hamster named Phillip who had disappeared shortly after she'd gotten him.

Yet another memory her father had managed to ruin.

"I really needed this," Margot admitted as they left the bar. The street was still bustling with people, everyone enjoying the unexpectedly warm and clear night after the clouds from earlier had moved along.

"Margot, you know it's OK to want to hang out, right? I'm always happy to listen, or give advice that you'll ignore, or whatever you need. But if you just want to get noodles, that's OK too. I'll still say yes." Wes looked at her as he held his passenger door open and she felt her face flush, uncertain if she was being called out for something, or if he was simply trying to be nice.

"O-OK."

He stared at her for a moment before giving his head a shake and shutting the door on her, then getting in the driver's side.

"We're friends," he continued, buckling his seat belt. "You know that, right? You know I care about you more than just as my partner. I would hope that was obvious enough by now."

Margot felt a lump forming in her throat. She knew Wes wasn't pushing her, he was only trying to be kind, but she suddenly felt like she was being backed into a corner, and her default reaction in moments like this was to panic.

Her pulse quickened and her head began to pound. She tried to take calm, steadying breaths, because she didn't need Wes to realize that words meant to comfort her had somehow triggered the exact opposite reaction.

Unfortunately for her, Wes Fox was *also* a very good detective.

They pulled up in front of her building and her hand itched to grab the door handle.

His hand touched hers, but pulled back when she jerked away. She hadn't meant to, but she hadn't been expecting the touch. "Sorry," she whispered.

"No, I'm sorry." He sighed, and the one sound carried a lot of different emphasis. Frustration, empathy, so many things it could have and probably did mean all at once.

Margot let out a breath to steady herself, because she knew him well enough to know that if she got out of the car without saying something, she was doing just as good a job of ruining what they had as she would if she decided to sleep with him.

There was more than one way to kill a friendship, and that was the last thing she wanted to do here.

She needed him.

She put her arm across the distance and took back the hand he'd pulled away, giving it a firm squeeze. Despite the fact that her pulse was still running a mile a minute and her fight or flight was telling her to get the hell out of here, for once she wasn't going to listen.

Because this was not a dangerous situation, and she needed to learn that not everything was life or death.

"I think my two most natural responses right now would be to bolt from the car without saying goodnight, or to make a joke out of this because sarcasm is the second easiest thing for me aside from avoidance. But both of those things would be sad and pathetic and I like to think I'm a tiny bit tougher than sad and pathetic."

Wes's face was mostly obscured in darkness, but she saw his lips turn up in a smile. She could feel his eyes on her.

"Wes, you are quite possibly the best friend I've ever had. And I don't want that to go to your head, because as you might have noticed, I do not have all that many friends."

"Sarcasm," he warned.

"I'm not sure that counts as sarcasm if it's just a fact."

At that he laughed. "Fair enough."

"I want to be able to ask you to dinner without having an excuse. And I'm going to work on it. But it also scares me, because I'm not used to needing people, and…" She sighed and broke eye contact, glancing out her window.

Then she lost her train of thought.

"Margot?"

"Justin?" She narrowed her eyes, looking through the glass doors into her lobby, where a familiar figure was sitting on one of the couches.

"Who's Justin?" Wes asked, obviously confused by the sudden turn their heart-to-heart was taking.

"My brother," Margot whispered.

SIXTEEN

Margot insisted on going in alone, but the second she hit the lobby, she wished she'd asked Wes to stay with her. She was so accustomed to compartmentalizing her personal life and her professional life that it didn't even occur to her she might want some moral support for what was about to come.

She loved her brother, and she was glad to see him, but she also knew he hadn't come all this way unannounced on a purely social call. That wasn't how they operated. He was aware she needed time to adjust to the idea of having someone in her space.

He could also rarely afford to make the trip without a little help from her financially.

She thought of all the pleading text messages she'd ignored over the years, practically begging for her to listen about some movie or series that was being made about their father. By this point he should have known better. But for some reason this one had been a real bug up Justin's ass.

He couldn't have come all this way merely about *that*, could he? Justin lived in Arizona now, and while that wasn't *far* it wasn't exactly a quick trip.

As she walked through the doors, Brody, the night concierge, looked up. "Evening, Ms. Phalen. I know he's been a guest before, but you do have instructions not to let anyone up without permission except for Mr. Fox, so I asked him to wait here until we could reach you."

Margot was surprised she had missed Brody's calls, but she had been otherwise occupied. Maybe it was a good thing she'd been too distracted to let this ruin what had almost been a nice night.

She could see at a quick glance why Brody might have been hesitant to let Justin come upstairs without permission. Her brother looked like shit. He was pale with dark bags under his eyes and his skin had a sallow almost waxy sheen to it. He sported several days' worth of stubble on his gaunt cheeks, and the moment she got within ten feet of him she could smell the radiant stink of booze wafting off of him.

Jesus, so he'd definitely fallen off the wagon, then. But was it just booze, or was it something harder as well?

"You want me to call anyone, Ms. Phalen?" Brody seemed like he might have been poised to call the police already, but Margot had arrived before he'd made that decision. She was glad he hadn't, but a teeny tiny part of her almost wished he had. That would have given her brother time to sober up before she had to deal with him.

It would hardly be the first time he'd had to sleep one off in a drunk tank somewhere.

"No thanks, Brody, I've got this." She came to stand in front of her brother. "Ju— David you have to get up, OK? I don't want to have to carry you upstairs."

Justin turned his glassy eyes toward her as if only now realizing she had entered the lobby. A molasses-slow smile turned up the corners of his mouth. "Heyyyy," he slurred, and his head wobbled slightly.

Margot sighed. She couldn't leave him sitting out here, he

would probably end up throwing up all over Brody's nice couches, and that would certainly get taken out of her damage deposit.

"Come on, bud, I've got you." She helped pull him to his feet, surprised by how much dead weight he could manage to be for having such a slight frame. He let her lead him to the elevator, though he literally dragged his feet the whole way. Margot gave Brody her most apologetic smile as they passed. She knew this would get reported to the building's owner in the morning, and Margot hated the idea that her brother's presence might reflect poorly on her otherwise perfect tenancy. She didn't want to have to look for a different apartment. She could never afford another building that offered what this one did.

Her building's owner was a kind man, but he also had his own rigid sense of what was proper.

Margot got Justin into her apartment without any issues. He was thankfully a very somber drunk, not prone to any fits of joviality or other kinds of outbursts. She had to lean him up against her wall to get all her locks open, but when she finally got him onto her couch, he seemed to be half asleep.

"What are you doing here?" she asked once her locks were engaged again.

She had the burning desire to pour herself a cold gin, but she knew it wouldn't mix well with the margarita, and just looking at her brother made alcohol seem considerably less interesting.

However, a Xanax *did* seem like an idea she didn't want to say no to, especially given that she'd already been on the cusp of a panic attack even before Justin showed up at her door. She went to the cabinet above her fridge and grabbed a familiar bottle. She'd been reaching for it more often the last few months, when something as innocuous as a ringing phone could set her anxiety off.

This was definitely not turning out to be a low-anxiety week.

Justin's head was lolling, his chin dropping down to his chest before jerking back up almost violently. He blinked rapidly, desperately trying to feign alertness before his chin would begin to droop again.

Margot sighed. There was no sense in interrogating him right now, he was more than useless and any answers she got from him would be colored by the liquor in his system.

"Lay down," she instructed, pushing his shoulder to tip him gently to the side. He went without any effort. She undid his shoes, putting them by the front door, then folded his legs up on the couch and put a crocheted blanket over top of him. He was already snoring.

"God, J, he did a number on you, too, didn't he?" Their father might not be out in the world causing harm anymore, but that didn't mean the lingering effects of his presence weren't still coloring their day-to-day lives. Margot pinched the bridge of her nose, trying to pretend the migraine she felt coming on wasn't real and that if she ignored it she might be able to get a proper night of sleep herself. That thought almost made her laugh, because there was no way she was going to get any kind of real sleep tonight and she knew it.

She left her brother sleeping on the couch and headed into the bathroom, desperate for a shower that might hopefully shake her free of the feeling that was clinging to her, or better yet, might lull her into a calm enough state that she could close her eyes briefly.

Maybe.

She stripped down and caught a glimpse at her reflection in the mirror. The bruises on her neck were now almost black, with halos of greenish yellow on the edges. When she pressed a finger to one of them, she was surprised by how tender the skin felt under the pressure. Margot grimaced, then got into the shower.

Ten minutes later she felt cleaner on the outside, if no more refreshed on the inside. She settled into bed and checked her phone where a message was waiting from Wes.

> Everything OK

She paused, struggling with how best to answer that question. Wes had gone out of his way tonight to tell her that he was her friend, he was there for her. Lying wasn't going to be necessary, though her shame over Justin's condition made her consider dampening the truth. She hadn't told Wes about her brother's constant struggles with addiction.

> No. But I think it will be.

> You need anything?

Margot smiled wryly to herself.

> If there are any more surprises this week I might need a temporary vacation in a padded room, but no, right now I've got it all handled.

Three dots appeared, then disappeared. Appeared again, then vanished. He was reconsidering whatever it was he wanted to say.

> Good night, see you in the morning. I'll make your coffee a double.

> What would I do without you?

He didn't reply, but she knew the answer.
She didn't want to find out.

SEVENTEEN

1993

Desolation Wilderness, California

"Why aren't we taking the regular trail?" Justin asked, his voice high-pitched, edging toward tears in a way that made Ed grit his teeth.

Ed had taken him into the trees after they packed up their tent, and now they were traipsing through rocky underbrush, moving adjacent to the trail but not on it. Ed wanted to be able to see anyone walking, but have them not see him.

Unfortunately, a whining child would ruin any element of surprise that he had won by moving into the limited treeline that thickened as they moved down the rocky slope. Justin had been huffing and puffing the whole way, and now he was adding bitching and moaning to the mix.

"This is supposed to be an adventure," Ed reminded him.

"I think the path was pretty adventurous," Justin countered.

It wasn't talking back, *per se*, and Ed had wanted his son to learn to have a backbone, but he still came up short, turning to face the boy. Justin seemed to realize he'd made an error, overstepped, and he stopped walking, staring up at his father with a pinched expression on his face like he was flinching away from something that hadn't happened yet.

Ed didn't hit his kids, never had, so he wasn't sure where this fear was coming from. He knew what it was like to have a parent hurt him, to be vicious and degrading. He could see little bits of his mother sneaking through sometimes, with sharp words, insults that could cut, but he would never raise a hand against his children.

He stared at Justin for a long time, until the boy seemed to realize that nothing bad was about to happen to him and his whole body physically sagged. The boy said nothing, though Ed thought an apology was owed, but when none came he let it go.

"I want you to learn to be strong, Justin. I know you think this is pointless, that I'm a prick for bringing you out here and you'd rather be at home watching cartoons or playing with your friends. I know this isn't something you wanted to do, but there are lessons from my life I want to give you, things that I think will make you a better man, a more confident man. And to do that, the path isn't always going to be an easy one, do you understand what I'm telling you?"

Justin nodded. There was a thin sheen of tears in his eyes and his lower lip was wobbling. Ed wanted to shake him until he could be a functional human, but he didn't think that would work for his son.

"Do you want to know why we're taking this route instead of the main path?" Ed crouched down so he was eye to eye with the boy. The change in perspective showed him how small and delicate his son really was. There was so much Kim in him that Ed almost couldn't look at the kid for too long because her judgmental eyes might start glaring back at him.

Justin just looked at him, not bothering to answer, because he knew Ed would keep going.

"I want you to learn to see people before they see you."

A look of confusion clouded the boy's features, his brows forming an animated V-shape. "What?"

"My uncle Stewart taught me when I was your age that one of the greatest defenses a man can have is the ability to hide in plain sight. To be able to see those around you without being noticed yourself. He told me it was the best way to assess risks, to know how to approach a scenario, because you already know what to expect." Ed's gaze bored into Justin's and the boy seemed to sense that he had to say something or risk frustrating his father more.

Ed wasn't a man of many words, usually, so when he spoke this much, he expected anyone listening to be paying attention.

"W-we're watching the trail?" he asked.

Ed patted him on the shoulder. "Exactly. Because we know that whoever is out there is probably on a nice hike like we are, but that isn't always going to be the case, is it? Sometimes there might be someone behind you who means you harm, or someone waiting around the bend looking for people not paying attention."

Ed was, in fact, counting on the people ahead of him on the trail to not be paying attention.

"OK." There was an edge of fear to Justin's tone now and he turned to look behind them, like he thought a madman might be just around the last tree.

"Hey." Ed took hold of his chin, forcing the boy to look at him directly. "You're safe with me, OK? This is just practice. For today I don't want you to think there's anything out there. For today I want you to repeat after me, are you ready?"

Justin nodded.

"I'm the scariest thing in nature."

Justin's nose wrinkled and Ed thought he might laugh, but instead he puffed out his little chest and did as he was told.

"I'm the scariest thing in nature."

"One more time, a little louder." Ed wasn't worried about

being heard, he assumed the girls were still a mile or more ahead of them.

"I'm the scariest thing in nature!" Justin crowed, an unexpected smile breaking out over his face.

Ed grinned back at him.

"And don't you ever fucking forget it, kid."

EIGHTEEN

Margot woke to the sound of rattling in her kitchen and for one horrifying moment she forgot there was someone else in her apartment. Someone she knew. She had reached for her gun before the events of last night came back to her.

Stupid, she chided herself.

She got out of bed and wrapped her big robe over her usual pajamas before heading out into the main living area of the apartment. Justin was up, the blanket she'd put over him in a heap on the floor, and he was milling around the kitchen opening cabinet doors and looking in the fridge multiple times as if he thought closing and opening the door might make food magically appear within.

When he turned his head he jumped, clearly startled, and held a hand to his chest. He started to chuckle. "My God, you scared the shit out of me."

Justin looked so much like their mother, Kim, it sometimes made Margot's heart hurt to look at him. He had her soulful dark eyes, her sandy hair. Lately he also seemed to have the same lost look about him that their mother had right before she gave up on everything, and that spooked Margot when she recognized it.

She'd been pushing him away the last month or so, annoyed by his request, but seeing him in person she realized that he'd needed her and she'd ignored him. What if she'd ignored him when his self-destructive tendencies were at their worst? They'd already lost their mother to her personal demons, she didn't want to risk losing Justin, too.

The last few years had been hard on him. He'd bounced around jobs, been sober and then very much not sober, gotten into a long-term relationship, had a baby, then had his girlfriend leave him because he was so volatile. Not violent, just unreliable.

Sure, he was an adult and it was his life to mess up.

But he was still her baby brother, wasn't he?

"Why are you standing there like a ghost, and why don't you have any food? You always have food when I visit, is this how you normally live?" He glanced back at the fridge.

Margot felt the moment of reflection pass and her scowl deepened. "*Normally*, I know when you're coming to visit, and I plan ahead to have food. *Normally*, I'm too busy with work to let things rot in my fridge, so I tend to eat takeout. There's a frozen dinner in the freezer if you're hungry." She moved over to the couch and angrily picked up the blanket from the floor and folded it, putting it back in its place over the arm of the couch.

She fluffed her throw pillows like they were hostile witnesses.

"OK, so you're obviously pissed." Justin opened the freezer and took out the TV dinner she had inside. The box was covered in ice crystals. Justin wrinkled his nose but wisely said nothing and just dusted the ice into the sink.

"Now why would I be pissed? Would it be because you showed up unannounced? Or maybe because my little brother who is *in recovery* was drunk off his fucking ass and couldn't even walk himself up to my apartment? The night manager was this close to calling the cops on you." She held her fingers a tiny bit apart.

Justin didn't have the common decency to look embarrassed. He simply put his meal in the microwave. "Yeah, but you're a cop, so it would have been OK."

"You don't have a get out of jail free card just because I'm a cop, Ju— David."

He heard it, the mistake, and his shoulders stiffened, but he didn't call her out on it.

Margot knew it wasn't fair, that she had moved on from her old name but she simply couldn't make her brain let go of his. He'd been David for decades longer than he'd been Justin, but for her she wasn't sure she'd ever be able to make the mental switch.

"You didn't answer my texts, and the production company wants an answer. I thought if I came to see you in person I might be able to convince you it was a good idea."

"It's *not* a good idea. We shouldn't be giving him the time of day, let alone helping glorify his legacy." She wasn't sure she had the energy to humor this argument again. He knew how she felt about these things.

Justin stopped what he was doing and braced his hands on the counter of the peninsula between them. Margot could tell he was just as angry as she was, but that only made her madder. What right did he have to show up, disrupt her life, and then get mad at her for calling him out on it?

She wasn't their mother; she wasn't going to handle him with kid gloves.

"You're not even going to hear me out? Somehow, it's fine for you to go visit him, but it's not OK for me to even talk to you about this project? I think if you listened to what they were saying—"

"Going to *visit* him? I'm not having lovely little afternoon chats with Dad, David. I'm going there because he fucking *murdered* dozens of women and I'm trying to help find justice for the victims he kept hidden. We're not having a goddamn family reunion. What, do you *want* to go see him?"

Justin wouldn't look at her, he stared down at his hands, his knuckles white. If it had been anyone else, Margot might have been afraid of his anger, but she just couldn't be scared of him.

She'd used up all the fear she had for her family a long time ago.

"You do, don't you? You want to see him."

He shook his head, and the beeping from the microwave provided a momentary distraction for both of them to regroup and chill out a little. Justin got his meal out, peeling back the plastic film, and he pulled out a fork to eat it while standing at the counter.

Margot sat in the armchair next to her couch so she could see him still, but simply by sitting down she felt less combative.

"I don't want to see him," Justin said finally, poking at a macaroni noodle. "That's not what this is about. I think the series is going to be different from everything that has been made before, this group is different. I feel like they really want to hear our side of things."

She picked up a pillow off the couch, needing something to do with her hands. "They don't want our side. Us being human helps make him human by extension. They'll just twist whatever we say to make us look stupid for not realizing sooner. They'll make Mom look bad. You've seen all the other ones, you know how this goes."

Justin pushed his food around in the plastic container. "I talked to the producers personally. Everything they've said makes me believe they want a full and honest portrayal of what happened."

"We know what happened. Why would you want to relive

that on camera for millions of people to watch? Is it the money? I can give you money." She didn't have a ton in her savings account, but surely he couldn't need that much to get his life back on track again. A few thousand? What could these snake oil salesmen be offering him?

"It's not that, Margot. I mean, sure, there's money involved, but that's not the reason I want to do this so badly. I'm sick of hiding. I'm sick of pretending that wasn't a part of our lives. Aren't you tired of living a lie?"

She laughed, but it was a hollow, ugly sound. "How is that any different than the lie we were living when we were still under his roof? It's all lies. At least *this* lie I'm in control of."

He set down his fork. "Do you know how that sounds? It's insane."

"I'm not going to do the interview. I won't stop you if you want to, but I'm not doing it."

"They want us both."

"Then they're going to have to learn to be disappointed, or they're going to have to adjust their expectations, because I'm not going to do it. Not ever."

"This is important to me. Can't you be even a little bit flexible?"

"*Why?* What could possibly make this matter so much to you? It's not even about you, it's about him. Do you really want to live in his shadow your whole life?"

"*No*," he snarled, tossing the half-eaten tray into the open garbage can. "And that's exactly why I want to do it. So I can finally be free of him."

NINETEEN

Margot was in a bad mood.

Normally, the cup of coffee waiting for her when she arrived—a daily treat from Wes—was enough to lift her spirits if she was feeling a bit tetchy. But today, even a perfectly brewed cup of Philz wasn't doing the trick.

That meant this was a *really* bad mood.

She was self-aware enough to recognize it, even if she wasn't able to control it.

"Are you OK?" Wes asked from the desk opposite her.

"No."

He sat back. "All right, we love an honest reply."

She looked up at him and glared, and he clutched his hands to his chest like he'd been shot. "Oh shit, I picked the wrong day. Looks *can* kill."

That, at the bare minimum, made her crack a smile before she turned back to her computer screen. At least things between the two of them didn't feel fraught after their little heart-to-heart last night. The one where she'd almost had a panic attack in his car when he told her he cared about her.

Really nice, normal response. Not at all something she needed to unpack with her therapist later.

"I take it things weren't all sunshine and rainbows with your brother. You didn't know he was coming?"

She shook her head and typed her password into a database, pressing each key with furious resolve. "I did not."

"He's visited before though, right? You had him stay with you for Christmas."

"I did. But we're not really the kind of family where surprise drop-ins are welcome."

"Yeah, you don't really strike me as someone who *loves* an unexpected guest."

That made her snort.

"He's really pushing me to do that documentary I was telling you about yesterday. He's obsessed. He thinks it's going to give him some kind of release. I don't know, like it's what he needs to separate himself from Ed, but I think it's going to do the exact opposite and just keep them bound forever."

"Well..." Wes drummed his fingers on the desk and took a long pause before speaking again. "Look, is this one of those things where you want to stay mad and you don't want any outside input?"

"Now who's the one talking like they spend too much time in therapy?" Margot sat back in her chair, curious what he might be about to say. She took a sip from her coffee—enjoying it for the first time that morning—and made a *go on* gesture with her hand.

"That one was actually life advice from my sister, who told me when I was a much younger and dumber man that sometimes women just want to be mad, and you've got to let them."

"That's solid wisdom, I'm glad younger-you absorbed it."

"I'd love to tell you I always remember it, but I don't."

"All right then, if I did want your perspective on this, what would it be?"

"It's just that—whether you see it as closure or not—you've been able to talk to Finch since the arrest and trial. You've been able to see him, to tell him to his face to go fuck himself, all those lovely cathartic things your brother hasn't been able to do."

"I'm not sure if I'd call my meetings with Ed *cathartic*, they're more *traumatizing*, but I can kind of see what you're getting at."

"I read all the letters Finch sent you, remember? The ones even you haven't read. All I know is that if your brother has been getting anything like that, then he probably has a lot of pent-up feelings about your father and nowhere for them to go. Maybe he sees this documentary as a way of finally talking back to your father in a way that he can't talk back."

Margot nursed her coffee, keeping an eye on Wes but not replying right away. She chewed the plastic lid on her cup, her mind processing his words and trying to put them into context with her reality.

Surprisingly, she found that she wasn't pissed off anymore.

But that anger had been replaced with a painful sadness.

"The letters were pretty bad, weren't they?" She'd only read one, selected by Wes, because it had contained information about Ed's second wife, Rhonda. But there had been dozens of other letters that had all sat unopened in her closet for decades.

Wes lifted a shoulder. "They weren't warm and fuzzy thoughts from dear old dad, I'll say that. He certainly has a high opinion of himself."

Margot laughed—really laughed—for the first time all day.

"A narcissistic sexual psychopath having a high opinion of himself. Imagine that."

Wes smiled. "I don't recommend reading them."

"I won't. But you're right. I don't think Justin... David... I don't think David would have been able to resist it."

Margot thought about her own statement for a long moment, her fingers drumming on her coffee cup. She had taken a very specific approach to Ed and their connection to him: no contact. She didn't read his letters, didn't accept phone calls—until recently—and didn't let her lawyer share anything with her that she didn't request. He had passed things along to her over the years just in case, letters, notes that might have some legal use later, but she kept all of that in bankers' boxes in her closet and tried not to think about it.

It had simply never occurred to her to ask her brother what he'd been doing with his own letters and documents. Obviously he was more willing to speak to crackpots about their books and TV shows, but for some reason Margot hadn't imagined Ed writing Justin any letters. She'd noticed in her meetings with Ed he often behaved as if he only had one child. Margot had perhaps foolishly assumed Ed hadn't cared enough about Justin to write to him.

But maybe he had. And maybe the contents of those letters were a big part of what had shaped Justin into the man he'd become.

"God, I'm such an asshole," Margot said at last, putting her coffee down.

"Nah, you've got your own trauma to deal with. That's not selfish, it's just life." Wes offered her a small smile. "But maybe knowing it can make you go a little easier on him."

"I get that, but I'm also not going to participate in this stupid documentary."

"I would never tell you that you had to."

"Well *he's* telling me I have to."

"Is that actually what he's saying?"

Margot shot Wes a look across their desks. He was being a little *too* insightful today. "Did you talk to your therapist about me?" she asked suspiciously.

Wes laughed. "I have, as a matter of fact, but not since

yesterday. This is just perception, kid, I don't know what to tell you. But I can stop being perceptive if you want."

"Please, it's annoying when you're this self-aware. Or whatever self-awareness is when it's about other people."

"I will return to being a grunting caveman immediately. Oog, agh, boobs, beer. Oohooh." He mimed ape-like gestures and Margot finally had to laugh for real then threw a rolled-up wad of paper at him.

"How does *anyone* find you attractive?"

"It's the face. They all run screaming when they get to know my personality."

While this was impossible for her to imagine, because she had only become *more* attracted to him as she got to know his personality, she said, "Smart women."

A knock on the door distracted her from needing to make any additional barbs, or learn any other hard truths about her relationship with her brother.

Harvey Farlane was standing in the doorway holding two cups of coffee. "You're an awfully hard woman to track down, Detective," he announced, then handed her the coffee. Margot accepted it gratefully, even though she had only recently finished the one Wes had brought her and probably didn't need any more caffeine.

"I'm not sure who started the rumor that people had to give me coffee before speaking to me, but I'd like to thank them personally." The coffee from Harvey was from Dunkin, and seeing the label seemed to appease Wes, who knew he had her preferred order down pat.

Men were silly.

"I wanted to check in and see how you were doing after that shitshow on Friday."

Margot wasn't about to start showing off battle scars in the office. She didn't need anyone's sympathy, and didn't want anyone to think she wasn't able to handle herself.

"I'm fine," she said, because anything else would be too much information.

Harvey obviously wasn't in a mood to pry, so he bobbed his head and said, "Glad to hear it. Look, I'm just stopping in because I'll be going toe-to-toe with your pal Chris in a few minutes, and so far he's been tight-lipped but also hasn't asked for a lawyer. I've leaned on him a few times, but I have a funny feeling sitting you across from him might rattle something loose."

Margot gave Wes a quick look that asked the question without words. They weren't immediately needing to go anywhere. Their victim was still alive, so a trip to the medical examiner wasn't needed, and the fire department was planning to release the car to them later that afternoon when they gave it the all-clear to be searched safely.

So for the moment, rather than looking up possible iterations of Angela's name and work on older cases, she *could* participate in the interrogation without throwing them off course.

"Be my guest. Poor motherfucker won't know what hit him." He turned his attention to Harvey. "Just so you know, when it's good cop, bad cop she is always bad cop."

"I play to my strengths," Margot countered.

"That you do," Wes agreed as she left the room with Harvey, now glad he'd bribed her with coffee first.

She'd need all the caffeine she could get to deal with the prick who'd attacked her.

TWENTY

Margot headed to the interrogation rooms. She'd spent hours in those rooms, learning to decipher body language, tone, everything that could help her pick the weak points in suspects' stories and goad them into giving her the truth.

Chris Smith wasn't her suspect, though, which did complicate things. She had enough information about his case to know why she'd been asked to participate in the undercover sting, but she wasn't a detective on his case, she didn't *know* him the way she knew her own suspects.

Maybe that would help her, though. Because right now the only preconceived notions she had about him were the ones she'd gained with his hands around her throat.

She and Harvey stood in the observation room, watching him. He looked placid, unconcerned. His hands were neatly folded and resting on the tabletop, and he stared straight ahead. There was no nervous fidgeting, no clock-watching.

"Was he like this for all your other interviews?" Margot asked.

Harvey nodded. "He's irritatingly chill."

"I know the type." She took a long sip of her coffee even

though it was too sweet. "What are you trying to get out of him right now?"

"I want to know who his employer is, because we know he's not our big fish. But even just getting him to admit he was using those girls would help us keep him locked up for a long time. His assaulting you means he's not going to be on the street again anytime soon, but maybe you can work that angle, like if he talks you won't press charges."

Margot snorted. "Fat fucking chance of that. I'm already in line to testify the second the DA calls me and I'll be there with bells on. But I get you. He doesn't need to know that."

"Exactly."

"All right, let me see what I can do. But no promises. This guy hates women, he's not going to be as shaken by me as you're hoping."

"I'm not so sure about that. I think it's worth a try."

"I'm always willing to try."

Margot left the observation room. She was used to having something with her, a thick file, even if it was fake, or crime scene photos, things she could use to rattle a suspect. But all she had on her was the bruises around her neck, and that wasn't going to spook this guy. If anything he'd be proud of his handiwork.

No distractions, then. Just a true one-on-one.

Margot opened the interrogation room door, and immediately she knew Harvey had been right to try this approach. Chris's smug grin vanished and he looked around the room as if trying to determine whether or not this was a trick being played on him.

"What the fuck are *you* doing here?" he said, his lip curling. He leaned further back in his chair as she took a seat across from him.

"Oh, I just missed the pleasure of your company." She set her coffee down and took up his previous posture, her hands resting on the table's surface, staring right ahead at him. She affected a sweet smile. "You didn't miss me?"

"Fuck, I don't even know you."

"Then let's get to know each other. I think that'll be fun. See, when we first met I think we were both doing a little bit of lying. I told you my name is Jasmine, and it's not. It's Detective Phalen and I work for the homicide department."

Chris visibly stiffened. "Homicide? I didn't fucking kill anyone."

Margot quirked a brow at him, interested by the vehemence of his denial when she hadn't actually made an accusation. "No one said you did. But not for lack of trying, right?" She gave him a meaningful stare.

He shifted in his seat, suddenly unable to sit comfortably. "Where's the other guy?"

"He's busy right now, so I thought I'd spend a little quality time with you when no one else is around to bother us. Chris, you told me your name was Dustin, that was a little fib, wasn't it?" She stared at him, not moving a muscle, as he continued to squirm.

"Who cares? Are you some kind of crazy bitch? I want to talk to the other guy."

"I *am* a crazy bitch, yes. You're not the first person to mention it recently. There's some kind of a theme. Maybe I should look into that. I'll go get the other guy, Chris, but I think I'd still like to talk to you alone for a minute if you don't mind."

"I do mind."

"Well," Margot laughed and looked around the room, gesturing at the empty corners, "that's too bad, isn't it?"

Chris eyed her warily and she knew she'd hit on that fine line between a perceived threat and an active one, a place where she could happily live because it meant her suspect was uneasy but not afraid. Uneasy was usually enough to get them to say something they didn't mean to.

"What do you want?" he asked.

"I want to know where you were going to take me on Friday night?"

He shrugged, trying to regain the composure he'd had before Margot entered the room. "I was trying to take you home, I think that was pretty obvious. Unless you were too drunk to remember it."

"I think we both know I wasn't drunk."

Again he shifted in his seat, but he said nothing.

"I think we also both know you weren't planning to *just* take me home."

"I don't know what you're talking about."

"Of course you don't." She leaned back and looked at her fingernails as if her ragged cuticles were vastly more interesting than anything Chris had to offer in this conversation. Which was at least partially true. She continued to look at her nails as she spoke again. "You know, an assault record is bad. But assaulting a police officer?" A low whistle escaped her lips. "That doesn't tend to go very well for most people. Especially not with how many witnesses there were. I think a few of them might have even caught it on bodycam. Not sure there's going to be a lot that can help you there." Raising her chin, she looked across the table.

Chris was furious. His features were twisted and his hands balled in to fists on the table. She could tell he wanted to say something, but his restraint was almost commendable.

"Of course, if that police officer were to drop the assault charges, things might look a little different."

That caught his attention. He leaned back further in his chair, so far he risked tipping the whole thing backwards. "What do you want?"

"I want information."

"Isn't this bribery?"

Margot smiled and took a sip of her coffee. "Bribery would

be if I was offering to give you something in return for information. I'm not giving you anything. I'm just saying that your life would look a little different if I *didn't* press charges, that's all."

Chris watched Margot with a mix of curiosity and repulsion. He was very clearly weighing what to do next, because he knew perfectly well that his time as a free man was entirely measured on her watch.

"What do you want to know?" he said finally, after Margot had been almost certain he wasn't going to speak.

This was where Margot trod into murkier water. She didn't know the insides and outsides of this case, and calling Harvey in for an assist here would almost certainly result in Chris backpedaling and shutting down all over again. She needed to see what she could get him to own to, and what names he might drop, without really knowing what she was talking about. Her limited knowledge was entirely based on the dossier she'd read on this one man.

"Who do you work for?" she asked.

Chris smirked, snorted a quick laugh and then looked up at the ceiling.

All right, too soon for that question, then.

She pretended not to be bothered by his deflection. "You know, your loyalty is kind of admirable. Because the people you're protecting don't seem to care a whole lot that you're locked up in here. They're letting you rot. So either you don't know anything, or they know you're like a little vault. Loyal to the bitter end."

Chris lifted one shoulder in a bored half-shrug. "Or maybe there's a third option and I don't work for anyone. Maybe you're projecting a whole shadowy network onto things, and I'm really just a shitty dude that likes to pick up drunk women."

"Well, that part is true, but I think there's more to it than that."

"Maybe, or maybe you guys want everyone to be a lot bigger

and badder than they really are. Not everything is a seedy underground crime network, you know. I'm not sure what you and your buddy are looking for, but you're barking up the wrong tree."

Margot gave him a thin smile. "Then I guess you don't really have any information I need, do you?"

She let the meaning of her words linger in the air between them.

If Chris had no information, there was no reason for her to do him any favors.

"I mean, just because I'm not involved in anything doesn't mean I don't *know* anything," he countered quickly. "There's some stuff I think you guys would probably like to know."

Margot was willing to bet anything he told her now would likely be related to different groups running trafficking in the city rather than anyone he was connected with, but any information was better than him sitting on his hands pretending he was mute.

"I'm listening," she said.

"Can I get a cup of coffee?" he asked, his eyes darting toward her cup. "I mean, if you're feeling so generous about getting this information and all."

Margot shoved her cup across the table to him. "Have at it."

Chris gave her a look and she wondered if he might make a complaint about the offer, but instead he picked up the cup, his cuffs jingling, and then made a face. "Jesus, you'd think a woman who drinks this much sugar would be a little sweeter."

Margot couldn't help but laugh. "Beggars can't be choosers. Now how about you share the sweetness and tell me something worthwhile?"

Chris sighed and took another sip of the coffee, looking no less disgusted the second time around. "Look, I can't give you much, because it's my fucking ass on the line if you go flaunting this shit around OK?"

"Yes, that would be terrible."

He looked as if he might reconsider before he said, "You know the club down on Howard Street? Odyssey?"

Margot was familiar with it in a peripheral way. The club was notorious for having drugs run through it and frequent arrests were made there, but it was also one of the most popular venues in town. The two things decidedly went hand-in-hand, but it meant the police were constantly having to revisit the same place over and over. Hearing Chris mention it in this context was unsurprising.

"There's this group, they're partial owners of the club, but like, under the table, you won't find them on the letterhead. They make sure the place is bustling with girls every night, and they take home a pretty sizable chunk of the door."

"You're talking about club promoters, man. Don't waste my time." She gave an exaggerated sigh.

"No, no. Look, I know promoters, lots of promoters work that club, and the place is always packed with babes, but those are models, y'know? Girls who live in promoter apartments and have to show up to meet their monthly quota for free rent. I know the difference, babe."

Margot shot him a look and he shrank back from it; she didn't think he'd be calling her *babe* again anytime soon.

"How is it so different?"

Chris leaned closer for the first time since they'd started speaking. She wasn't sure why he was so keen to keep things hush-hush now, but she leaned in enough to humor him.

"The girls that Riga is running out of that club aren't just models. They're escorts. Buddies of his, high-rollers from all over the city, these guys will get a specific VIP package. You go in and order a specific bottle for bottle service—it changes every week—and you get the company of the girl of your choice. Full service company."

Margot raised an eyebrow at him. "Who is Riga?"

He looked startled for a moment, almost as if he hadn't realized he'd said the name. He paled and looked around the room, his mouth clamping shut.

"Oh, come on, man. You can't drop a name like that and then expect me to let it go."

"Then *you* look it up, you're the cop."

Margot snatched the half-full coffee cup back to her side of the table. "If you don't give me somewhere else to look then I'm just going to focus all my attention on you, and I don't think you want that. I bet if word got around you were talking to the police, the people you work for would be a lot more interested in collecting their pound of flesh from a rat than whoever this Riga guy is."

Chris snorted, though it was more out of surprise than derision. "Fuck, you're a homicide cop and you don't know who Riga is? That fucker must be protected better than I thought."

This comment made Margot unexpectedly annoyed with Chris. He was literally in police custody, and yet he felt like it was OK to be a little shit about which criminals he was name-dropping?

Margot chewed on her inner cheek. At least Riga was a name, no matter how she'd gotten it, and that was something more than Harvey's team had before she came into the room.

"Who is Riga?" she asked again, pretending Chris hadn't said anything.

"Riga's the fucking bogeyman. He runs drugs, guns, girls, you name it."

"And he's running girls at the Odyssey?"

"Among other places. Look, with Riga it's all fucking ghost stories. He never gets caught for *anything*. Half the shit people say about him I don't even know if it's true. I think my favorite one I heard about was this website where guys could pick their girl online, but it was disguised. So like, the page looked like it was for a women's softball league or something? And the team names were all subtle ways to tell prospective buyers what the girls were willing to do." Chris chuckled.

Margot had gone stock-still, her blood running cold.

Because the website wasn't for a softball team.

It was for rec league soccer.

And so far, at least three women on that website were dead.

TWENTY-ONE

After Margot finished with Chris, getting little else except rumors and finger-pointing, she couldn't leave the interrogation room fast enough. Harvey thanked her for her efforts, but all the sound in her ears was a constant ringing tone, as if she'd been to the firing range and forgotten to wear earmuffs.

She wanted to go back to Wes immediately, but there was someone who needed this information sooner.

Detective Leon Telly was seated at his desk as usual, a napkin tucked into the top of his shirt collar, and a loaded meatball sub laid out in front of him.

Margot plunked down into the chair beside his desk and Leon almost jumped out of his skin.

"Goddamn, Phalen, do I need to put a bell on you?"

"Maybe you should turn up your hearing aids, old man," she countered lovingly.

"Don't be rude, it's unbecoming."

Margot rolled her eyes and Leon chuckled, then lifted up the sandwich to take a big bite. Perfectly on cue, a dollop of marinara sauce plopped onto his bib. "Aw, hell," he grumbled as he put the sandwich back down.

"Hey, that's why you put the napkin on, I guess. Know your weaknesses. But maybe also don't order the messiest sandwich on the planet to eat while you're wearing a white shirt. I don't know, I'm just a detective. Deductive reasoning isn't my strong suit."

Leon licked some sauce off his fingers. "Is there something I can do for you, Margot, or did you come here to pester me?" This was said with warmth, as Leon Telly loved Margot like a daughter, and she loved him significantly more than she did her own dad.

"I might have something for you about the Redwood Killer case."

Leon groaned. "I thought we weren't going to call it that."

"I've tried, Leon, but the press have won. They've named him, and it stuck."

"It's catchy, I'll give them that. But catchy is bad for us. Makes it stick in the public's mind. We don't want that shit to stick in the public's mind."

"Don't worry, I'm sure some celebrity will say something racist on Twitter any day now and we'll have a reprieve."

Leon huffed a laugh. "What'd you find?"

Margot had gotten the last big break in the case when she'd discovered that all three of the known victims of the Redwood Killer had worked for the same escort service. They hadn't been able to definitively connect the victims before that, despite their eerily similar MOs, and the fact that all three of the bodies had been discovered in or near Muir Woods park.

Since that discovery, though, they'd been hard pressed to make any additional headway. The names of the women on the escort site were all fake, and the pictures were all duds in terms of a reverse image search to help them connect the faces to their real names. Someone had done a bang-up job of making it almost impossible to trace the group responsible for the site. The registration was a foreign shell company, none of the names attached were linked to real people they could talk to.

But now Margot had a name.

"Have you ever heard of a guy, some spectral crime figure, with the name Riga?"

Leon almost choked on the bite of the sandwich he'd just taken. He dabbed at his wiry goatee with one of the napkins in a stack beside him, then leaned way back in his chair, taking the bib napkin off and putting it in the trash. He had evidently heard of Riga, and her mentioning the name had made him lose his appetite.

"Emmanuel Riga? Where did you hear his name come up?"

Margot quickly explained about Harvey's sting, and her interview with Chris Smith, and Leon seemed to mull over each new tidbit with total focus.

"I would almost think it was total bullshit, except for him bringing up the website. Low-level thugs love to throw Riga's name around because he's basically a scary bedtime story for criminals. People would blame the Kennedy assassination on Riga if he'd been old enough at the time."

Margot bobbed her head in agreement. "I know, if he'd just said that Riga was running girls out of the club, I wouldn't have thought twice about it, I'd have let Harvey go after this Riga guy for his case. But Leon, I think we need to talk to him."

Leon was already shaking his head before she'd even finished what she was saying. "I'm guessing you've been lucky enough to not come across Riga's name in a case before."

"I've never heard of him."

"I wish I'd never heard of him. He came up for me the first time about ten years ago. Guy was shot to death over on one of the piers, really nasty situation, kind of obvious it was a hit. But when I started to dig into it, no one wanted to talk to me. Not that wild with killings like that, I guess, but anytime I did get a whisper of an answer from someone, they'd all just say they weren't going to mess with Emmanuel Riga's business. On paper the guy is above board. Clean. He owns—I kid you not—a chain of laundromats, and a few diners over in Filmore and Pac Heights. Real businesses, clean accounts. But what I've learned in the years since—and you can ask your buddy Harvey from Major Crimes—is that this guy is deep dark organized crime. Drugs, guns, prostitution, and the kind of hits that go along with that line of work. Everyone knows he's the man on top, but no one can touch him, he's that well protected."

"Like... official protection?" Margot arched a brow at him.

"I don't know how deep it goes, but I know that no one has ever been able to pin anything on him. I won't say that anyone tried to steer me away from him, but I will say that when my files went to the DA to prosecute the actual gunman on that murder, there was no trace of Riga's name anywhere to be found." His mouth was set in a tense line, telling her that he hadn't liked that any more than she would have.

That also meant it was possible Riga had protection from within the department, or likely even higher up.

Which meant they'd need to tread incredibly lightly if they were going to find a way to talk to him.

"Well, fuck," Margot said, breaking off a small piece of the meatball nearest to her. "Here I thought I was bringing us good tidings, but it sounds like it might just be one more wrench."

"Au contraire," Leon said, slapping her hand before she could go back for another bite. "You've given us knowledge. And even when that knowledge is complicated, it's still power. If Riga is connected to these murders, he's not the only person we can talk to."

Margot stole a napkin to clean her hands.

"What do you suggest?"

"You're a detective, kid. What do you think? We start from the bottom and work our way up."

TWENTY-TWO

Margot returned to her office where Wes was immersed in something on his computer, and she settled into her own desk chair, staring at her monitor briefly before realizing she wasn't seeing a single thing that was on the screen.

"How'd that go?" Wes asked, looking up over his monitor at her. "You were gone so long I thought I might need to send out a search party."

Margot offered a soft smile, but wasn't sure how to answer.

"It went... unexpectedly."

This was evidently enough to pique Wes's interest and he wheeled sideways to get a better look at her. She was accustomed to scrutiny from Wes, so the attention didn't bother her.

She quickly recapped what Chris had told her, and then what she'd learned from Leon. And evidently, she was the odd one out for never having run across Riga in her history, because as soon as she said the name, Wes let out a low whistle, his eyebrows rising.

"I think our serial killer case just got a *lot* more interesting."

Margot gave him a quick look as if to say it had been plenty interesting—and complicated—enough before adding the potential organized crime connection into the mix.

"All I'm saying is, if Riga is involved then an already tough solve probably just edged its way to almost impossible."

"I don't agree with that," she countered. "Now we have a direction. If all these girls worked for Riga in some capacity, then he very likely has a connection to why they were killed, or who killed them."

Wes shook his head, and it infuriated her. She didn't think it was naive of her to consider this a good lead, but apparently everyone else involved in the case did.

"This is a man who knows how to cover his tracks, Margot. He didn't stay out of prison for as long as he has by letting his hands get dirty."

"Well, *someone's* hands got dirty, and I think knowing this connection helps us find that person." She returned her attention to her computer, but she was so frustrated she couldn't be bothered to actually look at her email or reopen any of her databases, she just furiously clicked on things without actually accomplishing anything.

Wes seemed to realize he'd set her off, but rather than apologize for it—which would have made her more annoyed in that moment—he went back to his own work. After a few minutes she calmed down and found herself back on the soccer rec league site where she had first found profiles for two of her victims, Leanne Wu and Frederica Mercado. A third—and the first they'd found—she had connected to the others by a small bird necklace that had matched their third victim's tattoo, and the "team" logo on the site.

Margot didn't know what she was looking for, she had scoured the Larks' profiles over and over, even using an internet archive site to find old profiles that were no longer listed.

She knew all of these faces with the familiarity of high school friends she might look at in a yearbook.

What was she hoping to find by revisiting them?

As she stared into the smiling face of a cheery-looking blonde with the fake name Steph, her phone started to buzz. She checked the screen with a spike of anxiety, not sure which prospect was setting her off more, that it might be Ed or that it might be Justin.

It wasn't either of them, it was Andrew.

Since Wes was fully versed in what was going on in her life, she didn't bother leaving the room to take the call. "Hey, Andrew," she said, keeping her voice clear of all the heightened emotion she'd been dealing with that morning.

Wes lifted his head for a moment, clearly curious, but then looked back down. She had no doubt he would keep listening, though.

"Hey, Margot, I just wanted to circle back on our conversation yesterday. I talked to the prison. Finch has evidently been on a strict no-visitation list since they busted him with that phone, but they're willing to let us go in tomorrow if it's under official business. I'm not sure if we're going to get as much leeway with them as we previously did, so I'd really like to jump at this if we can."

And there it was, a full circle that brought her right back to where she'd been a few months earlier, when she'd insisted she was washing her hands of this case and she would never set foot in San Quentin prison again.

Ed had called her bluff.

And he was going to win.

She sighed, hating that her resolve was corruptible, but knowing that the reason she was giving in was not due to Ed's irresistible appeal, as he certainly wanted to believe, but because she couldn't ignore him if there actually *was* someone out in the world still connected to those crimes.

"What time?" was all she asked.

Andrew paused, like maybe he was waiting for her to

change her mind, but when she didn't say anything else, he said, "Ten o'clock. Do you want to review anything before we go?"

"No. He's not going to be led. He wants to tell us something and he's going to make it as painful and frustrating as possible for me. There's nothing I can do to prepare for that that I haven't been preparing for my whole life."

Andrew cleared his throat, at a loss for words. Margot suspected he wanted to offer her some comfort or perhaps thank her for agreeing to do the interview. He did neither of those things, though. "All right, I'll see you at ten, then." And then he hung up.

There'd been a time in Margot and Andrew's history that they'd been close. He'd been a source of comfort to her when she was younger, a man she could look to as a good example of what a father could be. Now, with their complicated recent history, things had gotten fractured between them. Andrew moved between seeing her as the girl she'd been and the woman she was, and it was difficult for both of them because he could be both patronizing and then also treat her as an equal.

Margot wasn't agreeing to the interview to appease Andrew, though, nor would she agree to the documentary for him or for Justin or for any other power under the sun. But her sense of justice was as finely honed as a knife, and if sitting down across the table from Ed might afford her an opportunity to lock someone else up, make someone *else* face a jury of their peers, then that might be worth all of the myriad ways it would suck.

At the end of the day, her job was to make the world a safer place.

So the choice was made for her.

TWENTY-THREE

It wasn't often that Margot felt like a workday was wasted, but when she got into her car to head back to her apartment, she didn't feel a sense of accomplishment.

While she had made some headway in the Redwood Killer case—at least on paper—she didn't feel any closer to solving it. Everything Leon and Wes had told her made it clear that having Riga's name was about as useless as having no name at all.

She didn't agree, but she also didn't know how to take the next steps.

And now she needed to prepare herself to return to the prison to face her father for the first time in months. Deep down she must have known she would be back, because she hadn't thrown out the outfit she normally wore.

Prison visitation rules were strict about what could and couldn't be worn. Jeans were not allowed. Khakis were fine.

As a result, Margot now hated khaki pants with the fire of a thousand suns.

But she'd kept hers.

Because somehow, she knew.

On her way home she allowed herself to do something she almost never did. She justified it by telling herself that the rarity with which she did it meant it was actually the opposite of creating a pattern. She was breaking any other standard pattern she had. She stopped for drive thru. Knowing Justin was home, and knowing he was basically helpless to feed himself—she had no idea how he managed in his own home—she grabbed In-N-Out before heading back to her apartment.

She sat in the parking garage for as long as she could before mustering up the will to go inside while the food was still somewhat hot. Justin was basically where she'd left him, forming a union with her couch and watching the Giants game on TV.

"Hey," he said, barely looking up from the TV.

Margot felt something tug at her insides as she stood in her doorway and looked at her baby brother. It was a witches' brew of feelings, things she had trouble giving name to. She loved him, but in that moment, she hated him, too. She hated him for being too weak to get through his life without her help, for still needing some kind of approval from their father, for not being a good enough father to his own son.

And in that, she pitied him, too, and pity was a feeling even worse than hate in Margot's mind. She didn't want it from anyone else, but she couldn't help but feel it for the man sitting on her couch.

He was falling apart at the seams, and no matter how many times she managed to sew him back up again, he was still going to rip himself open.

She knew he was hurting from wounds that were decades old, but she was so *mad* that he didn't seem to want to make the effort to heal them. Were her own wounds healed? No. But she still went out into the world every single day doing something, *anything*, that might help set the scales right and make her feel slightly less broken inside.

What was Justin doing?

And maybe that was part of the problem with him being here, part of the unnameable thing she was feeling. Because looking at Justin made her wonder if she was really getting any better herself, or when people looked at her, did they see what she saw in her brother?

Was she just as broken as he was?

"I brought food," she said. Her throat wasn't bothering her as much today, though she still sounded raspier than she normally did. At least now it was more Kathleen Turner, less strangulation victim.

She could handle that. The bruises were still going to be an issue, but hopefully in another day or two she'd be able to cover them with makeup rather than continuing to wear the turtlenecks.

Justin roused himself from the couch and stood across from her at the peninsula as she pulled food out of the bag and set it all out onto plates. She was surprised that he took his plate to her small dining room table rather than returning to the couch, and she decided to listen to what Wes had suggested earlier and to treat her brother with some grace.

She didn't want to ruin their meal by getting into an argument, so she approached dinner conversation with the same careful tread she used to when they were seated alongside their parents, which always felt like having a meal between two live landmines.

"What did you do today?" She kept her tone mild, friendly.

Justin dipped a skinny fry into a pile of ketchup before stuffing it into his mouth. Everything about the action made her feel like she was sitting across from a nine-year-old version of him. She could practically see him with sunburned cheeks and his hair almost white blond from the summer sun. Now everything about him was darker, emptier, but there were glimmers of who he'd once been.

"I went for a walk down to the Pier." While there were literally dozens of piers along the bay, she knew he was talking about Pier 39, Fisherman's Wharf, which was arguably one of the biggest tourist traps in the whole city. He'd been to San Francisco so often she couldn't fathom why he'd be so interested in seeing that place again, but rather than ask him she just nodded with her best smile.

"That's nice. I haven't been there in a while. Good people-watching?" The last time Margot had been there was in the aftermath of a sniper assault, and she doubted she'd ever be able to look at it the same again.

"Went to the coin game museum, you know the one by the ship?"

"The Musée Mécanique? Wow, I haven't thought of that place in *years*." The museum was housed in a large warehouse on the wharf, near an old Second World War submarine, not a ship. There *was* an old ship on the piers, but it wasn't near the coin machine museum.

The Musée Mécanique was actually a little removed from the Pier 39 area, a bit of a walk to get to, and it was such a niche museum it was actually something Margot would consider worth a visit. It housed dozens of antique coin-operated games, and someone could get lost there for hours just enjoying the sounds and humor of what had been considered the height of gaming in the twenties.

She'd been once or twice, but was surprised it was somewhere Justin would find himself in his daily wanders.

Margot finished her burger and cleared their plates, but she knew she was going to have to tell him about her plans for tomorrow—there was no way to avoid it without outright lying—and she also knew that by disclosing those plans she would open herself up to a new discussion about the documentary.

Once the dishes were finished, she considered making them both a drink to dull the edges of what was sure to be an uncomfortable discussion, but Justin was in recovery, even if he'd fallen off the wagon hard the previous day. If anything she should be locking her alcohol up.

Instead, she grabbed two cans of Coke out of the fridge and set one across from him before opening hers.

"I need to talk to you about something," she said as she watched him take a long swig.

He raised his eyebrows, then let out a burp.

She couldn't help but smile.

"What's up?" He seemed too eager, too interested, like he might believe this was her about to change her mind about the documentary. He should have known better. No positive conversation has ever started with the sentence *I need to talk to you about something*.

Margot steeled herself, playing with the little silver tab on the top of her drink can so she didn't have to look at him directly. It was cowardly, and she hated herself for it, but she was doing what she needed to do to get through this.

"I have to go see Dad tomorrow," she said, almost too quietly to be heard.

But Justin heard her just fine. "I thought you said you were done with that. Wasn't that your big stance, your moment of power over him, that you gave him one last fuck-you and walked out?" He was raising his voice a little, his tone edging into an uncomfortable kind of anger.

Somehow, even though it was uncalled-for and unfair, she'd known this would be how he'd react. He'd been weird about her visiting Ed since the first time she'd told him about it. He wanted to know if their father asked about him, if he said anything that she should be telling him.

How to tell him that Ed almost never acknowledged that he existed? How to break an already broken heart by saying that a man with nothing but time on his hands still didn't have the time of day for his only son?

Margot didn't rise to the bait in his tone. Her brother

wanted to pick a fight, and she had plenty of experience with that. They'd known each other their whole lives. The reason he did it these days was because he was positively radiant with anger, and he lashed out places he thought were safe. At people who would love him unconditionally.

His son's mother, ultimately, had enough and left him.

So now he directed it all at Margot, and right now she was willing to take it. She looked up from her drink to meet his eyes finally, and it was obvious to see that he was angry and in pain, two feelings she understood all too well. She felt them herself whenever she needed to visit Ed in prison.

But explaining to her brother that this wasn't something she enjoyed hadn't seemed to work to this point. Justin was bitter, and maybe a little jealous, that she had seen Ed in prison, while he had never been afforded the opportunity.

It was evident he felt like he had something to say to their father, and now Margot was denying him that on two different fronts.

She sighed. "I wish it had been the last time. I wish I never had to see him again. But no matter what I do to bury him in the past, he always manages to find a way to come crawling right back into the present. And I know you're mad about it, you're allowed to feel what you're feeling, I'm not going to tell you you shouldn't. But it's important that you know I don't *enjoy* these visits. The first time I went to see him I threw up in the parking lot. Whatever you think these visits are like, they aren't father–daughter bonding time. Though, who knows, that might actually be how Ed sees it. For me, I have a job to do. And it's like having my skin sliced off one inch at a time for every second I'm there, and then him salting the wounds until I can leave again. It's not *fun*, it's not cathartic. It doesn't *heal* anything in me. So if you think I go in there and get a little jolt of free therapy by sitting across from the man who ruined our lives, then I hate to break it to you, but that's just not what happens."

Justin stared at her, apparently gobsmacked, and she watched the anger on his face morph into a dozen different emotions before it went back to anger. Albeit a much dimmer version of what it had been previously.

He was still mad, but this was a low-level rage he probably managed throughout his day-to-day existence.

"I didn't know, Margot," he said finally. "You don't talk about it, not ever. I don't think you even wanted to tell me you were going."

"Can you blame me? You handle the knowledge with such a level head." She offered him a soft smile to let him know she was just poking the bear in a loving way, and this time he smiled back, though it appeared to be almost painful for him to do it.

When Margot had told Justin about Ed's second marriage—a conversation she hadn't wanted to have, but knew she couldn't avoid—he'd gone eerily quiet over the phone. He hadn't talked to her for almost a full week after that, as if somehow she was the one to blame for Ed taking a new wife.

She'd expected this conversation to go about as well as that, but was glad to see it was a slight improvement.

"Why do you go, then?" Justin asked her. "You've gone to see him so many times, if you hate it as much as you say you do, why keep going back?"

Margot took a long sip from her Coke, the fizzy bubbles going all the way to her head, making her feel momentarily woozy.

Why did she do it?

It was a question she'd asked herself every time she made the long drive from North Beach to San Quentin.

Why did she do it?

She gave Justin a smile that she knew didn't reach her eyes.

"Because, kid. Someone's got to."

TWENTY-FOUR
1993

Desolation Wilderness, California

Justin was asleep.

Ed had learned the specific cadence of sleeping breath when he'd been only a boy, because knowing that sound had often been the difference between a night of peace or getting beaten for having to get up to use the bathroom when he should have been in bed.

He knew the importance of being sure.

And he was certain his son was asleep.

The tent was the next problem, because Ed wasn't a particularly small man, and any major motion was certain to push an elbow or knee into Justin and wake him, ruining his plan entirely.

But Justin was a heavy sleeper, nothing like Megan. Megan could be woken by a sneeze in someone else's house. She was proving to be more of an issue than Kim in terms of getting home late. Between the two of them, he'd learned it was a lot easier to do his dirty work when no one was expecting him.

Right now, the women in his life weren't here.

And Justin was asleep.

The flap on the tent tied closed rather than zipped, which wasn't ideal for keeping out insects at night, but did do him a big favor now as he wormed his way forward on his belly, moving inch by precious inch, grateful he'd slept with his boots on, not just because he'd need them outside, but because the rubber soles gave him extra purchase against the slippery surface of his sleeping bag.

It took him a long time to get out of the tent. Full minutes, as he had to pause every few inches to listen for Justin, to make sure he was still asleep.

If he got caught leaving the tent, he wasn't worried. He'd tell the kid he had to pee. But then he'd be stuck. Justin wouldn't fall back to sleep after that, because he'd be nervously awaiting his father's return.

What Ed needed was the time *outside* the tent. So, to have that, he couldn't have Justin awake.

After the longest ten minutes of his life, Ed was free of the tent, free of his son, and for one perfect, wild-eyed moment, he wondered if he could just disappear into the woods and never come back. Change his name, change his life, vanish and become someone new entirely.

It wasn't the first time he'd considered it.

In a lot of ways it would make his life easier, not to be tethered to his wife, his kids, and the crushing expectations put on him by the path he'd chosen for himself when he was barely old enough to call himself a man.

But every time Ed considered it, he knew he wouldn't follow through. For one thing, there was Megan. He simply couldn't do that to her. He knew how girls turned out when they had no father in their lives, and he didn't want that to happen to her.

Second, it made things easier in a lot of ways to have a family. Sure, they could frequently put a damper on his plans, but the truth of the matter was, people didn't give a second look to a man with a family. A guy with a wife and kids and a mortgage, he was safe. Steady.

If someone died or went missing, the cops didn't turn their immediate attention to a doting husband and father.

What happened below the surface didn't matter, as long as the image was upheld.

If Ed ran off and started a new life on his own somewhere, he'd be the new man in town, the single guy, the one whose history wasn't known. An easy and obvious target for pointed fingers.

Right now he was just Ed, he mowed his lawn every Saturday morning just like half the other dads on his block. He had a BBQ apron he'd received for Father's Day that read *Chillin' for a Grillin'*, and while he didn't really *get* the joke, he wore it every time he grilled. He would fix his kids' bike tires in the driveway and wave to his neighbors as they passed.

Ed was above suspicion.

He had picked up on the fact that his wife had her own doubts about him, but so far she hadn't come anywhere near to figuring out what it really was he did in his spare time. But because she was such a hawk about it, he hadn't been able to hunt nearly as often as he would have preferred.

He wasn't going to do anything to these girls, not with Justin so close by, but that didn't mean he couldn't watch them for a little bit. Chase that thrill of being near someone when they had no idea he was within arm's reach. It wasn't the ultimate satisfaction he craved, but it would scratch the itch a little.

Might be nice to know he still had it.

It wouldn't do to let his skills get rusty, because who knew when an opportunity might present itself. He had to be ready.

He *couldn't* kill these girls out here because it would be too obvious. People knew where he and Justin were hiking, there would be questions asked, attention pulled in their direction. This was just a hunt, and not the kill.

They'd trailed the women all day, just out of sight. He didn't think Justin had caught on to what they were actually doing. All the while, Ed had imparted little bits of wisdom he'd gleaned from his own hikes with Uncle Stewart. He pointed out various piles of scat, explaining to Justin how to tell the difference between the rabbits' pellets, the hairy remnants from a wolf, the impossibly large plop from a bear. Ed pointed to where a number of feathers had all fallen together, and explained how it likely indicated that a hawk or other bird of prey had managed to catch and pluck a songbird.

Justin hadn't liked that one, particularly, but that was the circle of life.

"Everything dies," Ed had explained. "Just some deaths can be a little more violent than others. That's OK. We might not understand it, but hunters need to kill to live, that's just part of nature."

Justin had nodded his understanding, and poked around in the fallen feathers, collecting an especially pretty one to add to his pack. Ed noticed Justin had taken a lot of tokens over the days they'd been hiking. A rock that had quartz in it, a large pine cone, and now the feather.

Ed was never one to deny the boy a trophy, even though the rule of the land was to take nothing with you, Ed didn't particularly see the harm. A feather and an acorn that would mean something to the boy were not going to be missed.

Now that it was night and he was alone, he couldn't help but think about what he'd told Justin and how it had been more true than the boy could ever know.

Hunters need to kill to live.

He felt those words deep in his bones.

Overhead, the sky managed to be both dark and bright, the black tapestry punctuated by an impossible number of stars.

The air smelled of cedar and pine, and damp earth, things that made Ed feel more animal than human.

He'd already figured out where the girls were camping when he ventured out under the guise of gathering kindling for their fire. They had their tent set up about a half mile up the trail, in a little clearing near the water. It was a nice spot, picturesque.

The running water of the river would also go a long way to cover any noise Ed made as he approached, a bonus gift from the heavens.

Though it was late, the fire was still burning. They had strung their T-shirts and bikini tops over the guyline of the tent, and Ed's fingers itched to reach out of the darkness and snag one of those too-small triangle tops.

But no, it was too risky, and what good would it do him? He couldn't take it home.

He crouched in the bushes, and moved slowly, so slowly he made no perceptible sound, and the girls were too busy chatting to be listening. There were two of them, one plump with blond hair and the kind of compact figure that told him even though she was stocky, she was strong. A real dairy maid, farm girl type. The other was tall and slim, her black hair cropped into a boyish cut that Ed would normally find unattractive, but for her it managed to make her face look almost otherworldly in its arresting beauty.

Ed wondered what she would look like crying, and the thought of it was almost enough to make him hard.

They had taken their hiking boots and socks off, the socks placed a bit too close to the fire, but neither of them seemed worried about it. Each of them had a can of beer in their hands, and they were laughing at something Ed hadn't heard in his approach.

Though they were not afraid to be heard, they also seemed to have some respect for the woods, and for anyone else they might not know was around. They kept their voices low, like every word was a secret, and Ed couldn't make out the words, just the tone.

It was all light, fun. They were enjoying themselves out here, in the prime of their lives.

They had no idea someone was sitting only yards away, watching their every movement, mentally cataloging all the ways it might be possible to incapacitate them both without them getting the chance to scream.

He had intentionally come unprepared, with only his pocket knife on him. He knew if he'd brought a real blade with him, the temptation to use it might prove to be more than he could resist.

Right now, watching the women dip their heads close together as they sipped their beer and shared trail stories, he knew he'd been right to avoid the risk.

They were just making it so easy. He was astonished at the frequency with which women made themselves easy to kill. An open window on a hot night, a sliding door with a broken lock, walking home alone in the dark, putting a thumb up to hitchhike. The latter was happening with less and less frequency, but there were still enough women out there putting themselves at risk that Ed never had to work too hard for the thrill of the hunt.

Weak prey would always exist.

These two young women had probably come out here for a few days in the woods to get away from it all. Maybe they were ditching their boyfriends for the weekend. Hell, maybe they were dykes, Ed didn't care. But what they were was oblivious.

They might have protected themselves against bears, against bugs, but they hadn't thought to protect themselves against him.

He watched them for a long time. Longer than he should have. When they finally climbed into their tent for the night, Ed shook off his stupor and left the protective cover of his bush to go back to Justin and his own tent.

Even though he had only watched the girls, the heady rush of the opportunity was still there. He felt high, euphoric, because he knew if he'd *wanted* to, he could have butchered both those women as they slept.

Ed climbed back into his tent, less careful about jostling things, as it wouldn't matter if he was caught now, he could easily just lie about going to the bathroom.

Just as he was getting settled back into his sleeping bag, Justin stirred beside him. "Where were you?" the boy asked, his tone pinched, tense.

"Taking a dump," Ed replied crossly, annoyed the boy would even question him, though he'd been prepared for it.

Justin was quiet.

As Ed lay staring at the canvas roof of the tent, his thoughts were not of the girls, or the gratification of sinking a knife all the way to the hilt in their sunburnt skin.

Instead a new thought was haunting him.

How long had the boy been awake?

TWENTY-FIVE

Margot had already told work she would be in late. They understood she worked alongside the FBI, and no one made a stink about it. The only people who needed the detail were Wes and her captain, and they both knew who she really was.

If anything, the captain felt bad for her, that she had to keep doing this.

Wes probably felt similarly, but knew her well enough not to show it.

Instead, he said, "Bring us back some lunch when you're done."

His smile had said more than his words, and Margot got that he cared, he was just giving her a way to avoid talking about it.

Margot had never known anyone who understood her the way Wes did. Most people started to get a look at the psychological mess lurking under the cool and collected surface, and they went running for the hills. So after a while, she just stopped showing people the mess. She stopped showing them anything at all. There'd been a time she would let herself enjoy a one- or two-night stand, purely for the release of it, but in the past few years even that desire had fallen by the wayside.

Margot didn't like to get close to people, because she didn't like to lie, but she also didn't want to show them the ugly truth of who she was.

And then came Wes. Wes, who knew the truth. Wes, who had seen her meltdowns, her freak-outs, her avoidance. He knew what was buried under the surface.

He hadn't run.

Not that he could leave their partnership, it had been mandated from above. But he could have pulled away a thousand times, kept things purely professional, ignored all the other messiness.

Instead, he just kept getting closer, letting himself get into the muck with her, and helping pull her back out.

Guys like that didn't come along often.

People like that didn't come along often.

It was terrifying.

But it gave Margot something new to worry about, and there was a weird kind of thrill to being worried about something that was *good* for her. It gave her a new topic to delve into with Dr. Singh, and frankly she thought even her therapist was happy about a change of discussion.

Margot was familiar with the route to the prison, she'd driven it often enough by now. When she'd gotten up that morning to dress and leave, Justin had been asleep on the couch, an arm cast over his eyes, the other drooped off the side of the sofa, his mouth open and a thin dribble of drool at the corner of his mouth.

Again, she was struck by how young he looked, and how there were times he didn't seem like he'd ever been touched by the truth of what their father had done.

Maybe she looked like that in her sleep, too.

He knew where she was going, but she left a note anyway, along with forty dollars in cash telling him to go out and enjoy the city, that they'd talk more when she was back from work that night.

They still hadn't settled things about the documentary. Margot had decided while trying and failing to sleep that she would at least offer to hear out the producers. She knew her answer would still be no, but at least she could tell Justin that she'd listened and declined from an educated place.

Hopefully if she talked to them, she could tell them one sibling was more than enough for their story.

The thought of that conversation followed her the whole drive to the prison, which was actually a nice change of pace. Normally she spent the drive worrying about what Ed would do or say, working herself up into a near panic state.

Now she was already parking and had barely thought about her father once. Perhaps that wasn't ideal, it meant she wasn't mentally preparing herself for him. But in her experience, no matter how much advanced planning you put in before a visit with Ed, it was never enough to actually *prepare* you. He knew how to play people too well.

Margot locked her personal items in the glovebox and headed into the visitor center where she would stow her keys with the guards and meet Andrew and their escort.

She hated how well practiced she was in this dance.

She'd never wanted to come back here again.

Andrew was already inside waiting for her, looking like he was the manager of a Radio Shack in his chinos and polo shirt. He usually looked like a professor, in blazers and suit pants. Today, only his tortoiseshell glasses remained as part of that life uniform.

Andrew Rhodes was a handsome man, in his fifties now, and he had actually gotten better looking with age, as his beard filled in and got grayer. The lines around his eyes spoke of someone who smiled and laughed often, it made him seem warmer, more approachable.

There had been a time in her life that being around Andrew had provided immediate comfort.

That time was long gone.

She gave him a smile, a nod, and he invited her to sit beside him while they waited. "It's been a while, Margot."

"It has," she agreed.

"We miss you at the office. Greg asks about you a lot."

This made Margot smile for real. She liked Greg Howell. The young FBI agent was obsessed with her father's case, to the point where he might know more about Ed than either her or Andrew combined. Normally that level of dedication to her father's legacy would prove off-putting for her. With Greg—who was often called *Gory* behind his back—she actually felt an affection, a kinship.

He was like the little brother she once had, before Justin had gotten morose and distant.

"Tell him I said hi. He has my phone number, he's welcome to use it."

The sentence struck her as funny for some reason and she couldn't help but laugh, a nervous response to being back here. "Unlike some people," she added.

Andrew looked momentarily hurt by her words, thinking she meant him, until he remembered what had happened months earlier.

"They check his cell weekly now, including *him*, to make sure he doesn't have another phone. He hasn't been allowed any visitors, and they now have his mail checked by two different guards just in case he's managed to bribe someone. He's not going to do that again."

Margot shrugged. After the call, she had been horrified. It felt like every shadow was just another place for him to hide, that he was lurking around every corner. She felt like Ed was in every closet, in the back seat of her car, there was simply no escaping the *idea* of him.

But Ed wasn't getting out. He was safely locked up in one of the highest security prisons in the country, he was sequestered away on Death Row, and he was *never* going to be standing outside her apartment door.

Dr. Singh had told Margot to remind herself of those certainties whenever she started to feel uneasy or afraid.

Besides that, the doctor reminded her, her father didn't want to kill her.

No, it was worse than that, she thought. He wanted to control her.

"I appreciate that," she said to Andrew. "I just wish we'd known about the phone before he'd been able to manipulate Ethan Willingham." Not the kid's real name, but his current legal one. The one he would go to prison under.

"That was a real fucking shitshow," Andrew agreed with a sigh.

"He probably would have acted out anyway. He's a psychopath." This wasn't an insult, it was a fact. The kid had been tested and was a clinically diagnosed psychopath. No wonder he and his stepfather got along so well.

Margot still had a hard time wrapping her head around the connection. Ed had married a woman named Rhonda, who had a young son. And Ed had managed to worm his way into that boy's brain and help shape him into something menacing.

"Not all psychopaths kill," Andrew reminded her.

"No, some of them start Fortune 500 companies."

Their guard arrived and they moved in silence through the familiar halls of the prison, which managed to simultaneously smell like disinfectant, piss, and ocean air. With that many men in one place it was impossible not to pick up the stench of them. The sweat and shit and semen and blood. It made her stomach churn.

They went into a dining hall, and Margot found her way by muscle memory to the metal stool where she normally sat. Ed's lawyer, Ford Rosenthal, sat at a nearby table, and Andrew joined him.

Rosenthal looked older than he had a few months earlier when Margot had last seen him. He had lost weight, his skin looked waxy, like being in the presence of Ed Finch had slowly started to suck the life out of him.

Like her father was some kind of vampire.

Margot adjusted herself in the seat. She'd forgotten just how uncomfortable the stool was. When she heard the doors on the far end of the room open with a *ka-chunk* followed by the jangle of wrist and ankle restraints, her whole body tensed. Fight or flight.

God, she wished she could pick flight.

Three people emerged from the shadows, two guards flanking a man in his late sixties who had evidently been taking very good care of himself in the months Margot had been away. Ed looked robust, his cheeks almost rosy, his frame less thin than she recalled. He looked good for his age, vital. Like he could live another twenty years.

God forbid.

The guards maintained impassive faces, settling Ed into his regular seat across from her, before retreating to the wings of the room where they would be on alert to move on him at any time.

Margot stared across the table at her father, and he met her gaze with an unflinching one of his own.

Then he smiled, and her skin crawled like she'd been covered in fire ants.

"The prodigal daughter returns."

TWENTY-SIX

Margot felt sick to her stomach, and that was exactly what he wanted. He was trying to get a rise out of her, and she hated how easily he'd managed to do it. But she wouldn't show him how well it was working.

She steadied herself, freezing her muscles to avoid any involuntary shudders, any uneasy fidgeting. She clasped her hands together and placed them on the table, then focused on the space between his eyebrows, rather than letting herself get absorbed by the icy, inhuman look in his eyes.

"Good morning, Ed," she said.

"Good morning, *Margot*," he replied, wielding her new name like a weapon. Like a toy he'd been desperate to possess. Now he had it, he wanted to flaunt it at her.

It's just a name, she tried to tell herself. *It doesn't give him power.*

But she wasn't sure either of them would believe that.

"You've been gone a long time," he told her.

"Not long enough."

That made him smile, a thin, menacing smile, something that actually pulled warmth out of the room.

"Yet here you are."

"Here I am," she agreed. "Against my better judgment. Against everything I told you and myself. Here I am."

"I didn't force you to come," Ed said.

Margot had to laugh. It was a sharp, mean sound, and she didn't like it. Didn't like the way it sounded coming out of her throat.

"You're better than that, Ed. Better than pretending like this wasn't all a well-executed plan. Do you want me to congratulate you? Tell you job well done, because you found the exact right card to play to get me back here? Well, all right then, job well done. You won. I'm here."

Ed assessed her, adjusting the way his wrists sat on the tabletop so that the metal bracelets of his cuffs weren't digging in. He was wearing a handknit cardigan, something she suspected he had made himself, since he'd told her once he had learned to knit in prison. It was well made, she could own to that. He had a lot of time to get good at things in here.

Ed looked old, now that they were face-to-face. Despite him looking healthier than he had in any of her other previous visits, she could also see how the texture of his skin had changed. It was thinner now, and saggy. There were deep bags under his eyes, dark circles that would never go away.

Brown age spots were on his cheeks and forehead, and Margot found herself thinking for the first time about her father's mortality, and how many years he might reasonably have left. She understood that realistically he was going to die here of old age before he was ever likely to get a date for his execution.

But she still clung to the notion that maybe one day the state would decide to strap Ed to a table and inject poison into his veins.

She would come back for that.

"You look good," Ed said, apparently assessing her the same

way she'd been assessing him. "I don't think I told you before but the nose job suits you. The weight loss, too. You were always a bit on the pudgy side, weren't you?"

Margot almost laughed. For all Ed's complaints about her mother, he sounded almost exactly like Kim in that moment.

And knowing it would bother him, she said so. "Mom thought so, too."

The smile faded from his lips. He thought he was going to throw her off by a jab at who she'd been, but she'd bested him for this round. Maybe she shouldn't keep score, but it was hard to resist relishing the little wins where she got them.

He didn't say anything for a long moment, recalculating, shuffling the deck to try again. While he was off-centered, Margot spoke first. "Can you be honest with me, since I'm already here, and you already got what you wanted?"

"I'm always honest with you, Buddy," he said, and he almost sounded earnest.

Ignoring that he'd lied to her for the first fifteen years of her life, and those lies had ruined any hope she'd had of a normal future.

But sure.

Honest Ed.

"Did you really have an accomplice or is this just some bullshit you concocted to get me back here? Because if it's a lie, I'm almost impressed. I'd give you a little round of applause." Margot had been thinking about this. About what would compel him to admit to an accomplice so late in the game. She'd come up with two options: it was just a lie, or he hadn't wanted anyone to know earlier because it would ruin his mystique as a perfect lone wolf hunter.

Regardless of which of the two options was correct, he'd obviously only mentioned it now because he wanted her to come back.

A thin smile crossed his lips. "You don't think very much of me, do you?"

Margot bit her tongue, because what she *wanted* to say would only set him off. As calm as he seemed in the moment, she knew his temper was permanently on a hair trigger. It didn't take much to piss Ed off, and she was hoping to keep things calm enough to get what she wanted from him so she never had to come back.

"I think I've been given a few reasons not to trust you," was the reply she finally managed.

Ed mulled this over a moment before nodding. "I suppose that's fair. But I wouldn't have made this up. I know you. If I lied about this, you'd never come back here again."

"I may never come back again, anyway," she reminded him.

"I think you will." He was calm, self-assured. She didn't like how convinced he was of this.

He already had a plan.

"So why talk now? Why not mention this accomplice years ago, during your appeal efforts? It might have helped you to have someone else to pin the blame on."

Ed smiled again, that slow, malicious smile that meant a thousand things other than being pleased. "I never felt the need before."

What an unbearable answer. Of course, he would only mention it when he *needed* it, but why was bringing her here more important than the potential for a lesser sentence, or to sow doubt in the mind of a jury?

Sure, Ed's case had been locked up tight long before the jury ever deliberated on it. When he'd finally been caught, they found trophies—not from every victim, but enough of them—hidden in the ducts of their suburban garage. It had actually been the most recent kills that had ended up doing him in, the ones he'd committed while they were visiting Kim's family in New York.

He hadn't managed to clean his shoes well enough, and the tiny drops of blood inside the grooves on the sole of his shoe had been enough to lock him up tight on at least one murder. From there on, it was like a row of dominos, falling one after the other.

But Ed had ample opportunity to point the finger elsewhere, to say it hadn't been his idea, that he hadn't worked alone. Throwing someone else under the bus could have been his hail Mary pass at trial, but he'd said nothing. His legal team hadn't even hinted at the possibility to get reasonable doubt.

It didn't make sense for him to wait this long to do it, but for some reason Margot believed him. She believed there was another person out there, and if she didn't she never would have come here today.

Still, it felt like an oversight on his part, an escape plan he'd never actioned, for reasons Margot couldn't fathom. Why would Ed protect this other person all this time, and only think about pulling their name out now, when it didn't benefit him in any other way than to get her attention?

Perhaps it didn't make any sense to try to understand the logic of a madman. Ed was always going to do what felt good and right to him in a moment, even if it didn't seem reasonable to anyone else. He had his own rhyme and reason.

Margot decided to approach this interview as she would with any other interrogation, picking away until she got the information she wanted. Only in this case it felt like she was handling a bomb, and one wrong move would set him off and blow her hands off with it.

She took a steadying breath to cling to whatever patience she had brought in with her, and stretched her fingers out once before refolding her hands neatly. She had a bad habit of balling her hands into fists when she was here, her nails ripping up the skin of her palms.

If she could walk out of here without bleeding, she would consider it a win. But her fingers and body felt stiff from keeping herself so still, and she knew getting up was going to hurt.

"Did your accomplice help you with every kill, or only some of them?"

"Very few, actually. You know me, I like to be by myself most of the time, and that was true of my kills, too. Killing is, for the most part, a solitary practice. When you bring someone else into the mix, you open yourself up to their mistakes, and you know how much I hate to handhold people through things."

Margot's mouth formed a thin line, and she thought about her father's paper-thin patience with her and Justin when they'd been children. Her mother had been the one to teach them to ride bikes, to lie in bed with them while they stumbled through trying to read passages out of storybooks. Margot had actually been shocked by her father's willingness to teach her to drive. He hadn't known that she'd been practicing with Kim for weeks already.

He wanted immediate results. He didn't like to see failure in others, because he seemed to think it reflected poorly on him. Margot had learned very young that Ed was someone to brag to after perfecting something, not one to ask for help to try it a first time.

She tried to imagine how that might translate to working alongside another killer, and she wondered seriously how he'd managed it.

"They had killed before then, hadn't they? Without you."

Ed's eyes *twinkled*. It was the most human she'd seen him look in all her visits, and she recognized the expression. It made bile raise in the back of her throat.

He was *proud*.

"You always were a smart girl, Margot, you know that? I don't think you got that from me or your mom. Both of us only finished high school. But you, you were smart right out of the gate. Still smart now."

She didn't thank him for the compliment. Growing up, her intelligence had felt like a survival skill. Even now her brain was trying to solve a puzzle so she could get out of this room.

"Was he ever caught?"

Ed tilted his head, observing her in a way that made her feel like prey. "I never said it was a man."

"You didn't, but you also don't think very highly of women. I don't think you'd trust a woman enough to have her be complicit in your crimes. You think women are too emotional. If you worked with a woman you'd be afraid she would get angry with you and weaponize her knowledge against you."

Ed laughed and, from the corner of Margot's eye, she saw Ford Rosenthal flinch.

"I don't hate women."

Margot rolled her eyes, she couldn't help herself. "Ed, please. You just talked about how smart I am, so don't treat me like an idiot now."

His mouth formed a thin line, but he wasn't a stranger to her backtalk at this point. What might once have set him off now rolled off his back instead. He finally gave her a little nod of agreement. "While I disagree with your premise, your conclusion is right. It wasn't a woman. I just want to remind you not to assume anything."

"It's not an assumption if it's based in observable fact." Margot shrugged. "Then it's just deduction."

"Ah yes, and you're my little detective, aren't you?"

"That *is* why the city of San Francisco pays me the little bucks. So, had he ever been arrested before?"

"Not for violent crimes, no."

But he *did* have an arrest record, then.

"And since?"

Ed shrugged. "I haven't really been keeping up with him, as you can imagine." He couldn't spread his arms apart, but he fanned his hands open to gesture to the room around him.

"And you haven't spotted him in the yard, I take it."

Another smile. "No."

"Younger or older than you?" She rocked her neck side to side to chase away a kink that had become painful.

"Age is more about what's going on up here, rather than how many years you've lived." He raised his chained hands to tap the side of his temple. "But since I know you're being literal, he was younger, but not by much."

So, similar age. Not a protégé, then, but a contemporary.

"How many victims did you kill together?" Margot asked.

Ed didn't even need to think before answering. "Five."

"Do we know about all five?" she shot back.

This made him pause, contemplating. Was he just drawing things out, or could he not remember? Did he need to go through a mental catalog of his victims just to remind himself which ones the police were aware of and which were still secreted away in his mind?

"No," he said finally. "You don't."

Margot shifted, her discomfort mounting. She didn't want to think of it as squirming, but she didn't like the way he was staring at her, eagerly awaiting each new question while his gaze stripped away all her carefully crafted layers of defense.

She suddenly felt like she was eight years old sitting across from him and this was just his way of teaching her a lesson.

"Do we know about *any* of them?" she asked.

"Yes. Two."

Great, so there were now an additional three unsolved homicides for Andrew and his team to connect Ed to. And they'd need to figure out which of his known kills were possibly committed by two killers instead of one.

Margot decided to go for the outright question instead of collecting little crumbs of truth. "Who was it?"

Ed was suddenly very interested in his cuticles, looking at the ragged dry skin instead of at her.

"You know, I'm not feeling very well. A migraine. They come on quite suddenly. I think that might be all the questions my poor head can handle." His lips formed a thin line, and if he'd been uncuffed she imagined he might mime zipping his lips and throwing away the key.

You son of a bitch, Margot thought irritably. He'd brought her all this way and now he was trying to back out of the arrangement?

"You can't just bail on this, Ed. You brought us here to talk to us, so *talk*," Margot said, trying to keep her tone calm when she felt anything but.

"No, I don't think I like your tone or your impatience today. You'll just have to come back another day, and I'll decide if I want to tell you anything then."

Margot wanted to explode at him, but she was well aware that was the exact reaction he was fishing for.

He sat silently and stared at her, one minute ticking into the next. She waited a full five minutes, just staring into his unblinking eyes before she relented and waved the guards forward.

The two men who had brought him in were suddenly at his side like they'd appeared out of thin air.

"I'm not playing games with you, Ed," Margot said.

He looked back over his shoulder as the guards led him out of the room.

"On the contrary, I think you are."

And the door shut with a heavy *ka-thunk* before Margot could say anything else.

TWENTY-SEVEN

Margot stopped at her apartment before heading to work.

Justin wasn't there.

The note was still on the dining room table, but the forty dollars were gone. He hadn't bothered to tidy up his space on the couch, and the cushions and blanket looked as if he'd just stepped out of them.

There were dirty glasses on her coffee table and in the sink, and several empty cans of Coke were littered all over the apartment, like he'd been walking around and just left them wherever he happened to finish one.

Margot's space might not be fancy, and it was largely furnished in second-hand items, but she *was* neat, and relatively meticulous about it. Having someone come into it and leave behind such a mess was enough to make her eye start twitching, especially after the morning she'd had.

Justin loved her, but he didn't respect her.

He was only here because he wanted something.

She took a deep breath through her nose and did a quick five-minute tidy of her space, loading dirty dishes into the dishwasher, tossing empty cans in the recycle bin, and throwing her note to him in the trash.

The sooner they had their conversation about this documentary the better. If she could appease him by agreeing to meet the producers, maybe that would be enough to send him home.

She had no real intention of doing the series, but ever since he'd been here pestering her about it, it had made her start to give the whole thing a lot more consideration than she previously had. Not necessarily that she was interested in opening up about her past in such a public way, but that *maybe* it was time to stop burying that part of the past like a shameful secret.

Now that Ed knew her real name, the primary reason she'd kept herself so hidden away didn't apply any more. So did it really matter if other people knew she had once been Megan Finch? She'd already seen with Wes, Leon, and even Captain Tate that no one thought less of her professionally for her past.

Maybe she didn't need to hide anymore.

But before she could think about that for herself, she needed to get her brother back to his own life.

And hopefully back to an AA meeting.

Margot didn't have the time or emotional energy to babysit her brother, and him being in her space was already starting to wear her thin. He'd told her he would only be here a day or two, but it was already starting to feel indefinite. She wondered if he'd lost another job, if he had nothing immediately pressing urging him home.

Once her apartment was somewhat restored and she had changed back into comfortable clothes that weren't suitable for prison, she left the apartment, though her mood was now even darker than it had been when she left San Quentin.

Andrew wanted her to stop by the FBI headquarters on her next day off to review things with him and his team, but she'd been non-committal. She didn't want to get roped back into this, though it didn't look like Ed was going to give her much of a choice.

When she got to work, there was a hot coffee sitting dead center on her desk, though Wes didn't look up to acknowledge her arrival immediately. She set a paper bag down in front of him, and another at her own desk. She wasn't hungry, but she knew she needed to eat.

Wes unwrapped the corned beef sandwich she'd brought him, then immediately held out his pickle for her, which she took and dropped onto a napkin on her own desk.

"How'd it go?" he asked finally, wiping a dollop of mustard away from the corner of his mouth.

"Just about as shitty as you might imagine," she replied, pretending to focus on unwrapping her turkey club. She knew Wes wouldn't be satisfied with that, even though he might not push her to say more. "He gave us just enough to make it convincing that there really was someone else, but then the second I asked for a name he shut down, got the guards to take him away."

"Forcing you to go back."

Margot nodded and took a bite of her sandwich. It was delicious, even if her stomach was still roiling from her morning experience.

"I'm sorry, Margot."

"Me too."

"On the flip side, Dr. Kaur said that Angela might be up for another brief interview today. She had a rough spell yesterday, but her readings have been strong today. The doc said she's been pretty lucid and said if we came by in about an hour we could have a few minutes."

That *did* brighten Margot's mood somewhat. Maybe they could at least figure out the girl's last name, see if she had any family or anyone who might be able to point them in the direction of a possible suspect.

"It gets better. The fire department has released the car. The CSIs picked it up an hour ago and said we could go have a look while they start trying to get fingerprints or a VIN off of it."

"Man, it's like Christmas in here today," Margot said, suddenly enjoying the taste of her sandwich much more. She picked up her coffee and looked at him. "This was still hot, how did you know when I'd get here?"

"Mental math and dumb luck?" he offered.

"Mmhmm, I don't need to check my car for a tracking device, do I?"

Wes chuckled and deposited his garbage into the trash can near his desk. He then presented his face in Margot's direction and she gave her head a quick shake to let him know there were no lingering dollops of mayo or mustard to be seen.

"No, no trackers. Let's just say that wasn't the first one I grabbed, and don't tell Leon the one I gave him an hour ago wasn't just a nice gesture."

That made Margot laugh out loud, something that felt incredibly nice after the shit morning she'd had. It felt good to be at work, better here than at home where there were all the reminders of her brother, and through him, more reminders of Ed.

She didn't want to think about Ed for the rest of the day, and blessedly, work was going to offer her distractions in spades.

"Hospital first, then car?" she suggested.

Wes nodded his agreement. "Probably the best idea. Not sure how much we're going to get out of either visit, but goddamn I'd really love to give this woman her name back."

"You and me both."

Margot stopped by Leon's desk before she and Wes headed to the hospital. She spotted the Philz cup on his desk and it made her smile. Leon glanced up, his glasses had slid low on his nose and he was going through a stack of files sitting in front of him. An open box of animal crackers sat beside his coffee.

"Hey, you missed some excitement around here," he said.

"Oh yeah?" She arched a brow, inviting him to continue.

"None other than Pressley Boyd came to grace us with his presence while you were gone."

Margot's brows now headed up toward her hairline. "The chief of police was here? What did that old stick-in-the-mud want?"

Pressley Boyd wasn't exactly the type of leader that rallied a lot of support behind him. Margot didn't envy him his job, and knew a lot of the bullshit from their day-to-day rolled downhill onto him, which couldn't be easy. But she also thought he was a pinch-faced weasel who cared more about politics than he did about good policing. She couldn't stand the guy.

"Talked to me and Tate about Redwood." Leon rubbed his temples to give her some indication of how well that was going. "Gave us the usual lecture on optics, asked what we needed. Seems like he might actually ante up for some extra manpower now that the newspapers have given the guy a name."

"Well, glory be, imagine Pressley Boyd *giving* money for something instead of taking it away."

"I'll believe it when I see it. He stayed for about twenty minutes, had a photo op planned outside, but notably absent was a press conference to announce funding a proper task force. So we'll see if he's just full of shit." He looked over at her and must have noticed how tired she looked because his tone shifted, his voice becoming soothing and a little too kind. "How'd it go with you guys?"

Margot groaned. "Don't ask."

"That good, eh?"

"Somehow every time is worse than the last. He's gifted."

"I've been thinking about Emmanuel Riga," Leon said, putting down the stack of files he'd been reading and pushing his glasses up on his nose. "I think our best bet, at least at first, is to make our investigation known. Go to the club, ask about our girls. That's going to get back to him in no time, and I'd like to see how he reacts."

Margot nodded. While she would have loved to drag Riga in directly and just start questioning the man at the top, she also knew that men in his position had not one but *many* overpaid lawyers, who would make sure he never had to say a single potentially incriminating word to them. Leon was right to suggest taking it slow.

"Wes and I are going to tackle a few things with the Golden Gate Park victim, but I have to stick around late tonight to do my penance for taking time off this morning. And night time is the right time to question anyone working at a club. You want to go over to Odyssey later?"

If she was being honest with herself, half the reason for volunteering for this was so she wouldn't have to go home and talk to her brother. She wasn't feeling quite up to the task yet, and was worried her annoyance at his slobbish ways might make her back out of talking to the documentary crew just out of spite.

She needed time.

"I don't promise to blend in," Leon said, gesturing to his tweed blazer and general being-a-sixty-year-old-manness.

"That's OK, I think blending in will be the least of our concerns."

In fact, Margot was counting on it.

TWENTY-EIGHT

Back at the hospital, and the smell of the place made Margot's skin crawl.

It was just too clean, and the overpowering smell of disinfectant reminded her of the prison. In both places the smell was doing a lot of heavy lifting to cover up something much worse.

In the prison, it was the stench of a life behind bars.

Here, it was death.

Dr. Kaur met them at the front nurse's station as she had during their previous visit. Once again, she somehow looked both flawless and harried, like she had no time for this, but also like she had just had a facial.

Margot's new goal in life was to look that radiant while also being crushed by the stress of her job.

"Thanks for coming, Detectives. I'm sure it's not easy to just drop what you're doing and come down here, but her lucid spells have started getting quite a bit further in between, and with the medications she's on they don't last long." The doctor paused outside of Angela's door and lowered her voice. "Between us, despite her having made it this far, I don't know how much longer she'll be with us. It could be hours, could be days."

Margot felt an overpowering blow of sadness that she hadn't expected. "So, there's no chance she's going to pull through?"

Dr. Kaur looked at Margot and must have read something akin to hope in her expression, because she offered a wan smile before speaking again. "If you'd asked me when I first saw her, I would have told you she wouldn't last the night. She's a fighter, and she's lasted a lot longer than I would have expected. I can't say with certainty. You never know, she might surprise the hell out of us."

The unspoken part at the end of this that Margot still heard was, *But don't count on it*.

Margot knew Angela's chances were slim, but they were still better than most of the victims she worked with in homicide. Being able to speak to her, however limited her ability, was a gift they never usually got.

If they had hours, or days, Margot would use them.

She just hoped that Angela would continue to defy the odds.

Margot's only pang of regret was that if Angela *did* survive, they could only pin *attempted* homicide on whoever had done this to her. And attempted homicide never carried the weightier punishments of an accomplished one. Margot never understood that logic. In her opinion, someone who failed at killing someone still wanted to do it. They should be punished the exact same as if they'd succeeded.

The justice system and Margot didn't see eye to eye on that one.

"You remember the drill?" Dr. Kaur asked, checking her watch to remind them she didn't have time to hold their hands.

"We do," Wes answered. "No undue stress, no touching, no pens, cover up."

Dr. Kaur gave him a thumbs up. "I wish my interns listened

as well as you two do. If you need anything else feel free to get the front to page me, but otherwise, good luck."

Margot and Wes donned the protective gear left outside the room and steeled themselves before entering. Margot had seen a lot of truly upsetting crime scenes, bodies in various states of decomp, things done to people that defied imagination. Yet somehow, speaking to a woman whose flesh resembled BBQ briquettes was much, much worse.

She felt guilty for feeling that way, because Angela's experience had to be a thousand times worse.

If the woman survived—a big *if* at this point—her life would never be the same. She was missing fingers and toes, her skin would be riddled with scar tissue. Margot remembered watching a documentary about a woman who had survived a volcanic explosion, and she imagined that the road to recovery would look similar for Angela if she did pull through.

But she'd be alive.

When they got to her bedside, she appeared to be dozing, but the sound of the curtain being pulled closed behind them was enough to rouse her. Blinking seemed to be an ordeal, and Margot wished she could give the poor woman eye drops or something.

"Hello, Angela," Wes greeted her warmly. "Do you remember us?"

Angela nodded. The bandages covering the bulk of her body had recently been changed, but there were still spots where the blood and other bodily excretions oozed freely, giving her bandages a wet look.

Margot gritted her teeth. In here, the room smelled of antiseptic creams and beneath that the faint but unmistakable scent of charcoal.

"We know it's not easy for you to speak to us," Wes continued. "But if there's anything you can tell us you weren't able to before—like your last name—that would help us a lot. Then we could figure out how to locate your family. I'm sure they'd like to know where you are."

A pained expression passed over Angela's features and a few tears trickled over her skin, with no lashes remaining to hold them in place. "*No. Fam.*"

No family.

Wes gave her a supportive smile. "OK, that's OK, but it would still help us a lot if you could tell us your last name."

Angela swallowed hard, like whatever she was going to try to say next was going to take some effort. She had obviously tried to share her name with the doctors, but must have known that so far they hadn't been able to decipher what she'd been saying.

If she could write it down, they would be in great shape, but unfortunately one needed to have fingers to write.

"Take your time," Margot urged, though time was really the last thing they had on their side.

"*Gr... Gru...*"

This was already different from their previous guesses of Good or Hood. Wes had a notepad out ready to write it down.

Angela sighed, tired and frustrated.

"Can you spell it?" Margot asked.

This seemed to brighten the woman's expression, like she had never considered to try this before. Perhaps the individual letters would be easier for her than the full syllables of her name.

"*G...R...O...M...A...N...D.*" When she finished speaking she took a huge breath, and Margot knew just those letters had probably pushed her nearly up to the limit of what she'd be able to offer them.

"Gromand?" Wes showed Angela what he'd written. She nodded, her eyes drooping.

"*Ooo,*" she answered back. She was correcting his pronunciation. It made Margot smile.

"Gromand?" Margot repeated, elongating the o so it sounded like *Groomond*, which explained the confusion with *Good*.

"Angela, do you know the name of the man who did this to you?" Margot said, hoping to get just a little more out of the woman before she slipped off. There was no guarantee when—or if—they'd get another chance like this.

The woman was thoughtful for a long time, so long Margot wasn't sure if she had heard or understood the question.

She might have even fallen asleep with her eyes open.

Then she spoke so suddenly it startled Margot, making her jump.

"R...O...B."

TWENTY-NINE

Wes had driven to the hospital, so they made their way back to his car, taking a moment for a quick debrief before they headed to check out the car.

"Rob isn't much to go on. And that's assuming it's the guy's real name," Wes said.

Margot took a sip of her coffee, which she'd brought along from the office. Even though it was now cold, she didn't mind. It still tasted good and delivered a jolt of caffeine she would need to keep her going through the evening.

"It's more than we had before. More than most victims are able to give us."

"I guess it would be out of the question to bring a sketch artist in," Wes mused.

"Considering it almost knocked her out just to spell her name for us, I don't think she'd be able to give Tula much to go on." Tula Sharp was their department's resident sketch artist and she was a whiz. She could turn even a vague description into something that at least passably resembled their suspect. But even Tula wouldn't be able to help Angela.

"Wishful thinking."

"I know. I want more from her, too. But I think we have to be grateful for even the little we're getting. It would be amazing if she could just wake up and tell us this guy's name and address, but at least we have *her* name now. And a starting point for him."

The corner of his mouth ticked up in a smirk. "I'm not used to you being the optimistic one, Margot. I'm going to need you to tone it down a notch."

She smiled back at him, still holding her cold coffee. All it needed was some ice, really, and it would be perfect again.

"It's funny, when you think about it. We see all these dead bodies, and every single time we think, *I wish you could tell me what happened to you*, and now we have a living victim and I'm *still* wishing she could tell us what happened to her."

"Makes you wonder how many of them would actually be able to tell us if they *could*," Wes said wistfully, navigating through traffic. It took them about twenty minutes to get to the crime lab, where they were quickly ushered into a large garage where multiple vehicles were being held for evidence inspection.

The room was large and sterile—a necessity for obvious reasons—and for the second time that day Margot and Wes donned gloves and booties to protect their evidence from any possible outside contamination.

The crime scene techs who were working on the car were clad head to toe in protective white suits, much the way they often were at crime scenes. The life motto of crime scene techs seemed to be to protect the evidence at all costs.

Just the slightest contamination—their own sweat or hair, for example—could make the evidence too compromised to be used at trial.

Margot could see the car at the far end of the garage, a burnt-out husk with very little left to tell them what it had once looked like. The wheels were melted, with ragged bits of rubber clinging to the rims. The whole exterior was coated in black from the smoke and fire damage. The windows were gone, small pebbles of breakaway glass glinted dimly, suggesting the heat had simply shattered everything.

The wreckage still stank of burning plastics and rubber, giving the whole thing a poisonous aura, like you didn't want to get too close to it. The crime scene techs presently working on it were wearing respirators.

Margot wrinkled her nose as they approached it.

"Afternoon, Detectives," greeted an altogether too cheerful young woman who seemed to be observing the work. She wore a lanyard with her name on it, suggesting she was DeAndra Leggitt. Margot and Wes shook her hand, which always felt odd when both parties were wearing latex gloves.

"I don't think we've ever met before," Wes commented.

DeAndra was pretty, and probably a decade younger than Wes, so just his usual type. Margot wasn't sure if he was being polite or flirting. Neither would have surprised her. Wes flirted the same way he breathed, involuntarily and to stay alive.

"Yeah, just transferred here from Houston about two weeks ago. Glenn Pearson retired."

Margot whistled. Glenn, the previous CSI lead, had been with the department for easily forty years. She wasn't surprised that he had reached retirement age, only that they'd actually managed to convince him to go. She thought Glenn would probably die in his office at the age of eighty.

"I'll have to send him a card," she said. "Wish I'd known to say goodbye the last time I saw him."

DeAndra nodded. "I didn't get to know him all that well, but I don't think he told anyone outside of his team he was leaving. Didn't seem to want to make a big deal out of it. I gather he was really well liked."

Wes nodded. "Big shoes."

The woman grinned. Her dozens of braids had been pulled

back in a thick ponytail and the ends swished as she moved. "I'll do my best to live up to the legacy. But take it easy on me, OK?"

Now Margot couldn't tell if DeAndra was flirting or just being nice.

"Have you guys been able to get anything so far?" Margot asked, hoping the topic shift wouldn't read as rude, but also not wanting to spend all day making friendly small talk.

If DeAndra thought it was abrupt, her expression didn't show it. Her cheerfulness simply rolled over onto the new topic. Glenn had been so stoic about everything, the new upbeat attitude was somehow both charming and off-putting.

"We've only had the car for about an hour since it was released into our custody, but so far we've been able to determine it's a mid-2000s Toyota Corolla, and we were able to get what we think is the license plate, though the plates have been pretty damaged." DeAndra wrote something down on a Post-It note and handed it to Margot with the plate number they suspected.

"Thank you." It was too much to hope that the vehicle would be registered to someone named Robert, but it was a little more information than what they'd previously had. Unfortunately, a mid-2000s Corolla was about as unique as the name John Smith.

Once they knew more about the possible color of the car, though, they could start asking nearby businesses to check security footage, perhaps they might luck into an image of their driver and Angela on the way to the park. If they knew what he looked like it could also help them see which direction he'd gone after fleeing the scene.

"Anything else?" Margot asked hopefully.

DeAndra shook her head. "It's going to be a painstaking process to get *anything* out of that car. Fingerprints and DNA I'd expect to be a no-go, so don't hold your breath, but of course we're always going to try our best. It does look like there are some unidentified items in the trunk and back seat, so once we're able to get those out and thoroughly looked at, I might have a little more to offer you." She gave Margot a smile that said, *patience is a virtue*, and then looked back at her clipboard as if to end the discussion.

Margot had been hoping for more, but the plate number and car model were better than a kick in the pants. They thanked DeAndra and her team before heading back out to Wes's car. It had started to rain, so they jogged across the parking lot.

Once inside, Margot felt breathless, a sure sign she needed to get back into some variety of fitness training again. The gym under the precinct was ancient and awful, but it was better than nothing at all, and Margot wouldn't join a regular gym—too much routine involved in that. Exercise tended to be something she dropped from her plate too often.

Right now, her body was screaming its discomfort at her, but she knew a big part of that had been the experience of keeping herself contained at the prison. Her muscles were sore, and she was exhausted.

Wes didn't say anything as they drove the short distance back to the station, but his expression was focused, there was something going on in his mind, even if he didn't say it out loud. They were both quiet all the way back to their office, though another jog through the rain left them silently cursing the San Francisco weather gods, among other things.

When they were finally settled Margot looked at him, a brow quirked. "It's not like you to be this quiet, what's going on?"

He shook his head to get rid of some of the excess water, then raked his fingers through his hair to tame it back into place. Margot probably looked like a sea monster right now, where Wes looked ready to sell her cologne.

"I don't know what it is," he admitted. "Just that itch, you know? The idea that there's something you should be figuring out but you haven't yet, and it's driving you crazy."

Margot knew that feeling well.

The great fictional detective Hercule Poirot would often talk about the work of his "little gray cells." What Poirot never bothered to mention was that sometimes the gray cells were working overtime, but they just couldn't give you the answer you were so desperately seeking.

Homicide was a lot like a puzzle being built upside down. It couldn't be turned over until that last piece was found, but in the meantime you understood the *shape* of the information you were missing. Only in the end did you get to see the complete picture.

What Wes was experiencing right now was the frustration of having a piece and not knowing where it fit.

Unfortunately for them, this case was a whole lot of pieces and nowhere to put them.

THIRTY

Wes tapped out for the night later than usual, donning his coat at seven. Margot was sorry to see him go, though he hadn't been his usual chatty self for the latter part of the day, but in fairness she wasn't a dazzling conversationalist either.

He'd worked on getting info on the car—a 2014 Corolla registered to a Helen Debicki and reported stolen a month earlier—and Margot focused on digging up details on Angela.

She'd been deep in her research when Wes flicked her ponytail like a ninth grader looking for attention. "You want me to come with you guys tonight?" he asked, almost like he was looking for an excuse not to go home.

While Leon was the lead on the case and Margot had gone with him to the original crime scene, Wes had been involved in the investigation since the discovery of the second body. It was as much his case to participate in as it was hers. Which was to say—as long as Leon wanted their help.

Margot paused, wondering if part of Wes's dour mood all afternoon was because he hadn't been invited.

If that was the case, there was a simple enough solution.

"Actually, yeah. Not to sound superficial, but we might have more luck talking to some of the waitresses if we have you along for the ride." She smiled at him.

Wes feigned a scandalized expression. "I'm going to tell Leon you don't think he's hot enough to charm information out of witnesses."

A throat clearing in the doorway announced the arrival of the man himself. "I think my wife would tell you that while my good looks were once a part of the reason she fell for me, I'm charming enough without them, Wesley."

"Hey, don't shoot the messenger, look at her not me." Wes was already settling back into his chair, and they turned to Leon to let him take charge of the evening's agenda.

Margot sometimes wondered why Leon had decided to become a homicide lifer like her. He had a natural gift with people that would have made him a remarkable leader if he'd opted to be. But instead he kept going out to crime scenes, kept standing over bodies, like it was the only thing in this world he was born to do.

She could relate, but at the same time, she thought he could have done more with his career. Wes, likewise, had the charm and people skills to climb the ladder, but as far as Margot had seen, he was content doing what he was doing.

For her, there was no choice, this was what she was supposed to do, and besides that, she had no people skills to speak of. She would have made a terrible leader.

It was astonishing to her most days that she'd managed to successfully work with a partner for as many years as she had. But that had more to do with Wes than anything else. When she'd first met him she thought he was cocky and a bit of a jerk. What she'd learned over time was that was just the special seasoning blend that made him who he was. And as she'd spent more and more time with him, she realized that was what she loved about him.

Liked about him.

It also helped that he wasn't too hard on the eye.

"Here's the deal," Leon said. "We aren't going to go in pretending to be something we aren't. If Riga is involved in this, which would not be surprising, then our ultimate goal is for him to find out we've been there asking questions. That said, this isn't a group of people who are going to be chummy with us or want to share any information. Riga might not own that club on paper, but he's involved, and no one wants to be the person who gave up information on Emmanuel Riga. So we're not going to lean too hard, we just stay friendly, stay professional, and assume everyone in that building is lying to us."

He handed each of them a small stack of photos, one of each of their known victims. The photos were taken from their social media profiles, and depicted the women as they'd been when they were alive. Vivacious, pretty, and thinking their whole lives were ahead of them.

A lot of people found it hard to look at photos of dead bodies.

Margot sometimes found it harder to look at photos of them when they'd been alive.

It was still light outside when they got to the Odyssey night-club. It was an unassuming building at first glance, situated in a SOMA with its tall glass office towers and shabby little parking lots everywhere. The building itself was a plain beigey gray from the outside, with only the neon sign over the door and some banners over the interior windows to give any indication of what was inside. This early in the evening there was no line outside, but a heavyset man in a tight T-shirt and wraparound sunglasses was bringing out brass posts and resting them up against the side of the building. Obviously, he was getting prepared for the onslaught that would come later.

Margot had never been a club-goer. She had completely bypassed the rebellious, up-until-two, party-until-you-puke life-style that most twentysomethings of her generation had gone through. The idea of standing outside in line, to go inside and drink while excruciatingly loud music played, sounded like hell to her.

But since Odyssey was only one of hundreds of similar clubs around the city, all of which were packed past occupancy almost every night, she was not in the majority on this.

Admittedly, she was also now pushing forty, so none of this was meant to be her scene.

The man who had been handling the stanchions paused in his work and swiped a meaty forearm over his sweaty brow, then watched the three detectives as they approached. He took them all in with one quick nod of the head, though Margot noted his gaze hold on her slightly longer than the others.

He crossed his arms over his chest, balancing them on the curve of his belly.

"Officers," he said.

"Detectives," Leon corrected. "Telly, Phalen, and Fox."

"Sounds like a law firm," the bouncer replied coolly, and Margot couldn't help but smile.

"Clever," Leon said, unmoved by the joke. "We're from SFPD Homicide and we have reason to believe that more than one of our unsolved cases might be connected to this bar."

The bouncer shrugged. "Could be. Lots of people come here every night. Sometimes people die."

Margot's smile vanished as a chill that shot through her body at the casual way he said this. The way someone might if they had *helped* someone die at some point.

"We'd like to talk to some of the staff," Leon said, unmoved.

The bouncer scratched his jaw, where dark stubble had formed since the last time he'd seen his razor. He gave the three of them another look, then grunted. "All right, but I gotta ask that you make it quick. No offense, but none of you exactly look like the typical clientele we serve. You look like cops. I mean, hot cops." He bobbed his head toward either Margot, Wes, or perhaps both. "But *cops*. And fuckin' no one wants to party with cops."

Considering Margot didn't want to party with cops, either—or anyone else for that matter—she wasn't about to argue with him. Police on site were bad for business, she understood that.

"We'll stay as long as it takes to find out what we need to know," was what she said out loud. Because if they wanted to hustle them off the property, then they were going to have to give them *something*. Perhaps the hint might help move things along.

The big man's jaw ticked, then he opened up the nightclub's doors and ushered them inside.

The club itself wasn't very big, especially not with the overhead lights on. Three of the walls were covered in mirrors, so when the lights were off and the club was lit by strobes and neon it probably looked a hell of a lot bigger. The pillars that lined the center of the room were painted in trippy white and black stripes that extended up to the ceiling, and Margot could imagine that, with lights flashing, they probably looked as if they were moving.

Right now, though, everything looked a little overworn, with paint chipping and streaks on the mirrors, as well as some permanent stains on the floor that no amount of bleach or elbow grease would ever be able to remove. The main bar was along the left side of the room, a DJ booth was built on a platform on the wall straight ahead, and next to the DJ there were two circular platforms on either side of the stage. On one of the platforms a girl in a skin-tight bodysuit with the same stripes as the pillars was adjusting her black and white wig in one of the mirrors.

A handful of bartenders were behind the bar, stocking glasses and checking alcohol levels. One was slicing lime wedges with the amount of focus Margot might expect from a heart surgeon.

At the end of the bar the mirrors ended, and a hallway extended further into the building. This was likely where the washrooms and office were located if Margot had to guess. Behind them, on the left side of the entrance, was an elevated area with thick velvet curtains and strands of faux gemstones giving the illusion of privacy. Velvet couches lined the area in a U-shape.

VIP.

A waitress in a short black dress and knee-high black boots was setting up ice buckets in that area. The bouncer paused in the entryway and jerked his chin toward the hallway. "Boss is back there. Talk to whoever you gotta talk to, then show yourselves out."

"And if we want to talk to you?" Wes asked.

"Then I suppose you know where to find me," the man said and headed back outside.

"Quite the charmer," Margot said once he was gone.

"I feel like that's about the level of welcome we're going to get around here. Let's divide and conquer out here before we head to the office," Leon suggested. "Wes, you go cozy up to the bartenders. I'll talk to Miss VIP, and Margot you go find out if the zebra knows anything." He waved a hand in the direction of the dancer.

Margot didn't have any strong feelings about who she wanted to chat with, so she made her way across the room to where the woman on the platform was now stretching, her boot-clad foot resting on the safety bar that surrounded her small stage.

She caught Margot's eye in the mirror, but her expression didn't change, she just leaned deeper into her stretch. She was in insane physical condition, her body toned without an ounce of fat to be seen, and her calves and thighs were muscular but still lean.

A dancer.

Like, a *real* dancer.

"Evening. You mind if I take up a few minutes of your time?" Margot asked, standing on the dancefloor and looking up at the woman slightly. Margot's height gave her the advantage of not feeling too dwarfed by the short stage platform, but the extra inches the stage provided were enough to make the woman taller than her. Not a common feat for this woman, Margot assumed, since she looked to be barely over five feet tall without the boots and the stage.

The woman stopped stretching and turned so she was facing Margot, draping her arms over the safety bar. Her skin where it was exposed was covered in glitter, and her eye makeup was severe but expertly applied.

"You have a badge?" the woman asked, her gaze raking over Margot in a way that felt like she was being judged.

Margot showed the woman her badge and the dancer nodded once before she started to stretch out her arms, lifting one long limb up in the air then crooking it over her head.

"What's your name?" Margot asked, pulling out a notepad and pen.

"Mistress Sparkle."

Margot raised one brow and the girl seemed delighted by her own joke, grinning broadly, her teeth so white Margot assumed they must glow under the black lights. Mistress Sparkle probably looked like a Cheshire Cat whenever that happened.

Follow me into Wonderland…

"My name is Fiona Thibodeaux." She instinctively spelled out her last name without being asked. "But in the club we just have stage names. Makes things easier, keeps us all safer."

"Safety a big issue around here?"

Fiona laughed, then grabbed the bar she'd been leaning on with both hands, dropped her weight and swung out toward Margot like a kid on the monkey bars at a playground. She ended up sitting on the edge of the platform in front of Margot, beaming that big toothy smile.

Margot wondered how old she was. Twenty-one seemed like a stretch just to look at her.

"Safety is an issue everywhere, isn't it, Detective?"

"I suppose it is. How long have you been working here?"

Fiona thought about this for a moment. "About eight months? Maybe a bit longer."

"Would you say you're pretty familiar with the regulars?"

"I mean, I know people to see 'em, but being up here isn't like being one of the waitresses. I'm not getting tipped or anything. I'm just here to help with the mood, make people want to get off their asses, you know. People who dance a lot, they sweat. People who sweat want to buy more booze. That's just drunk science."

"If you know faces, you might be able to help me anyway." Margot reached into the inner pocket of her jacket and took out the photos Leon had provided her, handing them to Fiona.

To her credit, the girl *really* looked at the photos, squinting, shuffling back and forth between them. Then she took one of the photos—Margot couldn't tell which—and held her own wig up to the image. This apparently helped, because Fiona tapped the photo aggressively and handed it back.

"I remember her." The photo was of Frederica Mercado, their most recent victim. "She used to come in a fair bit, always VIP. *Always*. But she had blond hair, cute little bob." Ah, that explained the experiment with the wig. "But like, you could tell it wasn't her real color, y'know? But I remember her. Those *eyebrows*." Fiona let out a dreamy sigh. "Just... chef's kiss, y'know?" She mimicked kissing her fingertips.

Margot glanced at the image of Frederica, having never really paid much attention to the woman's brows before. They were thick, dark, and full, but not in a way that overpowered her face. They *were* very nicely groomed.

"Did you ever talk to her?"

"Not really paid to talk." Fiona had pulled her knees up to her chest.

"Do you recognize either of the other women?"

Fiona looked at the two other photos again. "The blonde. Not a guest, though. She would sometimes come and visit with Jesse."

"Who is Jesse?"

The girl chuckled, then realized Margot wasn't kidding. "Oh. Jesse's the manager."

"And you saw her visiting Jesse?"

"I think so. But I haven't seen her in a long time. Maybe they were dating, I don't know. Jesse dates a lot."

Margot put the photos back into her jacket pocket.

"Fiona, do you ever do anything *other* than dance? Maybe you were asked by Jesse or someone else?"

There was a long pause as the girl stared right into Margot, her expression somehow both angry and hurt. "Oh, you think just because I'm a dancer, I'm also willing to do other shit?" She rolled her eyes. "You're just as bad as my fucking dad. *No.* I'm not a working girl, Detective. I'm a dancer. Not an exotic dancer. Not a sex worker. No shade if anyone is, I know some girls come into the club. But *no*. I just dance. I don't make a lot of money doing it, but I'm damned good at it, OK?"

Margot nodded, feeling like she should apologize, but also the question had to be asked.

"Have you heard anything about women coming to this bar and disappearing?" Margot asked, moving on from the last topic. She didn't fail to note that Fiona had mentioned knowing some girls did sex work out of the club, so there might be more she had overheard.

Fiona started to bite her nail, then let it drop, an anxiety response Margot felt a pang of sympathy for. Her own ragged nails were a testament to plenty of anxiety.

"I don't know anything about that. We have a lot of people who come into the club, they're around a ton for like a month, and then they never come back again. I can't assume they're all disappearing. Maybe they're just going somewhere else."

"The working girls, you mean?"

Fiona gave her another look, smoky eyes narrowed to slits. "Does it matter?"

This topic was obviously tender for the girl for some reason. Either she *was* involved in sex work and didn't want Margot to know, or the job touched her life in some other way, because she was more sensitive about it than most people would be.

"I'm asking because the three women in the photos I showed you are all known to have been connected to a high-end escort service. We have reason to believe that some of them were working here, specifically in the VIP lounge. I just want to know if you've heard anything about those girls disappearing."

"I don't know anything," Fiona repeated, but it was almost a whisper, and Margot felt certain it was a lie.

"Look, no one has to know you said anything to me. We can talk anywhere. You can call me anytime." She held out one of her business cards for the girl.

Fiona tilted her chin up, looking imperious, and repeated, "I don't know anything."

But she took the card anyway.

THIRTY-ONE

Margot left Fiona to finish her preparations, but the girl's words continued to nag at her, and the way she'd responded to some of Margot's questions. It seemed clear she knew more than she was letting on, but Leon had warned them that would be the case during this questioning.

It was frustrating how often it was obvious one of their witnesses knew something but fear or self-preservation kept them from talking.

The number of crimes that went unsolved simply because someone wouldn't share the smallest tidbit of information was a frustrating reality in her line of work.

She met Leon and Wes at the bar, and neither of them looked particularly enthused by whatever they had managed to learn, either.

"Can we speak to Jesse?" Margot asked.

"Your funeral," replied a handsome twentysomething bartender, inclining his head in the direction of the hallway at the end of the bar.

With that welcoming thought, Leon led them down the

hall, past the bathrooms, where Margot imagined they could probably find enough residual cocaine to make a cartel *jefe* blush, and Leon knocked on the door of a room marked *Office— Employees Only*.

After a moment a gruff voice said, "Come in if you're coming in."

Margot and Wes exchanged a quick glance, and he seemed to be thinking the same thing she was: they certainly weren't rolling out the welcome mat here.

Leon led the way, and they entered a decently sized office that was much less sterile than Margot had expected.

There were layered rugs on the floor, and a massive mahogany desk near the back wall. The room was dimly lit, no overhead lighting, just several lamps, including an old green-glass banker's lamp on the desk. Various abstract art pieces adorned the walls, and Margot wasn't enough of an art expert to know if they were worth anything, but based on the general vibes of the office, she wouldn't be surprised if they were.

"Good evening, Mister..." Leon let his voice drift, opening up for Jesse to give them his name.

The man they had come to see was seated behind the desk. He was in his forties, but fit and good-looking, dark hair cut recently, and a pair of wire-rimmed glasses slid to the end of his nose as he looked at his computer monitor. He had barely glanced up since they'd come in.

He took off his glasses and set them down, each small gesture pointed in a way to let them know they were interrupting him. "Simcoe," he said, even his syllables clipped and efficient. "Jesse Simcoe."

Margot spotted a series of small monitors on the desk to the man's left, and she could make out black-and-white footage of the club's interior, as well as one exterior view. So he had known they were here from the moment they'd walked up.

"We'd like to ask you a few questions, if you don't mind,"

Leon said, dropping himself uninvited into one of the chairs facing the desk. Wes gave the slightest tilt of his head to indicate Margot should sit in the other, which she did.

He wasn't being chivalrous; Wes had a keen eye and liked to wander the spaces they went into when speaking to witnesses and potential suspects. The incriminating things he'd found just lying out where anyone could see them was often surprising, to say the least.

Margot tried to match Jesse's posture, leaning back in her chair, an unimpressed scowl on her face. He looked over at her and it seemed to jolt him, like he realized what she was doing.

"I've got a few minutes," he said, his gaze not moving from Margot. She wasn't a fan of the new attention, but at least he was giving them a chance. Though she knew that Jesse more than anyone else who worked for him would be the least inclined to give them anything useful. Which was unfortunate because he likely knew the most.

Since he was focused on Margot, she decided she might as well lead the questioning and Leon could intervene if he felt like she was missing anything. She withdrew the photos from her pocket, knowing it would be a waste of everyone's time if she peppered him with warm-up questions.

"Do you recognize any of these women?"

Gamely, Jesse picked up the photos and looked them over, though he wasn't studying them the way Fiona had earlier. He slid Leanne Wu's photo back across the table toward them. "She was a bartender here probably four years ago. Haven't seen her since she quit. The other two could be just about anyone we have in here on a regular basis."

"Are you sure you don't want to have another look?" Margot asked. In light of what she'd learned about Rebecca Watson and her connection to Jesse, she was giving him an opportunity not to get caught in a lie.

He stared at her, then back at the photos again. His jaw

tightened and he wasn't a smooth enough liar to keep from darting a quick glance at Margot before handing the photos back again and tapping the photo of Rebecca. "She used to come around the bar sometimes. We might have hooked up once or twice."

This still didn't mesh with what Fiona had said, but better than having to call him out on the too-obvious lie.

"You hooked up with her but didn't recognize her photo?" Leon asked.

Jesse shrugged. "I work at a bar, Detectives, I hook up with a lot of women. I hate to sound cavalier, but I don't always recognize what they look like in daylight."

"Mmm," was all Leon replied.

"We have reason to believe that there might be some girls who frequent this club as a part of an escort business. You wouldn't know anything about that, would you?"

Jesse's expression hardened for a moment, his eyes darkening and a pronounced tension in his jaw making him look mean, then the moment passed. "I don't ask people what their job is. If they're hot, they get to come in. Sometimes hot women like to make money from being hot. Not sure that's a crime."

Margot was about to point out that it was, in fact, a crime, but she didn't think Jesse was looking for her feedback.

"I feel like you'd know if your VIP bottle service was being used to aid and abet sex trafficking," Leon said.

Margot gave him a quick look. So much for keeping things friendly and non-confrontational. Leon just went for the jugular.

Unfortunately, it didn't look like Jesse was interested in having the kind of anger-fueled reaction that might lead someone else to spill something in a rage lapse.

"Hey, I understand you're trying to do your jobs. I'm guessing you wouldn't be showing me these photos unless something bad had happened to these women. For that I'm genuinely sorry, but whatever happened to them it wasn't because of any connection to this club. At least not from a professional standpoint. I can't say that everyone who comes through our doors is psychologically well-adjusted. Maybe some nutter was coming in here to meet girls and something happened. But that could be true of any bar anywhere. Doesn't make me or my staff responsible."

"You knew two of these women personally," Margot reminded him. "One of them intimately."

"I don't know what to tell you that's going to satisfy you. Sometimes you fuck someone and they die. Doesn't mean you're responsible for it. You're barking up the wrong tree. Now, while I appreciate that you've got a job to do, so do I, and if you have any additional questions you can direct them to the club's lawyer." He put his glasses on and turned his attention back to the computer screen, efficiently ending the conversation with that one motion.

Margot and Leon got up and along with Wes they left the office and headed back outside. After Leon briefly questioned the security guard, they wandered into a nearby coffee shop to debrief. Since the club was downtown and it was after five, the coffee shop was almost vacant except for the two teenage girls working behind the counter. They were both glued to their phones, deeply uninterested in what three old people might be discussing at the corner table.

Leon drank an Earl Grey tea, while Margot was of the firm opinion that there was no bad time of day for an iced coffee. Wes ordered a small black coffee which he barely touched. They compared notes on what they'd learned at the club.

Evidently it had been fairly common knowledge that Rebecca and Jesse were an item, at least for a while. A much more involved relationship than he had alluded to, certainly, which did merit treating him like a person of interest.

Two of the longer-tenured bartenders recognized Leanne as

Jesse had. He likely hadn't lied about her because employment records were pretty hard to ignore. None of the bartenders thought Leanne had any enemies among the staff or management, and she'd left of her own accord after getting a different job several years earlier.

Was that job working for the escort service? Margot wondered.

The VIP waitress had been tight-lipped about activities that took place in her section, wouldn't name names, and while Leon was sure she'd had more to say, answered much the same as Fiona had. *I don't know anything about that.*

The trip hadn't been a total bust. They had one person to dig deeper into, and by now Riga would have certainly heard about their visit, so time would tell what the response from him would be. They had made it clear in their questioning they had known about the escort side-business, even if no one wanted to fess up to it. That would catch the big man's attention.

Despite the jolt of caffeine, Margot felt the weight of her day crashing in on her. She also knew she still needed to have a real conversation with her brother today, and hopefully it would get him off of her couch and back to his own life.

She had enough on her plate, she didn't need to deal with Justin's issues as well. Not right now.

After they made a quick pit-stop at the station, Margot collected her things and her car. But as she was leaving, Wes was lingering outside, and there was an expression on his face when he saw her come out that was altogether too serious.

"Walk you to your car?" he asked.

She considered pointing out that her car was only a block away, but bit her tongue since it was obvious there was something on his mind. Her pulse ratcheted up, and she took breaths in through her nose.

Having sat across from her serial killer father only that

morning and survived it, a moment of seriousness from Wes was not going to be the thing that set off a panic attack.

Not today.

She followed him over to her car. His form was more hunched than usual, shoulders rolled forward, head looking down at his feet while they walked. So it *hadn't* been the case making him behave oddly earlier, there was something else on his mind.

They stopped beside her car and finally she couldn't bear another second of him acting like this.

"What is *wrong* with you today?" she demanded. Her tone came out harsher than she'd meant to and she immediately felt terrible. She bit her lip and tried again. "I mean, you haven't been acting like yourself all afternoon. I thought I was supposed to be the surly asshole of our duo."

This gave Wes an excuse to smile, and finally look up at her. She almost wished he had kept looking at the ground, because his expression was too raw, too earnest. She suddenly didn't want to know what he was about to say.

"Margot..."

She swallowed hard, then pressed a palm to his chest. He let out a little sigh and she fought against a momentary desire to lean into him, to see if the things she often wondered about them could be real.

Her fingers twitched against his shirt.

"Wes, I can't pretend to know what it is you want to say, but can you wait? Wait a little longer. Until my brother isn't passed out on my couch, until I'm not fresh off of a visit with Ed, until—"

Wes looked at her, a moment of hurt giving way to something else, something warmer. Because she wasn't saying no. She wasn't saying *never tell me*, she was just saying, *wait a little longer*.

And she realized that was the real answer she wanted to give him.

She had worried that anything other than a no might be the end of them.

But now her worry was: what if it was a beginning?

THIRTY-TWO

Margot frowned, taking in her empty apartment. Justin still wasn't home.

Surprising, given how long she'd been gone, and how little money she suspected he had. But he was in San Francisco, there was plenty to do and see for free if one was motivated enough to go looking for it.

Justin wasn't unfamiliar with the city, they'd come here enough times when they'd been children.

Margot decided not to worry about him and take an opportunity to decompress alone. She felt as if she hadn't been alone in a very long time, though it had only been a couple of days since Justin had showed up at her doorstep.

She took a long shower, trying to wash the feel of her day away. When she got out, she spent a while looking in the mirror, inspecting the purple marks on her neck. They were starting to get more yellow than black, which was a good sign that they were healing, but it was ugly to look at.

She would definitely need to wait a few more days before she tried to go without the turtlenecks.

Sighing, she put on her pajamas—a pair of fading sweatpants and a Giants shirt with holes in it—and called down to the front desk. Brody answered on the second ring.

"Evening, Ms. Phalen," he said politely.

"Hey, Brody. Have you seen my brother at all today?"

The man was thoughtful. "I wasn't here in the morning, but I saw him around five. Came in briefly, then left again about an hour later. Didn't say anything to me."

Right around the time Margot normally might be getting home from her shift. Not that she had a typical nine-to-five, and her hours changed drastically when she was working overnights, but perhaps Justin *had* made an effort to be home to talk to her, and then left when it was clear she wasn't coming.

He hadn't texted her though.

"OK, thanks. You mind calling in an order for me?" This was part of her typical routine. She preferred Brody be the one to place food orders for her, so she didn't set up a routine with any restaurants or delivery drivers that gave them the impression she was a single woman, living alone.

"You got it, Ms. Phalen, hit me when you're ready."

She rattled off an order for her favorite Thai restaurant, adding a few extras for whenever Justin decided to come home. Thai was thankfully very forgiving to being reheated and eaten later on. Brody read the order back to her to make sure he'd gotten it right, then said, "I'll let you know when it's here."

"Thanks."

Once she hung up, she picked up her phone just to make sure she hadn't missed anything from Justin. It was getting close to nine o'clock. Which wasn't *late*, but it was getting into a time when a recovering alcoholic who'd recently fallen off the wagon could find himself getting into a little trouble if he was out and about.

She typed.

> Where are you?

Then, realizing how it might sound on its own, she added:

> I just got home, ordered some Thai that should be here in about thirty minutes.

For a while, there was no answer, and she started to wonder if she might need to call him or, God forbid, go out looking for him. She wasn't even sure she'd know where to start looking, and her brother was in his thirties, he would probably only be annoyed with her for making the effort.

About five minutes later, she got his reply.

> Be back in about fifteen.

The lure of Thai food was irresistible.

Margot went to the fridge and made herself a drink, mixing cold gin with a can of Fresca. She didn't want to be drinking when Justin got home, but after the day she'd had—that truly felt like a week of stress packed into only a few hours—she needed something to dull the sharp edges of her mounting anxiety.

She wanted to be able to sleep tonight.

Not that sleep was ever a given, and especially not after a day with Ed.

As if the universe had heard her thoughts, her phone pinged with a new message. Was Justin going to be delayed? She didn't want to have a serious discussion with him if they were going to be up past midnight, she just didn't have it in her tonight.

Instead she saw Andrew Rhodes' name on the screen, and finished her drink in a shot, before refilling the tumbler partway with just straight gin. Once steeled, she opened the message.

> Heard from the lawyer. Finch is willing to meet again. Wednesday morning. Prison has cleared it.

This wasn't a request, there were no question marks, no checking to see if she was OK with it. Andrew assumed she would go. She felt a flash of annoyance, then realized he was right. She would go. She had Wednesday and Thursday off ahead of her and Wes switching to the night shift, so it would be an ideal time for it.

If there was such a thing as an ideal time to see Ed.

She sighed and polished off the rest of her gin, and curbed the desire to pour more. She put the booze back in the fridge and rinsed the glass out, then picked up her phone.

A tart reply was on the tip of her fingers, but she found when the moment came, she didn't have the desire to send what she'd worked up.

Instead she just wrote, *Fine*.

Fine was a powerful word for those who took the time to hear it. Because it didn't mean *fine*, it wasn't a good word, it conveyed the weight of frustration, annoyance, and anxiety-fried nerves. But it also gave the recipient an out if they chose *not* to listen. Which she suspected would be the case with Andrew.

Justin arrived as close to on time as Margot could ever hope for, and the Thai delivery came ten minutes later. Once she collected it from Brody she set up the dinner table. Normally she would eat in front of the TV and watch something mind-numbing and funny, something to distract her from whatever horrors she'd witnessed that day. But circumstances wouldn't be normal until Justin went home again.

Margot turned off the TV when she heard the shower end. It was just local news, something they'd dragged good old Chief of Police Pressley Boyd out for, but it wasn't her beat, and it wasn't more help for the Redwood Killer case, so she didn't care to look at his weaselly little face right before she ate.

Justin came out of the bathroom, freshly showered, and

settled in across the small table from her. He looked better today, at least better than he'd been when he first arrived. He didn't stink of stale beer and whiskey, and his skin no longer had the waxy pallor of someone who looked like they were rotting. Justin had shaved, he smelled of her soap and shampoo, which were perhaps a little floral for him, but it was better than it had been by miles.

"How was your day?" she asked, and found that she was genuinely curious what he'd been up to. Also she longed for any excuse not to talk about her own day.

Justin shrugged. "I did the whole tourist-for-a-day thing, looked up landmarks I'd never actually seen, like the Painted Ladies and the Palace of Fine Arts, did a lot of walking." He paused as he piled crab Rangoons onto his plate. "Did a lot of thinking."

Margot thoughtfully chewed on a piece of chicken from her pad see ew, waiting to see if he would continue or force her to egg him on.

Justin sighed, pushing the deep-fried wonton on his plate around with his fingertip like he was a child. Margot wanted to grab his hand to stop the fidgeting, but resisted the urge, focusing instead on eating her own meal and giving him the time he needed to process whatever he'd been thinking about.

Honestly, it also gave her more time to put off what she had decided to say to him.

"My life is a fucking mess, Margot," he said. "I think that much is pretty obvious. I mean, ever since Tamara left me and took Cruz..." He paused, leaning back in his chair. "You know, probably a long time before that, actually. I mean, she didn't leave me for no reason. But whenever I'm with you I see how you've got your shit so together, and I wonder why it is that I can't do the same."

Margot laughed, she couldn't help it. "You think I have my shit together?"

Justin looked affronted by her laughter, staring at her like she was making fun of him. "Well, yeah."

"Oh my God, David. I am basically a train wreck just making it through day by day. My fridge is empty, I make my building manager call in food orders for me because Dad convinced me that any kind of routine is an invitation to have someone murder me. I don't have functional relationships, I freak out if someone puts the child locks on in a car, I drink too much, I'm *deeply* in therapy, and I wonder how it is I don't get locked up in a loony bin on a regular basis. But I'm glad my ability to shower and pay my bills on time makes you think I have my shit together. Maybe everyone on the outside believes it too." She wiped an unexpected tear from the corner of her eye and picked up a sauce-covered piece of broccoli, popping it in her mouth.

Justin watched her for a moment, taking it all in, and then smiling. "Jesus. I guess being fucked in the head is just the family legacy, huh?" He pushed some noodles around on his plate but didn't eat any. "Margot, I'm sorry I came here like I did," he said finally. "I wish you'd never seen me like that. It was a really low moment, and I let some big feelings get the better of me."

Had he been talking to his therapist while he'd been here?

Did Justin even have a good therapist?

It had taken Margot years to find Dr. Singh, just when she was about to give up hope that any doctor might actually be able to help her work through the trauma she had about her childhood. But she had, finally, and she hoped her brother had as well.

"I'm sorry that I showed up unannounced and put a lot of my shit on you. That wasn't fair of me. And I know that you and Dad have a different relationship than he and I do—"

"David," she said, careful to use his new name. "Ed and I don't *have* a relationship. Not good, bad, or otherwise. He's a fucking psychopath, you know that right? You understand that he doesn't have real relationships with anyone, he just changes whatever face he's wearing that day to be appealing to the person sitting in front of him."

Only he'd stopped pretending with her.

But that didn't mean it wasn't all still some sick game.

Justin's jaw tightened, and she felt bad for interrupting him. After a moment he continued with what he'd been saying. "I'm sorry I made you feel like you had to participate in the documentary. I know it's your choice, not mine."

He looked down at his plate, finally finished. It was evident to Margot he'd spoken to someone today, someone who had walked him through what to say. She was grateful for that, and for him making the effort. As Justin popped the crunchy crab Rangoon in his mouth, she took her turn.

"Thank you. That probably wasn't easy to say. I did a lot of thinking myself today, and I'm willing to make a concession."

He looked right at her, unable to keep the excitement off his face. Again Margot was struck by the way he managed to look so young sometimes, so innocent.

She held up a finger, hoping to caution him against raising his expectations too high, but she feared it was already too late for that.

"I will *talk* to the producers of the series," she said. "Just a meeting, totally confidentially. I am not going to do the filming, but if I talk to them, maybe I can give them some intel they can use and explain why it's not necessary that we are both filmed. I'll do what I can to make this happen for you, even though I don't think it's going to give you the closure you're hoping for."

Because wasn't that what she'd wanted—in part—from her own visits with Ed? Some way to find solace and put to rest her idea of who Ed *had* been. To perhaps bury her father as one of the many victims of Ed Finch? Since the man she had known simply didn't exist anymore.

Except in meeting with Ed, she had learned the opposite was true. He was still the man she had known.

Which somehow made it even worse, because how had she missed the truth for fifteen years? How had they looked into those eyes and not seen him for what he really was?

All she'd gotten from her visits with Ed was more guilt. She wondered what Justin would get when he went on camera and told millions of viewers that his whole family was made of fools who went to bed under the same roof as a monster. She wondered if Justin had thought about his *own* son in all of this. What would it mean for Cruz that his father's past was being made public like this? Would he grow up knowing his grandfather had been a killer? What might that do to him?

Or maybe Justin was doing this, in a way, *for* his son. Maybe by finding a way to exorcise the demons of his past, he thought he could be a better father to Cruz than Ed had ever been to either of them.

Justin, oblivious to her spiraling thoughts, was nodding his head, the excitement dimmed slightly, but not gone entirely.

"Thank you. That would mean a lot to me. But I do think you might reconsider when you talk to them."

Margot didn't want to give him hope. She didn't want to tell him that her own certainty on the topic had been wavering. That a *very* small part of her now wondered if the documentary couldn't be her own unique way of coming out. Not coming out of the closet—no one cared about her sexuality—but by coming out as Megan Finch. Finally letting that part of her past breathe so it didn't have to hold her back anymore.

But she didn't say any of this, because she knew the most likely thing to happen would be that the producers would make her skin crawl and she'd tell them precisely where they could take their documentary.

There was no need to get Justin's hopes up for more than the bare minimum.

What she did say was, "I hope you've really thought this through. Putting yourself out there like this isn't just about you, it will impact everyone in your life. *Everyone*," she emphasized, hoping he might be reminded of Cruz and reconsider this self-destructive path he was going down.

Justin fixed his eyes on his plate instead of looking at her. "I've done nothing *but* think about this, Margot. I'm not changing my mind."

So, she let it go.

They finished eating with basic small talk. Justin went to the bathroom after dinner as Margot cleared the table, but she almost tripped over his abandoned tennis shoes, discarded near the end of the couch.

He'd never broken the habit of just leaving his shoes wherever he took them off. He'd been doing it since they were children, and it had driven Ed up the wall. Margot finally understood why.

Setting the dishes on the peninsula, she picked up the shoes to put them by the door, but as they fell under the light of her living room lamp, she paused.

She stared at the shoes, barely breathing, both unsure and too sure of what she was looking at.

Dotted on the toe of the right shoe were two drops, so small they might have been easy to miss looking down at your own feet. But those red drops were unmistakable to Margot.

That was blood.

And though Margot couldn't be certain, it looked like it hadn't been there long.

THIRTY-THREE
1993

Desolation Wilderness, California

The day after Ed had gone to watch the girls, Justin was quiet.

Too quiet.

There was something tense and unnerving about the boy since he'd been awake next to Ed in the tent, asking in that quiet voice of his, *Where were you?*

Now that Ed was thinking about it, those words had sounded much the same as they had coming from Kim the night she caught him. What she believed to be infidelity had actually been disposing of a body, so he'd let her have the easy lie.

But now he heard that same tone from his son.

Where were you?

Not a question spawned by being alone and nervous in the woods, not a curiosity, but an accusation.

The longer Ed walked along in silence, with Justin trailing behind him staring at the ground, the angrier he got. He wanted to confront the kid, to demand where he got off asking questions, what right it was of his to have Ed in his line of sight at all times.

What if he *had* been going to the bathroom?

What if he'd just needed a little fucking alone time from the constant presence of an ungrateful brat who didn't appreciate the lessons his father was trying to teach him out here?

Would a little *gratitude* be so out of line?

Ed didn't think so. He didn't think he deserved to be questioned. However he did bite his tongue, because Justin hadn't asked any more questions about it, hadn't said anything at all, in fact, since they'd broken camp. Now they were circling back in the direction of the trailhead, a trip that would take them most of the day, and there was a chill to the air that told them they wouldn't want to be out here after dark.

So far the weather had been good for them, the nights pleasant in their small tent, but the chill around them now had a certain dampness, and while there were no clouds in the immediate vicinity, Ed knew a coming storm when he felt one.

Stewart had taught him the signs.

Instead of dwelling on his son, Ed thought about Stewart, about the life lessons his uncle had been able to impart to him. Stewart wasn't a man who wore his emotions on his sleeve, he was often chilly, never said the words *I love you*, which was harder for Ed's sister Sarah than it was for him. Ed learned to appreciate that his uncle demonstrated his affection in different ways.

He taught Ed how to throw a punch after learning the boy was being bullied at his new school, but more importantly taught him how to block one. He told him to never start a fight if he could help it, but to always be willing to finish one.

Stewart taught Ed how to survive in the wild, how to move quietly, how to cover your tracks.

Lessons that he had probably anticipated Ed would use differently, but that had served him well in adulthood nevertheless.

Ed wanted his own son to appreciate those lessons, because

they could help form someone who was self-sufficient, strong, and confident.

What he was starting to realize on this trip, though, was that Justin was a very different person than Ed had been as a child. Spoiled, coddled, but also innocent still. He hadn't been broken down the way Ed had been, hadn't been treated like a burden, like a curse.

Maybe Justin didn't need the same lessons as Ed did.

But without imparting Stewart's treasure trove of advice, Ed didn't know what else he had to offer the boy.

He glanced behind him and saw that Justin was staring down at the ground. Something in the detritus of the path had caught his attention. Ed waited a moment, wondering if it was a rock or pine cone that Justin might collect and add to his pack. He wanted the boy to hurry, they were going to be just ahead of a storm the whole way back to the car, and if they dawdled—if Justin dawdled—they risked getting caught in a freezing mountain deluge.

But Justin didn't pick up whatever he was looking at, he just kept staring at it, then in an unexpected motion, he stomped his foot down *hard*. Sticks cracked, the dirt ground against his shoe. Ed was surprised by the suddenness of it and almost said something, but Justin just wiped his shoe on the dirt path and continued on, his expression unreadable even to Ed.

Ed stared after him, then moved back up the path to where he'd been standing.

There in the dirt was the remnants of a bird nest that must have fallen from a tree. Ed hadn't even noticed it when he'd gone ahead of the boy down the path.

All that remained of the nest now was a scattering of twigs, and among the branches a red smear that had likely once been the nestlings.

Ed looked at Justin's retreating form on the path.

In his chest was a feeling, but for a man who rarely felt anything, he didn't know what name to give it.

Finally, after one last look at the mangled bodies on the ground, he understood what it was.

Fear.

THIRTY-FOUR

Margot couldn't stop thinking about the blood.

It could have come from anywhere. There were a thousand different reasons someone might end up with blood on their shoe, and almost all of those reasons were benign. Justin used to get nosebleeds a lot as a kid, there was a chance that was still happening and he'd simply never thought to mention it.

He might have cut himself at some point while he explored the city, might have encountered someone else who had cut themselves, might have walked somewhere and picked it up without realizing it.

This last one she was too well versed in blood splatter analysis to believe for herself. Blood didn't fall in drops if you got it from the ground.

But she told herself she was just worked up because of seeing Ed. She knew better than to let her brain wander down any of the paths it was poised to wander down. She was just looking for a worst-case scenario because she'd been to see Ed.

She was still telling herself that as she got ready for work next morning, because Justin was asleep on the couch.

He hadn't said anything about getting hurt, but maybe it had been so minor he hadn't even thought about it.

The blood was minimal, the tiniest little dots. So small she could almost convince herself it was something else entirely.

Almost, but not quite.

What else could it be?

A more sensible part of her brain told her to think this through. There were a *lot* of things it could be. Justin changed jobs a lot because he wasn't the most reliable, but he tended to end up doing a lot of construction work and building since jobs were constantly available. It could be paint, or rust, or hell, it could be pasta sauce. While it *did* look like blood to her, she knew the human eye wasn't perfect in judging what was and wasn't blood, so even though her gut was telling her one thing, her common sense tried to rein her in until she could really take the time to figure this out.

Once she got to work she would try not to let her worries show, especially not to Wes. If she acted differently toward him, especially after their moment the night before, he would most certainly take it personally. He'd misunderstand her. And the last thing she wanted to do was drive him away, but she also didn't want to explain what was going on.

If she was wrong... God, hopefully she was wrong... she didn't want anyone else to see Justin differently because of it.

She was going to have a hard enough time going back herself.

The usual coffee from Wes sat on her desk when she arrived, though the man himself was nowhere to be seen. She sat down and took a swig of the still-hot coffee and let the comfort of it wash over her. This, at least, this one small thing was still right, and normal, and unchanged.

Wes came in a moment later and grabbed his jacket off the coat rack. Margot had been poised to bring up her discovery, hoping that Wes might be able to talk her off a ledge and convince her that Justin *didn't* have potential crime scene evidence on his shoes. Instead, Wes handed her coat to her as he put his on, though she'd just taken hers off. "All right," she said, slipping her arms into the still-warm material. "I'll bite. Where are we going in such a hurry?"

He picked up her coffee from the desk and handed it to her, and she accepted it gratefully. "Caffeinate first, I need you to be nice."

"I'm always nice," she countered, but sipped her coffee anyway.

She was glad Wes was being *Wes* today, the stifling awkwardness between them gone, at least for a moment. There would be a day, she knew, not long from now, where she would need to have a reckoning with his feelings, and her feelings, and whatever that meant, but today was not going to be that day.

Today they were just Detectives Phalen and Fox. Margot and Wes would have to wait.

Once they got to Wes's car and he was pulling out into traffic, he said, "We managed to find an updated address for Angela Gromand."

Margot raised her eyebrows. The previous day their initial searches hadn't yielded anything worth digging into. "How did you manage that?"

"I spent about an hour arguing with people at the DMV before someone was able to tell me she had submitted a change of address form about a month ago that just hadn't been pushed out, so our search wasn't capturing it. Got the new address." He flashed a little grin at her. "All thanks to my above-standard charm."

Margot laughed. "I must admit, my standard-level charm, especially at seven in the morning with no coffee in my system, probably wouldn't have managed that." She gave a little mock round of applause. "Job well done."

He rewarded her applause with a bow of the head. They

were driving through an area of the city Margot rarely visited, where the street names were all nods to other famous cities or countries. Peru Avenue butted up against Vienna Street, and they passed streets named for Brazil, Madrid, Edinburgh and more before Wes parked in front of a house on Moscow Street, a stone's throw from McLaren Park. The street was on a hill giving them a good look down over the city, but the houses were all fairly small and nondescript.

The one they were in front of had been painted a deep red at some point, but time, fog, and sun had transformed it to almost a salmon pink. When they got out of the car Margot noted there was a sign in the tiny front flower bed that had the Pride flag on it, and in the window there was a sun-bleached Hillary Clinton "I'm With Her" sign.

Margot took the lead, heading up the small set of stairs to the front door. It was early enough in the morning they might be waking whoever was home—if anyone was home—but this was the first legitimate lead they'd had on this case since Angela came stumbling out of the woods, and she wasn't about to let it slip through her fingers.

She rang the doorbell and waited. There was a silver compact car in the driveway, one they already knew from checking the DMV reports wasn't registered to Angela. Angela had a red Nissan Versa that they had a BOLO out for but no one had seen yet.

After a moment of silence Margot rang the bell again. The silver car gave her hope that Angela didn't live alone, that there was someone else here. A boyfriend, a parent, someone who might be missing her. Someone who might know who Rob was.

Margot heard footfalls from inside, and a moment later the front door opened.

There was a pause, and a mutual moment of confusion and then realization.

For the girl standing in front of her, it probably took less time to make the connection, but Margot had to look past a missing wig, a makeup-free face, and a body clad in a floral pajama set.

"Detective?" the woman said, startled.

"Fiona?" Margot replied, once she realized it was, indeed, the same girl she'd spoken to at the club the night before.

Fiona looked from Margot to Wes, her eyes still clouded with sleep, and she was clearly trying to process what they were doing on her front step. Margot, likewise, was wondering what the odds were that they would cross paths with the pint-sized dancer a second time in less than twenty-four hours.

And then Fiona's expression changed, and a look of horror twisted her features. The sleepy smile she'd had when she opened the door was gone, and so was her confusion. In their place was pale skin and tears already wetting the girl's lashes.

"Oh my God, are you here because of Angela?"

THIRTY-FIVE

Margot stared at the girl as if she had almost forgotten why they'd come. Fiona was looking back at her, her blue eyes wide. Without her wig on, she had dark, curly hair which was pulled back from her face with a pretty scarf. Her skin was clear, though extremely pale at the moment, and she looked even younger than Margot had imagined her yesterday.

"What is your relationship with Angela Gromand?" Margot asked carefully.

"Angela's my sister," Fiona answered without hesitation. She must have seen the question in Margot's eyes, because she quickly amended, "Half-sister, technically. Different fathers."

Margot could see now how similar their eyes were, since eyes were really the only feature she'd ever been able to clearly see on Angela. They'd found photos of her yesterday while doing their preliminary searches, but it had been hard to reconcile the girl in those photos with the one in the hospital.

Those blue eyes were now digging an expectant hole into Margot, waiting for her to explain her presence. Every answer to one of Margot's questions came out in a rush, as if she was desperate to get through the preamble and find out what was going on.

"When was the last time you saw your sister?" Margot asked.

Fiona's gaze was darting from Margot to Wes and back again, like she was hoping one of them might tell her that this was actually a practical joke and they just wanted to talk about the club some more.

Something dawned on Fiona in that moment and she braced her hand against the doorframe, her other palm going to her stomach like someone had just punched her. "Wait, didn't you say you were a homicide detective?" the girl asked, her voice taking on a shrill edge.

Margot should have foreseen this reaction, should have led with the good news.

Even if it was the grimmest kind of good news.

"Fiona, Angela is alive," she said, putting a comforting hand on the girl's shoulder before she could start to spiral. It was clear from the panic in her eyes that she was on the verge of having a minor meltdown. That might still happen, but Margot hoped she could head off the worst of it.

"You're sure?" Fiona asked, her voice as thin as vapor, like the mere presence of a homicide detective meant this was an impossibility. Margot could hardly blame the girl for jumping to that conclusion, but still she nodded, squeezing Fiona's shoulder.

"I'm sure. Can Detective Fox and I come in?"

Fiona stepped out of the doorway almost mechanically, her hand still pressed to her stomach, the nausea of worry obviously not abated. Margot thought Fiona might ask to go change, but instead she walked toward the living room and fell into a large armchair by the window. She buried her face in her hands and her thin shoulders started to tremble.

The house was small on the inside, but also tidier than

Margot would have expected for two girls in their twenties. The living room was close to the front entrance, and was an open concept design that allowed lines of sight to both the kitchen and a small dining room. At the back of the main floor was a staircase, which most likely led to where the bedrooms were. The design of the houses in this area put primary living on the main floor and sleeping on the lower floor, which wasn't technically a basement because it was all still above ground.

Fiona and Angela's kitchen was tiny but outfitted with a butcherblock island on wheels to allow more workspace. The granite counters were outfitted with a Smeg toaster and coffee maker. Expensive appliances.

A metallic sound drew Margot's attention as she watched a fluffy gray and white cat emerge from the stairwell. It paused, processing that there were unexpected guests present, then immediately bolted back down the stairs, the bell on its collar tinkling as it went.

Margot led Wes into the living room, where there were some signs of the previous night on the coffee table. A wine glass—just one—and a few single-serve candy wrappers dotted the table. There was also an ashtray with the remains of a joint in it, giving the room the slightest lingering scent of weed, but nothing too overpowering.

Fiona must have gotten home in the early hours of the morning, considering her job. Margot wondered how much sleep the girl was running on.

"Fiona, when was the last time you saw your sister?" Margot asked again.

"Four days ago?" Fiona lifted her head from her hands, her eyes already red-rimmed from crying. She phrased her answer as a question. "We kind of exist on different schedules, it's not uncommon to go a day or two without seeing each other. But usually she leaves me little notes, like little Post-Its? She'll put them on the coffee machine to tell me to have a good night at the club, or to remind me how much she loves me. Just little stuff like that. And I haven't seen a new note since Friday. That was weird."

"Have you tried to contact her?"

Fiona nodded, "I sent her a couple of texts, but that's the thing, too. We're both *awful* about charging our phones, or losing them, forgetting them at friends' places and shit. That's why she does the Post-Its. Where is she?" she asked, this last question almost as an afterthought, like her answers to their questions were being run on autopilot, and only once she'd finished speaking did Fiona recall the reason they were here.

"Your sister was found near a burning car in Golden Gate Park early Saturday morning. She suffered extensive burns, and she's in the burn unit at Saint Francis right now."

"*What? How?* Oh my God, what happened to her? Why didn't anyone call me? Oh God, Angie," Fiona blurted, her tone somewhere between anguish and accusation.

"Your sister had no identification on her, and due to her injuries, it took several days for us to be able to confirm her identity. Once we had an address, we came here immediately," Margot explained. It didn't feel like enough, looking at the crushed expression on Fiona's face. She felt like she'd let down both Fiona and Angela somehow.

"Fiona," Margot said, to capture the girl's attention again. "Do you know if your sister had a boyfriend, anyone she was seeing?"

Fiona was confused. "Why? I thought you said she was in an accident."

Wes cleared his throat and Fiona turned her attention to him. "Your sister was with someone who we believe intentionally set the fire that caused her burns." This was perhaps gentler than saying *who set your sister on fire*. The phrasing was delicate enough that Fiona didn't immediately start screaming or crying again, so that was good.

She was looking at Margot, wary. There was something she wanted to say but she didn't know how.

"Angela..."

Margot nodded encouragingly, because she already knew what Fiona was trying to tell her, but didn't want to be the first to say it just in case she was wrong.

"Angela would sometimes go on dates. Professionally."

Had Margot not known what to expect from this part of the conversation, Fiona's gentle phrasing might have confused her. Instead, she understood what Angela's sister was saying, without actually saying it.

"Your sister did tell us that she was a sex worker," Margot said.

"Escort," Fiona replied. "I mean, I guess they're the same thing in some ways. But Angie worked with really high-end clients. She made good money and worked for a service, they vetted the people she was seeing."

"Did she ever mention the name of the service she worked for?" Wes asked.

Fiona shook her head. "No, we didn't really... She didn't like to talk about it. She just wanted to help take care of me." Her lower lip trembled. "You think one of the guys from the service did this to her?"

"We think, based on what little she's been able to tell us, that it was one of her regular clients," Margot explained. "Does the name Rob mean anything to you?"

Fiona stiffened. The girl would be terrible at playing poker, she was all tells.

"She was seeing a guy named Rob."

"Seeing like he was a boyfriend?" Wes asked, leaning forward and resting his forearms on his thighs.

"I thought so, but she never wanted me to meet him, and never brought him over here. So I guess..." She shrugged. "I guess maybe he was a client. He would buy her things, take her out to nice dinners a lot. It sounded like he really liked her."

"Buy her what kind of things?" Margot asked.

"Clothes, a few new purses... He took her on a trip to Napa a couple months ago, but I thought maybe that didn't go so well because she was a bit weird afterwards. Not her usual self. Angie is so bubbly, she's just the lightest, happiest person. And after the Napa trip she was really quiet, never wanted to go out and do anything. I think she might have been a bit depressed, honestly. But even though I asked, she wouldn't talk about it. She didn't mention Rob for a while after that."

Margot jotted all this down. "So you never met him?"

Fiona shook her head. "He never came to the house. Now, that kind of makes sense. If he was a client, she wouldn't want him to know where she lived, would she?"

Margot couldn't help but wonder if their new address was related to Angela being afraid of Rob finding her.

Margot had an idea, kind of a long shot. She'd already asked Fiona about the girls from the Redwood Killer case, but the connection to Angela now was almost too perfect to resist. She pulled out her phone and went through her pictures until she got to one she'd taken during Frederica Mercado's autopsy. It wasn't grisly, didn't show enough of the body to be upsetting, but it did show a very small tattoo.

"Fiona, did Angela have any tattoos or jewelry that might have looked like this?" She handed the phone to Fiona, whose eyes widened.

"Yeah. She had this tattoo right here." She pointed to her wrist. "Got it about two years ago, maybe?"

Wes and Margot exchanged a quick look, Margot's pulse was thrumming. There was a very real possibility that whoever *Rob* was, he might be responsible not only for Angela's attack but their three unsolved homicides as well.

Angela Gromand could have been intended to be the fourth victim of the Redwood Killer.

THIRTY-SIX

Before they left Angela's house, Margot gave Fiona the number for Dr. Kaur and tried to gently explain how difficult it would be to see her.

"She's covered in bandages, the burns were very severe, over her whole body."

Fiona nodded, tears welling in her eyes. "I need to see her."

Margot recalled, then, the way Angela had said she didn't *have* a family when they questioned her in the hospital. It was obvious now that she did, and that Fiona was very important to her. It made Margot wonder why Angela had hidden Fiona from them, if it was so the younger girl didn't need to see her sister in her current state, or perhaps she was trying to protect Fiona from the very people who had hurt Angela herself.

But she couldn't deny letting Fiona see her sister now that she knew the truth.

"She's not always lucid," Margot explained. "They have her on a lot of pain medications. And she can't say much. But I'm sure she'd want to see you. Do you need us to contact anyone for you? Her parents maybe?"

Fiona shook her head and swiped away a tear that had

fallen down her cheek. "No, her dad left when she was young, they don't talk at all. And our mom..." A loaded sigh. "Our mom had a lot of problems with drugs. We don't know where she is until she pops up asking for money. It might be easier for her not to know."

Margot nodded, understanding that parents were not always what people might hope them to be. Hearing about Fiona and Angela's mother issues, it made sense why Angela would have done anything she needed to to take care of her little sister.

Here, too, Margot felt a pang of sympathy, but she tried to tamp it down.

Thinking about Justin right now would only remind her of all the looming questions she currently had about her brother, and that was a mental tangent she couldn't afford.

"You have my card, OK? You call me whenever. If you need anything or think of anything, please call me."

This time around Margot didn't think Fiona was going to be so dismissive of the offer.

Margot and Wes left the house and headed back toward his car. Before they got there, Margot heard a screen door slam and looked back to see Fiona jogging down the street toward them, a piece of paper clutched in her hand. When she got to them her breathing hadn't even been affected by the jog.

"Angie kept this from that trip to Napa. I don't know if it will be any help to you in figuring out who Rob is, but maybe..." Fiona handed Margot the rumpled paper, and it was a receipt from a spa, Margot assumed it must be within the same resort or hotel Angela had been a guest at. The receipt was stapled to a glossy brochure that explained all the other amenities available at the location.

Based on the receipt, Angela had attended a couple's massage and couple's facial. It wasn't clear why she had the receipt, or whether she'd been the one to pay, but Fiona was right, it did give them one more place to track down a possible killer.

Fiona left them again and, once they were in Wes's car, Margot gave him a look, the pamphlet still in her hand.

"How do you feel about a little road trip to Napa Valley?" She waved the glossy pamphlet in his direction.

Wes considered her carefully for a moment as if trying to decide what to say, then raised an eyebrow and opted for, "Why, Detective Phalen, I thought you'd never ask."

The ride from San Francisco to Napa Valley was a little over an hour if traffic behaved. Which meant, since it was mid-morning on a Tuesday, it would take them two if they were lucky. Though the route took them north, Napa Valley was further inland than Petaluma, so much to Margot's relief they wouldn't be taking any detours through her old stomping grounds.

They stopped for coffee and breakfast sandwiches at a fast-food drive thru, and Margot suspected Wes had made the stop pre-emptively because he knew she could be a little bitchy if she hadn't eaten. It also meant she was able to focus on eating her bacon-and-egg sandwich rather than allowing the long drive to give Wes another potential opportunity for a heart-to-heart.

So far today he'd been in good spirits, with no sign of the quiet intensity of the previous day, and no hints that he was considering a serious chat. She hoped he'd taken her words from last night to heart. Not a no forever, just a no for now. With another Ed visit coming up the next morning, and her recent questions about Justin, she couldn't add anything else to her plate.

The problem for her—and for Wes—was she didn't know *when* the right time might actually arise.

What she did know was they had a promising lead, and she had a delicious sandwich in her hands, so if she could just focus on that, then she might make it through this day. One day at a time was all she was capable of at the moment.

She couldn't even think about Ed right now. That was a problem for tomorrow Margot.

Margot mulled over bringing up the situation with Justin. She'd been so ready to ask for Wes's take on it this morning before he'd dragged her out of the office, but now she felt herself suddenly unable to move her mouth and get the words out.

She needed Wes to be her true north, and he'd been by her side through a *lot*. But what if this was the thing that made him bail? What if killer father *and* killer brother was just more than one man could overlook?

Or worse, what if he thought she was just being crazy and imagining the whole thing? Having Wes dismiss her concerns would be almost worse than the worst-case scenario she was already imagining.

So, despite the fact that she knew he might be the very person to talk her off her ledge, she stayed out on it alone, preferring the uncertainty to the much grimmer option of driving Wes further away from her.

She caught him looking at her once or twice, registering her silence and the tension in the car, but took comfort in the thought he'd have no way to know what was really on her mind.

Absently, she chewed her thumbnail and looked out the car window.

The scenery started to change as they headed inland; gone were the forested coastal areas, replaced by brown mountainsides with patchy scrub, and soon the greenery returned but this time in the form of rolling vineyards. The verdant foliage almost looked at odds with the dry mountain landscapes behind them.

Margot had never been to a winery. Even though she'd lived in Northern California for much of her life, there had never been any reason to make the short drive that would have brought her into wine country. When she'd lived in Petaluma, she'd been too young. When she returned as an adult, she wasn't much of a wine drinker. Making a weekend trip, or even a day trip to the wineries wasn't really something that fit her lifestyle.

The areas they drove through were imprinted with the wealth of this region. Mansions were set back on hills, and gorgeous Spanish-style hotels were nestled in among the grapevines. Signs promised horseback riding, a small airport—for anyone who wanted to fly here on their private jet—and Margot saw more than one Porsche drive by them.

With her navigation, Wes turned at a paved driveway where there was a sign announcing the Bella Vista Hotel and Spa, proudly declared *Number One Resort in Northern California*.

Margot was never sure if those kind of claims had to be backed up somehow, or people could just wildly announce them. Could she say she was the number one detective in Northern California? What metrics could prove her wrong?

This thought engaged her all the way to the front entrance of the hotel, where she couldn't help but stare wide-eyed at the ostentatiousness of it all. Margot hadn't grown up *poor*, but especially after Ed's arrest things had been tight with the family finances. Even now she wasn't swimming in disposable income, and what little she had fed—literally—her takeout addiction and paying for therapy.

This hotel was the definition of luxury. The grounds were expansive and well maintained, looking greener than nature would ever allow on its own. The hotel itself was a mix of modern design with clean lines and a lot of concrete, but combined with an earthy vibe that included wood features and a lot of water everywhere, from ponds to fountains to small waterfalls. Everywhere she looked, water seemed to be moving. Koi fish swam in a pond near the entrance, and the burbling sound of running water was immediately soothing when she got out of the car.

They headed into the lobby and the smell once she passed through the front door further emphasized luxury and relaxation. The scent of eucalyptus and sandalwood filled the large room, but not in an overwhelming way.

Margot had to restrain herself from looking around the room with her mouth half-open in disbelief. For a second she wondered what it would be like to come here with Wes under different circumstances, before she moved that thought firmly to the back of her mind. They were here to find a killer. And just a quick view of the premises told Margot that Rob definitely had money, because even a high-class escort wouldn't make enough money to throw it away on a place like this.

They got to the reception desk and a woman in a tailored black suit smiled at them. Her long black hair had been perfectly straightened and Margot was willing to bet she had never had a blemish in her entire life.

"Good afternoon, welcome to the Bella Vista. Do you have a reservation?"

Wes plopped his badge on the front counter. "We were hoping we could speak to a manager."

The woman blanched on seeing his badge but she kept her smile plastered in place. "Of course. Can you tell me what this is regarding?"

"We have reason to believe one of your hotel's former guests might have been involved in a serious crime."

The woman nodded and reached for the phone in front of her. After a moment, she spoke. "Mr. Noru, there are some detectives here who would like to have a word with you."

Whatever the man on the other end of the phone said, Margot couldn't make it out, but he apparently didn't ask for more details. The woman hung up, her smile returning, though this time it was a little colder than before. "He'll be right up, you can wait just over there." She ushered them to the end of the counter, and Margot moved along as indicated.

She and Wes didn't need to wait long. An older man, in his sixties, appeared in short order. Like the concierge, he was wearing an impeccably tailored suit, and though his hair had started to gray at his temples, his complexion showed little sign of age. He was handsome in a severe way, and looked to be Japanese or Korean, though the name the concierge had used—Noru—made Margot think his heritage would be Japanese.

"Detectives, welcome to the Bella Vista. I hope you can appreciate that the hotel has a certain image to uphold, one that doesn't mesh well with perceived threats. Would you mind joining me in my office to continue this discussion?" He politely gestured to the hallway he'd just come from. Margot wondered if she should be offended that her appearance was so obviously police-like she posed a threat to their business just by existing in the lobby.

Once they were in Mr. Noru's office, his tense politeness continued. "Can I get you anything to drink? Sparking water, coffee?"

Margot and Wes both declined.

Wes spoke first. "Mr. Noru, we're investigating the case of a woman who was intentionally lit on fire last week in Golden Gate Park."

"How horrible," the man said quickly. "But you'll excuse me if I don't understand how an incident so far away could involve our establishment. Are you even in your jurisdiction out here?"

Wes's jaw ticked in annoyance. "It's within our scope to explore all leads, even those outside the city limits."

Margot set down the brochure and receipt for spa services and slid it across Mr. Noru's very expensive-looking desk so he could get a better view.

"We know our victim was here, and we know which

services she was participating in on which date. What we need is the name of the man who paid for those services."

Mr. Noru looked immediately uncomfortable. "Detectives, I need to impress upon you that our hotel's reputation is rooted in our customer service. And part of that service is our discretion."

Margot smiled at him, leaning against the desk. She knew her smile was not a comforting one. "Would you agree that all your guests are owed the same level of care?"

"Of course," Noru said, almost bristling at the suggestion that it might be otherwise. "All of Bella Vista's guests are treated equally. We want everyone to experience the resort in the same way."

"Then I'm sure you want one of your guests, who is currently fighting for her life, covered head to toe in third-degree burns, to receive the ultimate gift you can give her, which is to tell us who she came here with."

Mr. Noru looked momentarily shocked, then briefly sick, a flurry of emotions going over his face in the span of seconds. "She *survived*?" His stunned pronouncement was not that different from how Margot had felt when she'd first seen the burnt figure emerge from the trees.

"She did. For now."

"Oh my God," the man whispered. "But certainly, if she's alive she could tell you this information herself?"

Rather than try to explain the nuances of Angela's condition, Wes interjected. "Ms. Gromand is barely clinging to life. I'm afraid she's not in a position to tell us things. We believe this man's first name is Robert or Rob, so that should help you narrow things down."

"We wouldn't want to have to make any public statements that indicate a potential killer might have been a guest here," Margot said, making the point that would speak to Mr. Noru the most.

He chewed on his lip. "I suppose, given that you already know one of the guests' names, it wouldn't be a conflict to give you the other." He was convincing himself of this more than them. "But I can't give out any contact information, no addresses or phone numbers."

He probably wasn't supposed to give out the name, either, but Margot was glad he was willing to bend on hotel rules enough for that. They *could* get a warrant if they needed to, they had sufficient evidence to ask for one, but it was always so much easier to go right to the source and see what they'd be willing to give you without one.

A small part of her also wondered if the warrant was such a sure thing, because she was beginning to realize Leon hadn't been kidding about Riga's connections and protections.

Mr. Noru turned to his computer. "How did you spell her last name?" he asked. Wes spelled it out for him.

When the results of his search fielded on the screen, Mr. Noru went pale, his expression suddenly bordering on genuine fear. He cast a quick glance over to the detectives.

"I would *personally* be very grateful if you didn't make public how you learned this information," he said, his voice trembling.

Margot's brow furrowed in confusion. "You're just giving us a name," she reminded him.

"Yes, well. Depending on the name, that can mean a great deal, can't it?" Mr. Noru replied. He wrote something down on a plain piece of paper—no hotel logos—and slid it across the table to them, along with the brochure and receipt. "I understand you're just doing your jobs, Detectives, but I have a family. And while it may just be a name to you, these are people who don't necessarily want their names known—do you understand me?" He swallowed hard, and Margot felt like his anxiety had become an airborne virus, something she was starting to feel inside her bloodstream.

Wes glanced down at the paper, and the bug caught him, too.

"Thank you, Mr. Noru. We won't share this publicly."

Wes jostled Margot, indicating they should leave, and she was still baffled by the turn this interview had taken. Weren't they going to ask to look at security footage? Shouldn't they try to talk to hotel staff?

She was about to voice this when they reached the lobby and Wes handed her the paper. Once she saw it, everything became clear.

There wouldn't be any footage.

No one else was going to say a single word.

The name Mr. Noru had written on the paper in neat cursive was Roberto Riga.

THIRTY-SEVEN

Margot was quiet for much of the ride back to the city, and Wes seemed equally lost in his own thoughts. They knew certain things to be true: Angela worked for the same escort service as the girls who had ended up dead in Muir Woods, and now Angela was barely clinging to life.

Emmanuel Riga was almost certainly involved in that service to some capacity, and his brother—which Margot assumed was the connection with Roberto, though she would need to confirm—was directly connected to Angela through a long-standing business arrangement.

So Angela's case and the Redwood Killer case *were* connected, meaning they would need to loop Leon into the investigation.

But something was bothering her, still.

"You know what's bugging me about this?" Wes said, like he was reading her mind.

"So many things," Margot said. "But tell me what's topping the list."

"How Angela was attacked."

Margot mulled this over, because it had been nagging at her

as well. There was a good reason they hadn't immediately made a connection between Angela's assault and the other deaths they'd been investigating.

For starters, it was the wrong location.

But more importantly, the MO was so wildly different from what they'd seen in the three other murders. Those victims had been killed with a combination of strangulation and stabbing. There was nothing remotely like the assault they'd seen on Angela.

"*If* Roberto Riga was the one who killed all these women, then there's a chance Angela was just more personal," Margot suggested. "It sounded like she was with him regularly, so while they weren't a couple, he obviously had some kind of feelings for her. Fiona said he bought her a lot of gifts, and that resort wouldn't have been a cheap place to get a suite. You saw how much the spa services cost."

"And generally speaking, the more personal the connection, the more brutal the violence," Wes said. It was a sad truth. Typically, in the rare case of stranger murders, the method of homicide was equally impersonal. Murders where the victim knew their killer were the ones where they typically saw overkill—a flurry of focused violence—or personal types of attack focused on the face.

The viciousness of the attack on Angela, the intention it would have taken to douse her in gasoline and light her on fire, that was *deeply* personal. The attacks on the other women showed signs of familiarity, but nothing like this.

"I think we need to go do a little homework on Roberto Riga," Margot said. She would have loved to jump right to interviewing him, but after everything she'd learned about Emmanuel, she knew that wouldn't be such a simple task. And if he *was* the man responsible for three murders and an attempted homicide, he wasn't going to be the kind of man they just wanted to knock on the door of.

He likely wouldn't go in easily, not if his family history was any indication. And if Emmanuel had a team of lawyers, then certainly Roberto would be protected by them as well.

They needed more than just his name. They needed evidence before they could bring him in.

Margot hated that they couldn't just go talk to him, but she understood—though she suspected not to the same extent Wes and Leon did—that the Riga family weren't the same as other people, and they couldn't treat this as a case just like any other.

As they approached the Golden Gate Bridge heading into the city, the police radio in Wes's car crackled, and then a friendly female voice said, "Fox and Phalen, you available?"

"We're 10-8, Dispatch, go ahead," Wes replied into the handheld unit, indicating he and Margot were available for assignment. They were on call rotation, so if they were getting a dispatch notice it meant it was their turn for a new body.

"We got a 187 over on Via Bufano, between Greenwich and Columbia. Auto service shop called it in."

"10-4, Dispatch, we're on our way there. Patrol on site?"

"Two cars."

"OK, thanks. Fox out."

187, the code for a homicide. And Margot felt a tightening in her chest at the address. Via Bufano was a narrow lane in between two busy streets. It was also practically in her backyard in North Beach.

Wes affixed his magnetic siren to the car's rooftop and engaged it, and they weaved their way through traffic. As usual, the general disinterest of city drivers, coupled with the lack of places for cars to move, meant that the siren didn't add much in the way of time saving. Fifteen minutes went by before Wes pulled into the parking lot of an autobody shop called Greasy Pete's, where two police cruisers were already parked with their lights on.

"Here's to an easy one," Wes told her as they got out.

"Don't jinx it," she scolded.

She was trying to keep her tone light, but there was a nauseous feeling inside her. They had passed by her apartment complex on the way here, the curtains of her living room window wide open, which she would never do on her own. The distance from where she lived to this parking lot was no more than a ten-minute walk.

And she couldn't stop thinking about that blood on Justin's shoe.

She knew it wasn't normal to catastrophize this way; most people wouldn't jump from seeing a dot of blood to connecting their own brother to a murder. But in Margot's case, she had reason to fear the worst.

She'd lived through it once before.

Wes took the lead this time, and she wasn't sure if he had sensed some reticence in her, or if he just thought it was his turn. Either way she was grateful to follow him.

There were three uniformed officers standing near a taped-off section of the parking lot. A fourth could be seen inside the auto shop talking to one of the employees. One of the officers in the lot was talking to a couple who had a small dog on a leash and Margot immediately pegged them for being the ones who had discovered the body.

She touched Wes's elbow and jerked her head in their direction to let him know she was going to go get a read on them. He nodded.

As Wes began to speak to the two officers that were waiting for them, Margot headed over to the third, a young man in his early twenties, who appeared to be taking vigorous notes of everything the middle-aged couple was saying.

Margot approached the group and flashed her badge, and she could immediately see the way a level of tension and frustration faded away from the couple.

"You're the detective?" the man asked.

"SFPD Homicide. I'm Detective Phalen. Were you two the ones who called this in?" She gave a nod of greeting to the officer to let him know she didn't want to undo any of his work, but based on the flush of his cheeks that extended all the way to his ears, she got the feeling this was actually a rescue operation. Kid must be pretty green.

"Yes, my wife and I were taking Schnitzel for a walk." He gestured to the dachshund at their feet as if there might be any confusion about which member of the family was named Schnitzel. Margot smiled at the dog, which seemed to soften the couple more. The tightness in their shoulders eased and they both turned their bodies completely toward her, shutting out the poor officer entirely.

"I know you probably explained everything to Officer..." she quickly darted a glance at the young man's chest, "Rutherford here, but I hope you won't mind going over it again with me. Though I have no doubt he took meticulous notes." This time she moved her smile from the dog to the young man, and he seemed grateful for it.

She'd seen beat cops get frustrated when the detectives came in, as if there was some unspoken competition over who was going to be the one to solve the case. If this kid had managed to figure out who the killer was before she arrived, he was welcome to the collar. A solved case was a solved case as far as she was concerned. Unfortunately, not everyone saw it that way and there could sometimes be an undercurrent of competition that Margot didn't like.

The couple in front of her were apparently reacting to her perceived position of being in charge, and she let them go with it. They were in their fifties, white, both going gray but not quite there yet. He was incredibly tall, over six-five, and his wife was rounder and shorter, her head only coming to her husband's shoulder. They looked nice enough, but they also had the look of people who had money and the self-importance that came along with that.

Margot was willing to bet they weren't shy about asking for managers.

"My husband went to throw out a doggy bag," the wife explained. "You know... poop?" Margot nodded. "And when he lifted the lid of that dumpster, he saw something inside and told me to call the police."

Margot glanced over at the dumpster in question, a rusted, ancient-looking thing that had probably been in place since Greasy Pete's had opened. Which, according to the *est 1978* on the sign, had been a long time ago. There was a small plastic baggie on the ground next to the bin, and Margot assumed that was the doggy bag, dropped when the tall man had seen whatever he'd seen.

"Did you notice anything unusual about the area around the bin, anything stand out to you before you lifted the lid?" she asked.

The man shook his head. "No. I mean, it didn't smell great over there, but it's a garbage bin, I didn't expect anything different."

Depending on the state of the body, it was possible the victim had started to decompose, which would definitely lead to an increased scent of death in the air. But they couldn't have been around longer than a week, depending on where this place was on the garbage route. At Margot's building, which was nearby enough to be on the same schedule, it was a Friday pickup. So if this place was the same, the body couldn't have been in there longer than four or five days. It probably wasn't too rank just yet.

"And can you tell me what you saw, exactly? Take your time, I have no doubt it was an upsetting experience."

"It was pretty dark inside, but there was no doubt about it when I got that lid open. There was a woman's body. I think at first I wanted to think it was a mannequin, that's what my brain told me."

Margot nodded, this would not be the first time a witness assumed something was a mannequin. Which made Margot wonder how common people thought free-range mannequins were.

"But then I saw her face and I knew it was a real person and that's when I yelled at Annie to call the police."

"And I did right away," Annie declared.

"Did you touch anything in the bin?" Margot asked.

The man shook his head. "No, absolutely not. I did touch the lid itself, though, of course."

"We'll need to get your fingerprints, just to rule them out," Margot explained, handing him her card.

"Oh, my cards are already on file," he explained. "I'm a prosecutor, they did a background check for me."

"OK, that's really helpful to know, thank you." She wrote down both their names and told them to call her if they remembered anything else, before she sent them on their way.

The young officer had watched the whole thing without saying a word, but once the couple were gone he turned to Margot. "They didn't want to tell me anything," he grumbled, shutting his notebook.

"Don't take it personally. Sometimes they need to see a little gray hair before they're willing to open up. Especially a couple who wear Ted Baker and Lilly Pulitzer to go for a walk with their expensive designer dog, you know what I mean?"

"Lilly what?" He frowned.

"It's a clothing brand. They're rich."

"How did you figure that out?" he asked.

For Margot, it was just second nature, she wasn't sure how to explain it. She just looked at people and knew things about them. Which was probably why she was a detective.

"You'll learn to spot the signs," was all she could offer. Or maybe he wouldn't. Observational skills were not second nature to everyone.

Margot left Officer Rutherford and returned to Wes, who was discussing things with the first officers on the scene. Margot had missed the initial part of the conversation, but arrived just in time for the fourth uniformed officer to emerge from the auto shop and join the group.

His name tag said he was Officer Lemon, which was so unexpectedly delightful Margot smiled when she read it.

"Detectives," he greeted with a nod. "Just talked to the owner of the shop."

"Pete?" Margot asked, almost hopefully.

"Alas, no. Evidently hasn't been owned by a Pete since about 1984. Current owner is named Rick Newsom, and he's owned the place since 1998. Says there are security cameras, though they don't cover the whole rear of the lot, but he's going to get the tapes for us." He glanced at Margot and Wes, then amended, "For you."

Hurray, blurry parking lot security footage viewing party.

But footage was footage.

A lead was a lead.

"That's great news. He have anything else to offer?"

Officer Lemon shook his head sadly. "Said he hasn't seen anything unusual lately. Shop closes up for the night at five, opens again in the morning at six. He gave me the name of all his staff, but was a bit cagey about it. Thinking some of them might be illegals and he's pretending not to know."

Lemon handed the list over to Wes.

"He also confirms that the bins are emptied every Friday morning, so hopefully that helps you with a timeline, but he says they're used pretty consistently by people all over the area, not just the shop. He says there's a lot of foot traffic back here, sometimes not the best kind. Vandalism, a few times the shop has been broken into. People have also been known to dump stolen goods around here as well. So, basically, he washed his hands of the whole thing."

"We'll see if he sings that same tune when we ID the victim," Wes said. "Thank you, that's some real thorough work."

Lemon just nodded like it was all part of the job, but his attentive questioning had saved them a lot of work.

They'd covered all the preliminaries, so it was finally time to go see their victim. Margot had no doubt the chief medical examiner, Evelyn Yao, and her team would be here soon to help comb over the lot and take the body away, but Margot needed to see it in situ before any of that happened.

She and Wes made their way over to the dumpster. She pointed out the dog-poop bag to him so he could avoid stepping on it, since it was unfortunately technically evidence.

Wes pulled out a pair of latex gloves from the inside of his jacket and handed them to her, then donned a pair of his own. He lifted the lid of the dumpster and they both recoiled in unison at the stench that wafted out. It wasn't the telltale stench of death, though.

Yes, the earlier markers of decomp were there, but as Margot predicted, their victim likely hadn't been here very long. The smell came from the contents of the dumpster itself, a putrid mélange of motor oil canisters, frequent dog-poop dumpers, and what appeared to be the discards from a nearby restaurant. The combination of those fragrances was positively repellent and Margot already felt bad knowing the CSIs were going to need to take this entire dumpster with them for further investigation.

That was not a sexy job, despite how a certain television series had tried to pitch it.

Their victim was a woman, short brown hair in a pixie cut, two earrings in her right eyebrow, and a lip ring in her lower lip. Her skin was somewhere between white and purple at this point thanks to lividity and the side-effects of being dead. She had probably been Caucasian and in her twenties.

While there were no obvious signs of stab wounds or gunshots from Margot's current vantage point, that didn't mean they didn't exist. The woman was partly buried under bags of garbage and loose food waste. People had been dumping things on top of her since she'd been tossed in here herself.

Margot would think ill of the lack of attention being paid, but the walls on the dumpster were actually quite high and the dog-walker had likely only noticed her because of how tall he was. Even Margot had to stand on tiptoes to get a look inside, and most people weren't as tall as her.

There was also likely an element of situational blindness involved. Not many people took a good long look into a garbage can before they threw things in it themselves.

She still couldn't help but wonder how many people had used this particular dumpster without realizing they were throwing their garbage onto a dead body. Knowing that might actually help them figure out how long the woman had been in there.

While Margot couldn't guess at the frequency of use of the can, it looked to be no more than a day or two's worth of bags on top of the body. Enough that she was partially covered but they could still see her.

A few more days and by Friday she doubted even the garbage men would have noticed the body as they unloaded the canister, and then no one ever would have found her.

"Jesus, I hope when we track this guy down there's a way to tack on an extra charge of mistreatment of remains. This is fucking awful," Wes said, his nose still wrinkling from the stench.

Since they couldn't move the body until Evelyn arrived, they put the lid down and scoured the area, placing plastic evidence markers near anything that looked potentially relevant, like a few cigarettes, some discarded beer cans, and a used condom. The likelihood was that none of this was going to make a difference in their case, but it all had to be marked.

There *was* a spent shell casing on the ground that got Margot's heart rate going, but they wouldn't know if it was involved until Evelyn could get the body out and give them some idea of the cause of death.

Once the area had been checked the sun was starting to get low in the sky. Evelyn and her team had arrived and were working on the dumpster, photographing the body thoroughly before she was removed.

When she finally was, Evelyn's team laid her out carefully on the ground, ready to bag her before taking her to the morgue. They could only do an initial inspection on site; to get more thorough information she would be taken to a sterile environment.

The uniformed officers kept bystanders at bay while Margot, Wes and Evelyn's team formed something of a human wall to block anyone from seeing the woman. But people were still pausing nearby to see what all the fuss was about.

Laid out, Margot could see how the woman had been killed. There were stab wounds on her chest and down her torso, but she was also mostly still dressed. Her top had been a smallish crop top to begin with, and was still in place. Her pants were unbuttoned but still on, like someone might have tried to take them off and stopped.

Evelyn Yao came to stand between Margot and Wes. Compared to the two of them she was practically dainty in size, but she still commanded all the attention with her purple-streaked hair and general boss bitch aura. "She has defensive wounds on her hands and arms." Evelyn pointed out some deep cuts on the woman's forearms, and her bloody hands. "So, she put up a fight. Preliminary count is about sixteen stab wounds, and if I were a betting woman I'd say it was actually this one that killed her." This time she pointed to a wound on the woman's arm. "Looks like he got her radial artery. Don't take my word for any of this until we get her back to the morgue, but I think she bled out."

Margot swallowed a lump in her throat. What Evelyn was describing was an inexpert kill, probably by someone who had never killed anyone before. The woman had been alive when she was dumped in the garbage, but likely already weak from blood loss.

They hadn't found any significant blood pooling in the parking lot though.

So had she been killed somewhere else?

And then there was the question Margot simply couldn't stop asking herself, even if she never bothered to voice it out loud.

Had any of that blood wound up on the killer's shoes?

THIRTY-EIGHT
1993

Petaluma, California

Justin had been quiet in the three days since he and Ed had returned from Desolation Wilderness. The entire drive home he had just stared out of the car window, not commenting on anything, not seeming to see anything at all.

Now that they were back on home turf, Ed had been keeping an eye on the boy, watching him carefully. He was polite, he was obedient, but he was also so quiet.

Had he always been this quiet?

Ed had to admit he'd never paid enough attention to know. He didn't dare bring Kim's attention to it, because the moment he asked if she thought something was wrong with the boy, she would pivot her hawklike gaze over to him. While the reprieve would be nice, Ed didn't want to do anything that might make Kim ask questions.

He wasn't sure what Justin's answers would be, and that part was what spooked him more than anything else.

That last day on the trail, Ed had seen something in Justin

that he never had up until that point in the boy's short life. He saw himself.

Not just the similar noses, the similar eyebrows. He had had those pointed out enough by strangers and friends whenever they saw the pair together. Justin resembled his father enough that Ed knew he was the boy's father, even though he sometimes had his doubts, and everyone always commented on how much he looked like Kim. It would have been awfully rich if Kim had been unfaithful to *him* after all the viciousness she'd lobbed at him over the years for his perceived infidelity.

But now Ed was seeing something in Justin he recognized from his own youth, and he felt fairly certain he'd never noticed it before this trip. The boy was withdrawing, curling in on himself and putting distance between himself and those around him.

Normally he would be driving Megan up the wall. Insisting on going with her whenever she went to meet friends at the mall, or if she was going to get ice cream. And while Megan was almost thirteen and owed a certain bit of privacy, Justin seemed to recognize the opportunities where he knew his parents would be on his side and force Megan to let him tag along.

But since their return from the mountains, Ed hadn't seen Justin try this. He seemed content to sit at home, to read books, to potter outside in the yard or ride his bike alone up and down the block.

He didn't seem unhappy, and during Ed's constant observation he hadn't witnessed anything else like he had with the birds. Recalling his own early forays into violence, Ed kept a keen eye not only on Justin but all the cats that he knew roamed free in the neighborhood.

Just in case.

So far, there had been no changes in the feline routines of the cul-de-sac.

Ed wasn't sure what he was hoping for. That Justin was just in an off mood, or that he *would* try something. A sick little thrill lit inside him at the idea of being able to mold someone else like him, to teach him the way he'd taught him to follow the hiking trails.

But a more logical part of his brain knew just how dangerous this would be. Ed *knew* how to kill, he knew how to be careful. Having his own son lead to his ruin by some kind of careless violence would be the sickest joke the universe could play on him.

No, if Ed was going to be the father of a proper killer, it wouldn't be Justin.

Ed wondered if he should talk to the boy, see if there was anything in his head that he was just waiting for the right opportunity to ask or say. But then he thought of the long drive home, and the hours available for Justin to have voiced his concerns or asked his questions.

It hadn't felt like he was holding anything in then, like there was anything he was dying to ask and simply unable to give voice to.

Ed felt the strangest certainty that if he asked Justin if there was anything on his mind, the boy would simply say, "No."

And being disaffected, being unmoved by what he'd seen and done in the mountains was almost worse than being scarred by it. Because Ed knew what path that moved a man down. He'd walked it himself.

He had no idea if the thing he was—a hunter, a monster, whatever—was something that was in his blood. He didn't know if there was a gene, or whatever they were called, that he could pass on, the same way he'd passed on the nose, the eyebrows.

So if Justin *was* like Ed, then was Ed always meant to be this way?

Was Justin?

Ed didn't think it worked like that. He'd been pushed to become what he was. If anything, this had been all his mother's fault. She'd gotten what she deserved and he never regretted it a single moment of his life.

But no one had ever treated Justin like that. There was no reason for him to become anything so... unseemly.

Ed stood in the garage, the door open, and watched Justin go up and down the street with an almost lazy indifference to the activity. Ed tinkered with his lawnmower just to have an excuse to stay outside.

But the whole time he couldn't stop asking himself one question.

If he is like me, is he my responsibility?

And how far was he willing to go to make sure that his responsibility didn't become his problem?

THIRTY-NINE

Margot didn't love her days off. They left her with too much time to herself and not enough meaningful ways to fill it. She read sometimes, or watched TV, but normally even when she was away from the station, she was thinking about her cases in some capacity.

When she awoke on Wednesday morning, the girl in the dumpster was on her mind.

She got dressed in her prison outfit and then stood in the entrance to her living room and watched Justin sleep on the couch. He'd told her the night before that he was planning to leave today, and Margot couldn't think of a valid reason to insist that he stay. She knew the squirming unease in her gut was her own creation. The blood on his shoes couldn't possibly belong to the dead girl in the dumpster.

Yet, she couldn't stop asking herself, *But what if it does?*

That *what if* was malicious, nagging, and simply wouldn't give her a moment of peace. There was a very real possibility that Justin would be gone when she got back from San Quentin, and the part of her that relished her privacy was happy to know she'd soon have it back. But the part of her she thought she had spent almost twenty-five years healing... that part simply wouldn't let her go.

She stood over him, his arm covering his eyes in the already dim light of the room, his breathing soft and even, without a care in the world.

As Margot stared at him, she tried to look past all the ways he still reminded her of her baby brother, the *boy*, and tried to see who he was as a *man*. A man who was strong enough to throw someone's body into a dumpster?

"What did you do?" she whispered, as if he might answer her in his sleep.

Instead, he just adjusted his position with a grunt, and began to snore. That was not the sleep of a man with anything weighing down his conscience.

But then again, Ed never had any trouble drifting off at night, either.

The parking lot at San Quentin Penitentiary was almost empty when Margot pulled in, certainly the emptiest she'd ever seen it. She parked next to Andrew's familiar sedan and moved through her now well-practiced routine of stashing important items in her glovebox and taking only her keys in with her to the guest center.

"How are you feeling?" Andrew asked, but it was the kind of question where he was trying to dig into something deeper, except Margot didn't know what he was *really* asking. Did he want to know if she was prepared? If she was going to do what it took to get the answers in this visit so they didn't need to keep playing with Ed?

But now Margot was wondering if she *wanted* the answers.

Because what would she do if the name Ed gave her wasn't a name she wanted to hear? What if finding out the truth would just obliterate any remaining ability she had to trust?

What would she do then?

To Andrew, she said, "I'm fine."

Again, that word. That lie of a word.

Andrew either didn't understand the weight of *fine* or chose not to acknowledge it, because he just nodded. "All right, good. Let's hope we can make this one count. I'm sick of him jerking our chain around."

Margot gave him a look. Jerking *our* chain around? Was he getting nighttime calls from a serial killer? Was he being manipulated and mentally shattered by sitting across from the dictionary definition of *daddy issues*?

Andrew blanched at her expression. "I just mean it will be nice to not have to come back again. For a while."

For a while.

Margot mulled that expression over, and it felt like gristle, getting stuck in her molars where she'd spend the rest of the day trying to coax it out with her tongue. *For a while.*

It was very different from saying *forever*.

And Margot understood, then, the many facets of the mistake she had made in agreeing to come back. Not only did Andrew and his team feel like she was working with them again, she may have also inadvertently set herself up to learn something that she could never unlearn.

She had a feeling that once Ed was done with her today, she wouldn't be the same person again.

FORTY

The metal seat at the community dining table was more uncomfortable than Margot could ever recall it being before. It felt like no matter which direction she shifted, her spine was out of alignment, her tailbone was pressing into the metal, or the seat was simply trying to tell her she should get up and leave.

The latter was not an option, but it would have been her preferred approach.

She stayed as still as she could, so as not to show her discomfort, which would only please him, and she stared straight ahead, waiting for his arrival. If she focused only on her breathing, maybe she could clear her mind of anything else.

The familiar sound of the opening door and the shuffle of Ed's feet across the tile floor along with the jangle of his restraints made Margot think briefly of Scrooge awakening to the ghost of Jacob Marley. Was that what Ed was going to represent to her today, a foretelling of dire things to come?

Margot was desperate to chew on her thumbnail, but opted to dig her fingernails into the flesh of her palms. The pain would be better than this morose mental pathway she was letting herself wander down.

Ed took his seat, and his smug expression made Margot want to reach across the table and throttle him. Didn't he know what this was doing to her? Didn't he care?

She bit back a laugh at her own expense.

No, of course he didn't care.

"Back so soon?" Ed said with a chuckle, like this was all some funny joke he'd played on them. Because that's all any of this was to him. A joke. A game. Something to amuse himself rather than spending another day alone in his cell.

And it was working, because they just kept coming back whenever he called.

"There was room in my calendar," Margot replied dryly.

"Oh, I'm so glad you could find the time." His tone took on an edge, because suddenly he wasn't the one making jokes, and if there was one thing Ed hated, it was jokes being made at his expense. The absolute embodiment of *he can dish it out but he can't take it*.

"I want to know more about your partner," Margot said. "You said he was experienced, that he'd killed before you. Was that a lie?"

From the corner of her eye she saw Andrew stiffen and then turn his body more in her direction. He had no idea where she was going with this. Neither did she. But she knew the answers were important. Vital.

"Why would I lie about something like that?" Ed asked, sounding almost genuinely perplexed. "Why would I lie at all?"

Margot scoffed. "Why stop doing it now?"

Now that she was sitting across from him, all the worry she'd been carrying about Justin was twisting into something new: blame. She looked at her father and all she could see was the person responsible. If her brother *had* done what she was terrified he'd done, then it hadn't been an action he'd come to on his own. It was something dictated by years of living alongside this man, and even more years living alongside his legacy.

If Justin *had* done something bad... and maybe not for the first time... then he was guilty of his own crimes, but Ed shared culpability in that, too.

And sitting across from him now, she found that he was the only one she could aim her feelings at.

Ed stared at her from across the table, but instead of looking furious, as he normally would have when challenged like this, he seemed baffled by her. Curious, even. "Margot..." God, she hated the sound of her new name on his lips. Hated that he had that now. "In all the time you've been here, I've never lied to you. Have I been a little... careful with the truth? Probably. Can't make it too easy for old Rhodesy over there. But I wouldn't lie to you."

She slammed her fists down on the table in a gesture so sudden, so violent, that the guards at the periphery of the room took a step forward. The tension in the room was thick enough to cut with a knife. And Ed was all too gifted at that.

"You did nothing *but* lie to me," she snapped. "My whole fucking *life* was a lie because of you. Why in God's name would you think I'd believe you'd suddenly stop now?"

Ed blinked, took a breath through his nose, and seemed to actually consider his answer before he spoke.

"I never lied to you. I hid things from you that were too hard for you to know, that you were too young to understand. But nothing I ever said to you was a lie. I spent so much time teaching you about what I was, what I *really* was. I told you everything you'd ever need to know to spot a threat, to protect yourself, to keep yourself *safe*. None of that was a lie."

Margot's hands were shaking and she pulled them back to her, putting them in her lap so he couldn't see them tremble. Her heart was racing a mile a minute, still on the rush of her outburst. The guards, however, assumed the moment had passed, and resumed their original positions.

"I spent my whole life thinking you would keep me safe,"

she whispered, almost to herself, wishing she could keep from revealing too much but utterly powerless to stop herself. "But now I can't leave my house without wondering if I'm creating a routine. I can't get in my car without looking in the back seat first. I can't sleep with a window open. Never."

Ed considered this, considered her, and then he did the most devastating thing he could do.

He shrugged.

"But you're alive," he said.

Margot clenched her hands together under the table, took deep breaths, and tried with all her might to remember what Dr. Singh had taught her about how to fight back against a panic attack.

The tiles are gray. My shoes are brown. The man to my right is named Andrew Rhodes. There are sixteen kinds of chocolate bar in the vending machine. She listed, with as much detail as possible, all the things in the room she knew to be true. All the things that were mundane and factual.

When she had counted ten things, she no longer felt like she might open her mouth and an endless scream come out.

"Why would you decide to pair up with someone when you spent so long working alone? Why share that with anyone?"

"Because he asked," Ed said matter-of-factly.

A chill swept over her, and her palms were suddenly damp.

No matter how many times she came here, no matter how accustomed she was to asking suspects about the horrific things they had done, she would *never* find it easy to hear the man who taught her how to ride a bike be so casual about the act of murder.

"How did that conversation even come about?" Margot asked, hoping that he might drop some tidbit, some clue. Just *something* that would prove her most horrible theory right or wrong.

She could just ask him, she was here to get the answer one

way or another. But if it *was* Justin, if somehow he had been so young but a monster just like their father, what was she going to do?

Could she keep that truth buried for the sake of her brother?

Would she?

She didn't think she could.

Normally, Justin being so young when Ed was an active killer would have immediately made her think it was impossible. But a few recent cases had convinced her that there was no age too young for a killer to start thinking about taking those steps. She'd sat across from one boy so baby-faced and innocent-looking she'd wanted to hug him, only to learn that he'd manipulated and orchestrated the murder of his entire family.

No, there was no age limit for when evil could show its face.

Still, she wanted to know about Justin on her own before it became an inescapable fact, and she was trying to see if Ed might say something that would tell her before he actually *told* her.

"He caught me. Not in the act, of course—I'd never let anyone catch me in the act. But it wasn't long after, and he found me cleaning up after myself. He said he didn't want to tell anyone, and he wouldn't, as long as I let him join me." Ed gave another shrug, but Margot could tell from his expression how much it bothered him that someone had gotten the upper hand on him that way.

Ed continued. "He said he'd done it before, on his own, but he always wondered what it would be like with someone else. To take turns, to never know which of you was the one to land the fatal blow."

A small hint of a smile flickered over his mouth, then disappeared.

"It must have gone well if you did it five times," Margot said.

"I think that had more to do with making sure there was a

certain level of mutually assured destruction between us. The kills themselves were lackluster, by no means my finest work. He lacked a lot of finesse, had no control over himself in the moment. Once, I thought he might turn on me, that's how intense his bloodlust could be when he was in the throes of it." Ed sighed and it was almost a wistful sound, like he missed being in those moments and thinking about it was a fond memory.

"Did he stop?" Margot asked. "When you were finished, was he done with it?"

Ed smiled, slick as oil on water. "I don't think any of us can *stop*, Buddy. No, I sincerely doubt our short-lived partnership got anything out of his system. The best I can hope is that I taught him to be a little smarter about it."

"You're not still in touch?"

Ed scoffed and rolled his eyes, letting her know how little he thought of the question. But it *mattered* to her. If it was Justin, had he simply cut off contact, had he never written a single letter? Margot had never thought to ask her brother about that, and now she desperately wished she had.

"It's not such a crazy idea," she goaded. "Obviously you were once close enough to do something that... intimate... Together."

Immediately she regretted her choice of words because Ed's expression darkened.

"Look, there was nothing fucking *queer* about it," he snarled.

Margot, who considered herself to be queer, felt his tone like an unexpected slap to the face. She actually hadn't been implying anything by the word she'd used. She was thinking only of Justin, and whether or not the partnership her father was talking about might have actually been some twisted father and son bonding.

But hearing the vitriol in his tone took her by surprise. She knew Ed was hateful, hated women, hated most people, but for some reason this pivot toward homophobia felt personal, even though he had no idea.

"That wasn't my implication," she replied flatly.

"Well good, because it wasn't fucking like that."

Margot stared at him for a long moment, willing her face to be impassive and her pulse to still. She didn't need him to know what he'd said had resonated with her in some way. Didn't need to give him a new weapon to wield against her whenever it suited him.

She was mad at him now, which didn't help her approach. He was, once again, pushing all her buttons, only this time he didn't even realize how well he was doing it.

"Do I know them?" she asked, which was the question without being *the* question.

Ed nodded, and Margot felt her heart crash into her feet.

No.

No, no, no. She couldn't be right, she couldn't believe it.

She wished she'd never seen those spots of blood on Justin's shoe. Wished she'd never given herself a reason to start wondering.

Wasn't it a shoe that had been Ed's undoing as well, after all?

But then again, was being blindsided by it better or worse?

Tears were forming, but she blinked furiously to chase them back. She wouldn't cry in front of this man. She wouldn't give him the satisfaction of getting that much out of her.

Finally she just had to ask, because otherwise she would start shaking so badly someone would need to carry her out of this place.

"Was it Justin?" she whispered, almost hoping Ed wouldn't hear her.

"Justin?" Ed took in the name, the suggestion, and he was quiet for a long time. Too long. Margot felt the acid in her stomach rising at the back of her throat. "Justin," he said again finally, as if he hadn't thought about the name in a very long time.

Then he let out a half-hearted chuckle.

"You know, it's funny you should ask that. I was just thinking about your brother. Thinking about this trip he and I took one year up to Desolation Wilderness near Tahoe. Do you remember that? You were so mad that I didn't bring you."

Margot actually *did* remember the bitterness she'd felt toward her brother and father on being excluded from that trip, but she didn't remember much else about it.

She nodded, hoping he would go on, because he had said a lot, but he hadn't said *yes*. He also hadn't said *no*.

"There was a point on that trip I started to wonder about your brother, about what he might *become*. I saw a lot of myself in him on that trip, and I can't say I liked it very much." He laughed at this, mostly to himself, and he was barely looking at her now as he dipped his toe into the recollection.

"And was he your partner?" Margot asked. Her throat hurt and she wasn't sure if it was from the pain of getting those words out, or just a side effect of her recent choking.

Ed's focus sharpened and he looked back at her with the full force of his gaze. Margot didn't look away, she met it head on and waited.

"No, Buddy. Your brother wasn't my partner. I hoped you would know that without asking."

"How could I?" Her palms hurt from squeezing so hard.

He stared at her. "Don't you understand? If I was going to show anyone who I really was, it was going to be you. It was always supposed to be you."

FORTY-ONE

Relief and horror washed over Margot in equal measure.

It wasn't Justin.

It wasn't Justin.

The second part of Ed's revelation made her stomach churn, but she fought it. Now that she had the answer she needed—the only one that really mattered to her—she could do what was necessary to get the *other* answer she had come for.

"I guess, in a way, you did shape what I became," she replied coldly. "And aren't you proud?"

"Sometimes I think you're more his daughter than you are mine," Ed replied, looking over to Andrew. The FBI agent said nothing, just met Ed's gaze without flinching. It would have been a perfect opportunity for him to land a jab at Ed's expense. *Well someone had to be her father*, or something else. But Andrew said nothing. This was Margot's show, and he wouldn't intervene.

The fact that he'd let her do things the way she had this whole time was wild in and of itself. At certain points, Margot really wished he *had* pulled her back from the edge rather than letting her emotions get the better of her.

But she knew why. It was because her outbursts got reactions out of Ed, for both the good and the bad. Sometimes they set him off as well, like a chain explosion, but other times they seemed to be precisely what he was fishing for.

"You really thought it might be your brother?" Ed said, his voice bemused, his expression thoughtful. "No, I don't think your brother has it in him. That killer instinct is something you're either born with or you'll never learn it. You. You've got it. You just use yours differently than I did."

Margot frowned at him. "I'm not like you."

"Oh please. You're *just* like me. Except you eviscerate people with words and I just did it with a knife. Don't tell me you don't get a sick thrill sitting across from someone when you know they have a dirty little secret, using nothing but your brain and your tongue to get them to give you everything you want. You're still gutting them, kid, you just have a different weapon of choice."

This was a trap, she knew. Because he was right. He was absolutely fucking right. There were few things in the world that Margot relished more than getting a stubborn suspect to fess up. But Ed made it sound like an act of violence.

Maybe it was, in some way she didn't understand.

She already had far too much new material to take to her next appointment with Dr. Singh to begin processing that.

"If you say so," she replied.

This wasn't the response Ed wanted from her, but he didn't reply right away. "You're not very fun today," he said after a long pause.

Margot stifled the urge to laugh. "Well, sorry to be a disappointment. Maybe I just don't like wasting my time. And before you do what I know you're going to do, and try to play off some paternal guilt trip, like there's no such thing as wasted time between father and daughter, I can save you the trouble. I have some active investigations that deserve my attention a lot more than you do. Now, if I tell you that I'll keep coming back, keep letting you waste my time, will you stop jerking my chain and just tell me who your partner was?"

The whole room was quiet.

Margot wasn't even certain if she was lying or not. She felt drained by him, but somehow *not* visiting had been worse, because she lived in fear of her own phone. At least here she knew he was chained, and she controlled their interactions.

Mostly.

Finally, Ed cleared his throat. There was an expression on his face that Margot had a hard time deciphering, and she decided not to try. She didn't need to be the world's most knowledgeable expert into all things Ed Finch. That was FBI Greg's job. If Greg wanted to sit here and map all of Ed's facial expressions, he was welcome to them.

"You might not remember it, you weren't very old at the time. But I used to have a friend named Jim. I think you kids called him Uncle Jimmy."

It took every ounce of self-control that Margot possessed not to look over at Andrew.

Fucking Uncle Jimmy.

The FBI hadn't even known he existed until Margot had mentioned him a few months earlier. And even to her he had seemed like a distant memory. He'd also seemed much too obvious to be the man in this case.

Apparently it had been easier to believe her brother was capable of murder than to believe it was the man her father spent his bachelor summers with whenever Kim took the kids to New York for the summer.

Uncle Jimmy.

The FBI had briefly looked into him when he was first mentioned. But she hadn't known Jimmy's last name, and it turned out there was no shortage of men named James who owned boats in Northern California.

"I remember Uncle Jimmy," she said, not giving away that he had recently come up in her conversations with the FBI. "He had a boat."

Ed smiled at this, nodding his head. "Yeah, he did. And that's why your FBI friends only know about two of the victims he and I worked on together. We didn't do things right the first couple of times, got too excited, did the jobs in a way where we didn't have time to take them with us. After that we got smarter, more patient. Took them with us and killed them on the boat. A lot easier to clean up, dispose of things."

Margot remembered something Ed had said about one of his previous victims, whose body he dumped in the Bay.

She belongs to the ocean, now.

Apparently more than one woman did.

Remains washed up all the time from boat accidents and other marine mishaps, but often, if someone's body was dumped in the ocean, that's where it was going to stay. Animals would take parts of it, but the battering waves and rocks were a more common cause of bodies being lost forever.

There had been an unusual mystery further north about ten years earlier where almost twenty feet, still in shoes, had been found on the beaches near the Salish Sea. At first there had been murmurs of a serial killer. But the ultimate cause was simply ocean tides. The bodies had all gone into the water at different locations—several were confirmed to be suicides who had jumped from bridges—and the bodies had been battered apart by the sea. The shoes kept the feet buoyant enough for them to travel further, and they all found their way to the same stretch of water.

Margot wasn't expecting that these women's feet had wound up on a beach somewhere.

The FBI would cross-reference things, of course, but she was sure the two victims Ed was speaking of were bones at the bottom of the ocean by now.

"What's Jimmy's last name?" she asked. She hadn't been sure of it at the time, recalling only that it might start with the letter M.

"McMaster. James McMaster. If you see him, tell him Ed says hi." Ed's eyes twinkled at this, his grin broad.

Margot wondered if there was something she was missing. Had something happened recently behind the scenes that made Ed decide it was finally time for Jimmy to pay for his sins?

"Do you remember their names? The women." Her palms were itching like they were on fire. She was desperate to get out of there, to talk to Andrew. To figure out where they went from here.

If they were going after Jimmy, she was coming.

Ed leaned forward on the table, his cuffs scraping the Formica surface.

"Margot, if there's one thing you can believe to be true, it's this. I *always* remember their names."

FORTY-TWO

Margot took deep breaths of fresh air in the parking lot, the sea breeze more cleansing today than it had ever felt before. The air itself was cold, the wind turning her cheeks a ruddy shade.

The parking lot was full now as it was visiting hours, and she'd passed family members and groups on their way in as she headed out. Margot was currently waiting for Andrew, who'd gotten stuck talking to the warden about their visits. It took an extra twenty minutes, but she found she didn't mind the wait today.

The sea air was doing something to her, something healing.

It wouldn't last, but she was enjoying it for the time being.

Gulls screamed overhead, wheeling in circles above the parking lot in hopes of lost snacks dropped by little toddler hands on their way inside. She didn't like to think about the kids she could see coming to and from the guest center. She couldn't decide why, exactly, but they made her feel guilty.

Andrew nodded a greeting as he approached her. She noticed he was playing with his key ring, an unusual nervous tic for someone who was usually very composed.

"I'm coming with you," Margot announced before he could even speak.

"I don't know if that's a good idea," Andrew countered.

"The funny thing is, I didn't ask if you thought it was a good idea. I'm coming. Without me, you wouldn't have his name. And who knows, maybe a familiar face will be easier for him to handle instead of a full contingent of armed FBI agents."

Margot didn't bother to point out that her face wouldn't exactly be the same one that Jimmy would remember. Losing a lot of the weight she had carried in childhood, and a very professional nose job, had ensured that Margot didn't resemble any of the old family photos of herself.

Not that she had many of those left.

For a moment, she thought Andrew might put his foot down. If he wanted to, he could. She had no jurisdiction, no access to the case without him. But she could see him wrestling with what he should say next, and she knew why.

He needed her.

He might even admit as much.

Without her, none of this was happening, none of these women would have names, and they wouldn't be within reach of locking up a previously unknown serial killer who had worked alongside Ed Finch.

This was groundbreaking stuff.

This would mean national media attention and a massive feather in Andrew's cap.

Andrew's. Not hers.

"Fine," he said gruffly. "You're right, he might respond better to someone he knows, even if you are a hell of a lot older now." He added this last part with a wink.

"Ouch. Not like you're getting any younger, pal," she shot back.

"So I learn every morning when I wake up." He unlocked his car but, ever the gentleman, he waited for her to get into hers first. "I'll be calling the team in for an emergency meeting. If we can find his address and he's still local, we move today. No sense in wasting time. If he's out of state, well... Your coming along might not be up to me anymore."

Somehow Margot hadn't even considered the possibility that Jimmy might have moved. She had decided the moment Ed said the man's name that he would be right where she'd left him in her memory, at his marina slip, waving to them with a can of beer in his hand.

Margot nodded her understanding. "I'll meet you at the office."

The San Francisco FBI headquarters, where the team assigned to Ed's ongoing case were working day in and day out to tie potential cases to him, had never buzzed with such energy as it did when Margot entered alongside Andrew that day.

The air was electric with excitement, and every other monitor she passed had an image of an older man's face on it. It took her a few beats too long to realize it must be Jimmy.

Andrew guided her into their usual conference room, where the team managers were waiting. Greg could barely contain himself, pacing back and forth beside the table, while Alana Yarrow and Carter Holmes were seated across from him.

Alana looked impossibly chic as always, her peacock teal suit and silver blouse looking like something right out of the pages of *Vogue*, if *Vogue* accessorized with an FBI badge. Her platinum blond hair was in its usual blunt bob. Carter, meanwhile, looked as if he'd just left a practice as a linebacker for the 49ers and put on a suit on his way over.

They both nodded to Margot as she entered.

"Heard you did a hell of a job today," Alana said casually. "Good work."

Margot felt an unexpected flush of pride. She wasn't accustomed to getting complimented for the work she did, and it felt both very wrong, but also very nice.

It didn't hurt that she harbored a mild crush on Alana, the way a teenager might have a crush on a supermodel, in that unattainable, too good to exist kind of way.

Greg, vibrating like a puppy, fixated on Margot the moment she walked into the room. "Do you know how rare it is for two established killers to team up? I'm having trouble thinking of comparisons. I might need to re-evaluate my entire thesis. This is a completely earth-shaking discovery, Margot. Really incredible."

She offered him a smile, not because she agreed, but because she liked him, and she didn't want to dampen his enthusiasm, even though it was geared toward something she loathed with such intensity.

"All right, Greg, dial it down a few notches, you look like you're going to explode," Carter said, but his tone was gentle, not cruel. Greg could sometimes be the butt of some nasty adult bullying because his earnestness—and strangeness—made him an easy target. Margot was glad that the others in the room were learning to be kind to him.

"Greg, why don't you channel some of that energy into giving us a breakdown of what you guys have learned since Margot and I left the prison," Andrew said as he took his place at the head of the table.

Margot sat near Greg's spot, surprised to realize she had a usual spot, and that she didn't mind that much.

Greg jumped into work-mode, launching a PowerPoint presentation on the main monitor in the room. The efficiency with which someone in this department could create Power-Points was something that Margot would never cease to be amazed by.

"We found six men named James McMaster in the state. By culling those whose birthdates made them either too young or too old to be our guy, we were able to narrow it down to two potential men. Then using the information we had been provided by Margot previously, we found that only one of those men had ever rented a marina slip. James Dennis McMaster. He's still presently living in the state of California, though it appears he has moved from boat adventures to boat repairs. He owns a small repair yard in Healdsburg." Greg hit some buttons on the laptop and the next slide popped up, showing an aerial view of the marine yard from Google, and a picture of the building, a single-story unit that looked to be in dire need of a new coat of paint. The sign on the side of the building read *JDM Marine Repairs*.

This wasn't part of Margot's memory of Jimmy. She could only picture him adjacent to the water, caught in the reflection of sunshine on waves. Even when he'd visited their house, which hadn't been often, he'd smelled of salty sea air, like he'd sailed to get there.

As Greg advanced to the next slide, there were two photos. One was decidedly of the Jimmy she'd known, though an aged version of him. He was in his early seventies in the photo, his sandy blond hair gone silver, and his years in the sun on boat decks giving his skin a weathered, leathery appearance. But he was smiling, his teeth slightly yellowed from his ever-present cigarettes, deep smile lines next to his eyes.

Even knowing what she knew, Margot's first reaction to seeing the photo was to feel a surge of warm nostalgia. This was countered when she looked at the photo next to it. In this, Jimmy was not smiling, his expression was guarded and mean. He stared straight ahead into the camera and there was nothing in his eyes at all, no spark of life.

It was a mug shot.

"McMaster was arrested in the late seventies for fraud; he was caught passing bad checks, did a few months in a low-security prison for it. He was arrested again in the mid-eighties—the time we know Finch was starting to be his most active—for assaulting a girlfriend. She told the police he was going to kill her. He said it was just a lovers' quarrel. If Margot's timeline is correct, then he and Ed started their friendship in the late eighties, after those arrests. McMaster was questioned once or twice in relation to violent assaults, but he was never charged, and never arrested again."

Alana piped up: "Because of the dates of his arrests, his profile wasn't collected for NDIS submission, meaning his DNA never made it into CODIS. There's a possibility his DNA was collected at crime scenes and entered into the database, but part of our goal today—aside from bringing him in for questioning—will be to collect a sample so we can get that entered and see if there are any hits on existing cold cases."

Greg nodded his approval. "Based on what we can tell, McMaster was an avid traveler, especially anywhere that boating was available, meaning we could have cases linked to him up and down both coasts, as well as in Florida, Louisiana, and Texas. It's unfortunately a very wide net."

"Well, let's start with the easiest part," Andrew said. "Do we have a team ready to hit the road?"

Healdsburg was about an hour and a half drive north. And this time, unlike her luck with Napa, the path would take them right through Petaluma. Margot thought it was almost fitting, given what they were headed to do.

Greg bounced from foot to foot and Margot just *knew* he was included in the away team.

"Ready when you are, boss."

FORTY-THREE

Margot spent the drive looking over the file that the FBI had created on James McMaster. It was impressive the speed with which they'd been able to scour police databases, social media, newspapers, to establish a fairly robust history of the man they were on their way to see.

Based on the hours the repair shop was open, they were actually heading to McMaster's home, hoping to find him there and avoid making a scene. As if ten black SUVs pulling up to a suburban home in Healdsburg wasn't going to cause a stir no matter what.

But Andrew had a plan, and it would involve him and Margot going in first, with one armed backup unit flanking the house as they talked to McMaster. He would get the option to go in quietly, and if he didn't, the other units would be on standby.

Knowing that he was getting on in years, Margot hoped it would be a quick conversation followed by the old man willingly following them outside. There was always a chance this was a lie Ed had made up to get revenge on Jimmy for some kind of perceived slight. He was petty enough to do that.

Yet something about the way Ed had insisted he'd never lied to her kept creeping into the back of Margot's mind. He hadn't. So far, at least in all their interactions in the prison, everything he'd told them had turned out to be true.

Margot was almost surprised by the slight rock of the car as they came to a stop. She'd missed Petaluma entirely, and was grateful for it. She leaned over, looking past Andrew to the house she had only seen in a grainy photo in the dossier she was holding.

It was a squat single-family home that was painted a butter yellow shade, and much like Jimmy's business, could have probably used a fresh coat. The front steps had seen better days with ragged, peeling carpet on the steps and two dead flower bushes flanking the entry.

The lawn, however, had been recently mowed, and the place looked tidy, if a little worse for wear.

"How well do you remember him?" Andrew asked, following her gaze across to the house.

"Not all that well. He and Ed weren't close for long. Now I guess we know why."

"Yeah, nothing like a little murder to force a wedge between friends," Andrew mused.

Margot nibbled her thumbnail, continuing to observe the house. The curtains were open, but she couldn't see anyone looking out at them. The second black SUV that would wait in the block with them was parked right behind, and there were well-armed agents in there just waiting for the moment Margot and Andrew went into the house.

Local police were aware of their presence, because nothing could make neighbors quite as uneasy as a bunch of dudes running through their yard with assault rifles.

But he was always such a nice man, Margot imagined them saying of Jimmy.

People had said it about Ed.

The smartest killers were the ones you never saw coming, and Margot wondered how many women didn't see Jimmy coming.

Margot found herself needing to pause before they entered. She needed to distract herself, if only for a moment, because she worried if she went in now, she would give everything away by the expression on her face.

"Andrew, can I ask you something? Maybe it's a little personal."

His attention shifted from the house back to her. He was probably so accustomed to her being surly and a little defensive with him that this question might have felt out of the blue. He looked both intrigued and the slightest bit concerned.

"Sure, go ahead."

She had been thinking about the documentary more and more with Justin being around. And her visit with Ed today had brought it right to the front of her mind. She thought about Justin, and how, more than just the payment from the documentary, he wanted some kind of closure. While she had been steadfastly against participating, she was beginning to wonder if giving him this... this one thing might be enough to help chase his demons back into hiding.

She was beyond help running from her own.

Andrew's willingness to participate made her wonder if maybe the whole thing might be worth thinking about. Just thinking.

"Why did you decide to go ahead with the documentary series?" she asked. She wasn't looking at him at first, instead focusing on the house, but she finally shifted her gaze and met his, trying to hold it so she didn't let him see how uneasy this whole topic made her.

If Andrew was taken aback by this question at this moment, he didn't let it show.

"I get asked to do a lot of those things about Ed. I say no to most of them, especially when they're going for shock value, or sensationalism. But I've seen the work this crew has done before. They did a special on the Green River Killer a few years back, and last year they did one on the Long Island Serial Killer. They have a good way of balancing the dread of the crimes with the really important stuff, the focus on the victims, humanizing them. I trust that they're going to be fair in their storytelling, and they do good, thorough research. So I said yes."

Margot looked at him for a long moment, neither committing to anything or questioning his own reasons. Her thumbnail throbbed from where she'd been biting the skin.

Finally, she nodded, letting out a little sigh and jerking her head toward the house. The distraction had worked, it had given her something else to think about, and she figured she could walk up Jimmy's sidewalk now without looking as if she was there to arrest him.

"I'll go first," Margot said, though she wasn't feeling as confident as she was trying to sound. She didn't have her service weapon with her, since she wasn't on active duty right now. At best, she was a civilian helper. But she hoped that Jimmy would remember her with enough fondness to let them inside.

More than anything, she hoped he wouldn't immediately know why they were there.

Andrew looked as if he might argue, since he was the agent in charge, but even he had to admit that their chances of getting through the door with no violence were higher if Jimmy recognized the person he was talking to.

As they crossed the street to the little yellow house, Margot's heart hammered, her anxiety causing her pulse to pound inside her ears. This wasn't how she'd planned to spend her Wednesday.

She jogged up the three steps to his door, careful not to trip on the tattered carpeting, and rang the bell.

For one brief moment, she hoped Jimmy wouldn't be home.

Two seconds later, the door opened and a weathered-looking old man peered out the door at her. He was shorter than she remembered him, or perhaps that was because she had gotten so much taller, but they were now eye to eye, when once she'd had to crane her neck to look up at him.

"You don't look like a Mormon," Jimmy said, smiling at her, that familiar twinkle in his eyes, his crow's feet deepening. There wasn't, however, any spark of recognition.

He was just playing the part of a friendly old man.

"Jimmy?" she said, trying to come to terms with this man being the same one she had known when she was only a child. They were both the same but also completely different in so many ways. She wondered how much of that was the knowledge of his extracurriculars that Ed had given her.

"Sure, who's asking?"

"I'm Megan. Megan Finch." The name sounded *wrong* even as she said it. Though it had once belonged to her, saying it in the present tense felt like a lie.

Jimmy's whole bearing changed, and a million different things seemed to move through his expression all at once. Confusion, delight, worry, and things that Margot couldn't quite catch they flitted by so quickly.

"Well, I'll be goddamned. Look at you, Meg. God, the last time I saw you, you were probably as tall as my knee and just the chubbiest little thing." He paused as if realizing this might not be a kind thing to say. "Sorry, I mean, you look great now. So grown up. And you were a cute kid back then. Just..." He puffed out his cheeks.

"Yeah," Margot said, struggling to keep her smile in place. "I finally grew into myself, thank God."

"Look nothing like your pop, thank God," Jimmy said.

Margot felt the words as sharply as a slap. It was meant as a compliment, and one she was grateful to hear, but having him mention Ed so casually was somehow more than she could stand. Everyone else talked about Ed like he was the bogeyman. Jimmy said *your pop* like Ed was just any father.

"Jimmy, you mind if me and my friend Andrew come in for a minute, we just want to talk to you about something."

Jimmy's gaze moved over to Andrew for the first time since the door had opened.

"Jesus. You just scream *cop*, don'tcha?"

"Fed, actually," Andrew replied, and flashed his badge casually.

"Ah, you guys must be here because of those new bodies they've been pinning on old Eddie. You know, it's a funny thing, I thought you would show up at my door all the way back when he was arrested. Want to know what he got up to back then. But no one ever came."

Andrew nodded, forced a smile of his own. "Believe it or not, it took us this long to find you," he admitted.

Jimmy snorted and held the door open wide for them. "Guess the FBI *doesn't* know everything."

"No, sir," Andrew replied amiably. "But if you don't mind keeping that to yourself, we do have a reputation to uphold."

He and Margot exchanged glances as Jimmy led them into the house. If Jimmy chose to believe they were here to talk to him about Ed, then there couldn't be any harm in having that conversation first, before letting him know they needed to take him in to talk about his own crimes as well.

Jimmy's house was tidy inside, though it did speak to a lifetime of being a bachelor. There was no couch in his small living room, only a leather recliner and a very large flatscreen television. The dark paneling on the wall and framed prints of hunting dogs and sailboats suggested a woman had never lived here, and that Jimmy hadn't made a single stylistic adjustment since about 1979.

But the house smelled of fresh coffee and there wasn't a speck of dust to be seen.

An ancient-looking dog was sleeping in the recliner, a little white terrier who looked at Margot and Andrew with rheumy eyes that Margot suspected were mostly blind.

The dog gave her pause. Made her work through some of her own preconceived notions about killers. Most true psychopaths, even most narcissists, cared only about themselves. They didn't tend to have pets because they didn't see the value or purpose in them.

Jimmy having a dog, especially one that likely required regular medical attention, was something Margot hadn't expected.

The dog put its head back down and Jimmy never acknowledged its presence to them. He led them into his tidy kitchen, the same butter yellow color as the exterior of the house. It looked to have been designed in the fifties during the peak of the Mid-century Modern craze, and Margot doubted very much had changed in the intervening years except for the addition of some more modern appliances.

"I'm an afternoon coffee guy," Jimmy announced. "Picked it up back in my boating days, cause you can never be *too* awake going into the setting sun when you're on a boat. Anyway, I just made a fresh pot, you two want some?"

Andrew took the lead here. "Sure, Mr. McMaster, that would be nice."

Margot got the hint. They were just here to interview, that was the vibe they were going with. No hints at anything else. Just be friendly, be cool.

"I'd love one," Margot echoed.

"You can just call me Jimmy, Mr. Special Agent Rhodes. Megan here used to call me Uncle Jimmy, but that was a long, long time ago." He looked back over his shoulder and gave Margot a smile. "So, Jimmy is fine."

He poured them both cups of black coffee and didn't ask if they took anything, then gestured to the small table in the center of the kitchen. A stack of mail was sitting there awaiting his attention, and Margot noted the grease-stained coveralls hanging at the back kitchen door, as if he'd put them there on his way in from work to keep anything else from getting dirty. He was clearly a very meticulous man who had long ago found rituals that worked for him, and still stuck to them every day.

Margot sat next to Andrew at the table and took the cup of coffee she'd been offered, though a consistent churning in her stomach meant she didn't think she would be able to keep it down if she took a sip. She warmed her hands on the cup. Andrew, obligingly, drank a sip of his before setting it down.

"Jimmy, we just wanted to ask you a few questions about Ed," Margot said. "You've obviously read the newspaper reports about his newly discovered victims, and one of the ones he recently admitted to was a crime that happened during the summer Mom, Justin and I were in New York."

"Sure." He sat down. "How is Kim anyway?"

Andrew's gaze shot to Margot, but she managed to keep her composure, though her grip tightened on the mug to keep her hands from shaking.

"Mom... Mom passed a few years ago," she said. There was no need to explain how.

"Shit, I'm sorry to hear that, kid. She was a pretty cool lady."

This was kinder than anything Ed had ever said posthumously about Margot's mother, so she took the compliment and offered a tight smile in return. "Thank you. I told the FBI I remembered you and Ed spent a lot of time together that summer, and we were wondering if you might remember anything he said, or anything about his behavior that might have stood out to you."

Jimmy seemed thoughtful about this, and Margot watched every shift of expression on his face, trying to see if there was a trace of worry or fear, anything that might lead her to think he was aware of his own precarious position with the law.

But he just looked like a man contemplating long-forgotten history.

"That was a really long time ago, but you know, in the years since Ed got arrested I've spent a little time of my own thinking about that. Realizing he must have been getting up to his misdeeds at the same time he and I were friends. That's a tough thing to reconcile." He looked at Margot. "But I'm sure you know all about that."

Margot's jaw clenched. "Yes, I do."

"You think you know a guy." Jimmy shrugged. "But the thing is, even after I'd heard what Ed had done, I thought about all our time together, and I couldn't recall a single time that anything stood out to me as strange. Stranger than usual, anyway. Ed never was a really typical guy, he was always kind of a quiet one."

"How did you and Ed meet?" Andrew asked, then when he got an odd look from Jimmy, as if this question might solely be reserved for couples, Andrew went on. "We interviewed everyone Ed worked with, all his neighbors. Just curious how your circles ended up overlapping."

Jimmy nodded and sipped his coffee. "We met at a garage sale."

Margot smiled despite herself. "God, Ed *loved* garage sales. He'd spend most of his weekends going miles out of his way in search of garage sales."

Jimmy chuckled. "He was looking to buy a set of antique carving knives, but I had my eye on the same ones. Really pretty, mother-of-pearl inlay, the kind of thing you feel bad putting in a drawer."

The pit had returned to Margot's stomach to hear him describe the knives with such reverence.

The idea that two serial killers had met over a set of second-hand knives would have been funny if it wasn't the most horrible thing Margot could imagine Jimmy saying. She'd half expected him to say it had been through a classified ad since that was how Ed had found many of his victims and earned himself the nickname the Classified Killer.

"Who ended up getting the knives?" Andrew asked, his tone light, as if this was some fun story.

"Ed did," Jimmy said. "Can't say I ever quite forgave him for that. But he offered to buy me a beer to dull the disappointment, and we found that we got along pretty well. We didn't have much in common, him being married with kids, me a confirmed bachelor even back then, but somehow we ended up talking for about three hours that day. By the time it was over I told him if he was ever in the area again he should come for a boat ride. The next weekend he took me up on it."

Again, the tone here was all too light, too fondly reminiscent. Jimmy didn't seem to have any negative feelings associated with these memories, not even the knives—which Ed certainly didn't use to carve turkey—and that awareness didn't seem to bother him any.

"Did you and Ed ever spend time on your boat with any women?" Andrew asked. "We know that during those summers Ed's family was away, we're just trying to figure out if maybe he had a change of MO during those periods. Maybe he got to know some of his victims more personally. Or maybe he met them in a party environment."

Jimmy shook his head, sipped his coffee. "Nah, nothing like that. Honestly, I think time on the boat was Ed's opportunity to get out of his head, get away from the things in his life that were stressing him out." His gaze cut quickly to Margot. "No offense, kid."

"None taken," she said, though it most certainly was.

"Would you say you knew Ed pretty well?" Andrew asked.

"At the time, I would have said yes, but now I'd probably

say how well can you know anyone? He obviously had some pretty big secrets. And I generally believe a man is entitled to his secrets." Jimmy got up and headed to the coffee pot with his empty cup.

"But not in his case?" Margot asked.

Jimmy poured himself another cup, then opened up his cupboard and got out a little jar of sugar. He set it down on the counter next to his cup.

"To tell you the truth, kid, even him. But I can't stop him from telling you whatever it is he's going to tell you, I suppose."

He pulled out a drawer, cutlery tinkling.

It wasn't until Andrew stiffened beside her that Margot realized what he had: Jimmy hadn't taken out a spoon.

He'd taken out a gun.

Jimmy was still facing away from them, contemplating his coffee cup, but from the position of his arm, she could tell it was held in his right hand.

"And I can guess he told you some things about me. But, see, I'm an old man now, and while Ed might be content to rot away in prison, doling out little tidbits to the law, that's not how my story is going to go."

He turned toward them, black pistol in hand. Andrew was up from the table, unlatching the clasp on his holster. "Jimmy, put that gun down," he said.

Margot sat at the table, immobile, staring Jimmy right in the eye.

Then he put the gun under his chin and pulled the trigger.

FORTY-FOUR

Everything that happened next moved in slow motion.

Andrew's shouts came through muffled, as if Margot was underwater. She couldn't make out the words over the ringing in her ears. She understood, if only vaguely, that her hearing was a mess because of the sound of the shot.

The back door to the kitchen burst inward and officers in black Kevlar with big guns came spilling in, their weapons aimed at Jimmy.

Except Jimmy was on the floor, no longer had the top of his head and the corner of the kitchen was splattered with gore.

Margot stayed seated, vaguely aware that there was something wet on her face, but she couldn't make her hand move to touch it.

The front of her shirt was covered in blood droplets. Most of the contents of Jimmy's skull were on the yellow and white cabinets behind him, but since he'd shot straight up, some of it had come down on the table and on Margot herself.

She couldn't move.

She felt someone touch her shoulder, gently at first, then shaking her, but she just kept staring at Jimmy. His eyes were open, staring in her direction but seeing nothing. Margot tried to feel something, anything, but there was just a hollow place in her chest where any kind of emotion should live.

Why couldn't she feel anything?

The hand on her shoulder moved to her arm and yanked her up out of the chair. She tottered, unsteady. Someone took the coffee cup out of her hands.

It wasn't until she was facing Andrew, his hand squeezing her chin and forcing her to look at him instead of the dead man in the corner, that she finally felt anything at all.

Panic.

A small sound of alarm escaped her mouth, and Andrew guided her out of the kitchen and into the tidy living room. He sat her down on the only other chair in the room, an uncomfortable wooden one that was obviously intended more for decor than for actual sitting.

As Margot looked out the front window, she saw more SUVs pull up out front. People she recognized and people she didn't flooded onto the sidewalk, up the steps and past her. Navy-blue FBI windbreakers made everyone look the same.

Something touched her feet and Margot looked down.

The ancient white dog was staring up at her, seeing her, even if its eyes didn't work properly.

She bent down and picked it up, and the dog went willingly, so light she barely noticed the addition of its weight in her lap.

Margot held that dog the entire drive back to San Francisco.

Justin was gone when Margot got back to her apartment, still carrying the dog that no one had been able to get her to give up —not that they would have any idea what to do with it as an alternative.

Margot set the small, white dog on her couch, where it immediately curled into a little ball on top of one of her throw cushions and went to sleep. She had never wanted a dog, mostly because they forced her to create a routine since they needed to be walked.

She didn't think this senior pup was going to demand much more than a few morning trips out the apartment's front door.

She wasn't even sure why she'd brought it home, she just hadn't been able to let it go.

Justin had left the apartment, but there were little hints of his recent presence, in the pile of damp towels on the bathroom floor, the dirty dishes left in the sink, and the short note left on the table.

Thank you for being good to me.

Had she been good to him?

She wasn't so sure.

He'd never know the sickening certainty she'd felt in her gut, believing that somehow, even as a child, he had been helping their father murder women. That he was still doing it.

The blood on his shoe still bothered her, but she also knew if she was bold enough to ask him about it, he would want to know *why*.

And she could never tell him the truth.

Justin was the only family she had left, and she couldn't let her own paranoia fracture that relationship.

If there was evidence, real, hard evidence of a connection, she would do what had to be done. But after Ed had absolved Justin of a connection to those old crimes, Margot found it hard to hold onto the same conviction she'd had about him only a day earlier.

God, a day?

Was it really only that morning she'd stood over her brother and watched him sleep? Sat across from Ed and heard him admit that *she* was the child he wished had turned out like him.

That in many ways she *had* turned out like him.

It was dark now. Margot had gone through a debriefing with the FBI, they'd let her shower in the employee locker room, and given her a new shirt, though it had FBI emblazoned on it, so she wasn't sure she'd get much use out of it. They'd offered to give her her turtleneck back, but there was no way she wanted it.

She sat down on the couch and stared at her phone, wondering if she should call someone. An appointment with Dr. Singh was in order, but she didn't want his calm and steady voice right now. Briefly, she wondered if she should tell the captain what had happened, but she knew that by the time she got to work on Friday he would already be aware.

The lingering threat of desk duty was at the back of her mind. It wasn't unfair of him to want her to take things easy after what she'd just seen. And Margot couldn't pretend she was OK. Every time she closed her eyes, she saw Jimmy lift the gun to his chin. Over and over, she marveled at the ease with which one bullet could open up a human skull like a flower coming into bloom.

She was hesitant to reach out to Wes only because of the pause she had placed on them having any kind of a serious conversation. What was this if not serious? And how could she ask him not to open up to her when she was also asking him to be there for her?

She kept making demands of him that weren't those of a partner. Not a police partner. And he kept rising to meet them. But could she do that and then tell him *not* to want something more?

Especially when she knew *she* wanted more and was just afraid where it would take them.

She found, in that moment, she wanted his presence more than she was worried about what that meant.

He answered her call after only two rings, and the cheery tone of his voice was almost enough to undo her completely.

"Can you come over?" she breathed, her voice hitching on the last word, a dead giveaway to just how not OK she was.

Wes didn't hesitate. He said, "I'll be there in twenty minutes."

He was at her door in fifteen.

When he sat on her couch, he gave the small dog a questioning eye, but the dog also sent a questioning look back, somewhere in the direction of Wes's right shoulder. Its little tail thumped a few times once it seemed to decide that Wes's smudgy appearance or smell were suitable company.

The dog put its head on Wes's thigh.

Margot sat in the armchair, looking at her hands, and for a long time she couldn't bring herself to say anything.

Finally, Wes asked, "What happened?"

Margot let out a sob.

Wes shifted the dog aside and crossed the room without a pause, kneeling in front of her and wrapping his arms around her. She cried, her body shaking, until the force of her tears was almost enough to exhaust her, to break her. She thought she might fall to pieces if it wasn't for him holding her together.

And she thought, in that moment, that maybe it wasn't such a bad thing to need someone.

When she finally caught her breath enough to speak, she gently pulled herself away from him, though he stayed close, and explained everything that had happened since that morning. She talked about her visit with Ed, she confessed what she had suspected about Justin, she explained the meeting with the FBI and the drive to Healdsburg. Then in painstaking detail, as if she needed to relive it in order for it to be real, she told him what had happened in Jimmy McMaster's kitchen.

Wes didn't say anything the entire time she spoke, though

he did keep hold of one of her hands and would squeeze it whenever a particularly unpleasant piece of the story came up.

When she was done, Margot was whittled down to nothing. She was more tired than she had ever been. Yet somehow, she was lighter. The simple act of sharing the story with someone else, someone who might care enough to listen, gave her more relief than she had anticipated.

"Jesus Christ, Margot," he said after she was done. "I'm not even going to ask if you're OK. You're definitely not OK." He got up, giving her shoulder a squeeze as he went, and when he came back he was holding two tumblers of whiskey, one of which he pressed into her hand. "Normally I'm not an advocate for using booze to solve problems, but I think you need this."

She looked into the amber liquid in the glass, then let out a little laugh. "Why did I take his dog?"

Wes looked from her to the sleeping dog. "Who else was going to?"

She looked at the little creature, one paw in the grave already, and realized he was right. The dog would have ended up in a shelter if it was lucky, and more likely than not it would have been euthanized. The dog was not responsible for what its owner had done. No more than she was responsible for what her father had done.

Maybe, deep down, she knew it needed to be saved.

And maybe that was the same reason she'd called Wes.

Because she knew she needed saving, too.

But was she willing to let someone save her?

Without much thought, she realized that the answer *could* be yes.

She looked up at him, held his gaze. "Will you stay?" she asked.

He nodded once. "Of course."

FORTY-FIVE

The dog's name—according to a little heart-shaped tag on its collar—was Betty. Since Margot couldn't fathom coming up with a better name on her own, nor did it feel right to change the name of a dog who was probably 150 years old in dog years, Betty it was.

Betty did not require much. She ate a small scoop of senior kibble every morning. She went out to pee precisely twice a day and had no interest in going more than ten feet from the building.

If Betty missed Jimmy, it never showed. She settled into life with Margot in less than a day. And by the time Margot went back to work on Friday evening, she felt like the dog had been there a lot longer than just two nights.

When she got to the precinct, Wes intercepted her almost the second she got through the door, a gentle hand on her elbow, guiding her away from their office.

"Why do I feel like I'm in trouble?" she asked, but let him lead her, surprised to find that she wasn't anxious.

The night of Jimmy's death, Wes had stayed with her the

whole night. In her bed. While nothing had happened, Margot had been shocked to find that when she woke the next day to find him curled on his side next to her, that she didn't have a panic reaction to it.

It felt... nice.

It felt *right*.

And she had *needed* him that night. Needed someone to be a buffer between her and the enormity of what she was feeling. Wes was the only person who could do that.

They hadn't talked about it since, or what any of it meant. She got the feeling that he didn't want to use her moment of weakness as a bridge to whatever it was he'd been wanting to say to her.

But Margot realized that, despite all the walls she'd put up, all the boundaries *she* had established between them, she wished he would bring it up again. Maybe this time she wouldn't run and hide. Maybe.

"You're not in trouble." Wes looked intense, like a man on a mission. He wasn't his usual jovial self, which made Margot question if he was being honest with her, but she soon realized it was just that he was deeply focused. He slowed his walk for a moment and looked at her, his expression softening. "But the captain *did* tell me to send you to see him as soon as you arrived."

"Then why are you dragging me in the opposite direction of his office?" she asked, almost bemused. Was he planning to keep her stashed away in an interrogation room so she couldn't get officially relegated to desk duty?

"Before that happens, there's something I need to show you."

"OK." She drew out the word, making it into a three-syllable question. *Okaaaaay?*

He guided her into the media room, where they kept a variety of video players that could look at everything from memory cards to computers to old VHS if necessary. Wes pulled out a chair and Margot sat down, wondering what the hell this was all about, and more than a little intrigued.

It was a wonderful distraction, whatever it was.

"We got the footage from the auto shop where we found the woman in the dumpster," he said.

Margot stiffened and Wes placed a hand on her shoulder, close to her neck. He squeezed gently. "I think you'll want to see this."

The video was already queued up, and Wes hit play.

The feed wasn't very high quality, but it was good enough that Margot could make out the layout of the parking lot she'd been standing in only a few days earlier. At first there was nothing to see, just an empty parking lot. Car headlights passed by, changing the light from time to time, but the parking lot itself remained untouched.

Then, so suddenly Margot gave a start, a woman appeared, running onto the screen. She was limping, and Margot realized she must have lost a shoe, the other heel still strapped to her foot.

A moment later a man appeared, coming from the same direction. He was faster than she was and soon caught up to her, grabbing hold of her purse and yanking it from her shoulder.

The woman clung to the bag, obviously screaming something in the man's face, though the recording had no sound.

The two figures struggled for a moment and in Margot's head she kept telling the girl, *Just let him have the bag, it's not worth it.*

But she understood the animal instinct to protect what belongs to you. She knew why people didn't just let go of their things. That bag likely represented everything the woman had in that moment. Her money, her phone, her apartment keys. Giving it up would have meant letting him have all of that.

Margot got it.

The man finally wrestled the bag away from the woman and started to walk away, his strut proud, aggressive.

The woman shouted something at him, and Margot realized her mistake the same moment the woman on screen did.

The man came back at her, moving so quickly the woman barely had time to react, and he began pummeling her. Her arms went to cover her face as she tried to push him away, but soon he had her on the ground, and Margot saw the flash of a knife. Her stomach clenched, and Wes paused the video then, before Margot had to watch another person die in front of her.

"Look at him," Wes said, tapping the screen. "Just look."

Margot didn't understand what Wes wanted her to see at first, but then she did look. *Really* look.

Their killer was short, and while she couldn't say with absolute certainty, he was likely only about five foot seven max. He was stocky, with broad shoulders like a football player, and his head was shaved. She could even see the mark of a tattoo on the side of his scalp, though she couldn't have said for certain what it was.

What she knew, though, and what Wes was making sure she saw, was that this man was *not* her brother. Her skinny, tall brother so desperately in need of a haircut. The man she was looking at couldn't have looked less like Justin if he tried. She'd told Wes her fears and, rather than placate her with reassuring words, he'd known what she needed. Proof.

Margot looked up at Wes, who was staring down at her intently, watching as the realization clicked.

"Thank you," she whispered.

"Don't thank me yet," he said, giving her neck another squeeze. "You still need to talk to the captain."

She let out a long sigh and then nodded. "Can you just give me a minute?"

Wes regarded her carefully and then got up to leave. "You

know where to find him, you don't need me to hold your hand." He said this with a smile, though Margot felt that she might not mind him holding her hand right now.

But she needed comforting from someone else in that moment. Someone she hadn't been fair to, even when he thought she was being good to him.

She picked up her phone and called Justin. The line rang several times before he picked up, and when he did his voice was thick, like he'd been sleeping.

"You were gone when I got back," she said instead of a greeting. "You didn't have to leave."

"Margot?" he asked blearily. There was nothing in his tone that made her think he was drunk, no slurred consonants, no dropped letters. He was just tired.

"Yeah, just making sure you got home OK," she said. It was a lie, but she did want to know he was all right.

"Thanks. Yeah, all good here. Needed to get back because I get the baby this weekend."

Nerves clenched at Margot, recalling how he'd been at the start of his visit, but she also knew Justin's ex-girlfriend… separated baby mama—she wasn't totally sure of their current status and hated herself for not asking her brother more about his life—was aware of Justin's issues and wouldn't leave him alone with their baby if there was anything to worry about.

Justin had seemed better toward the end of his stay. Clearer. The lapse in his sobriety wasn't anything to overlook, but she hoped for his sake it was just a lapse.

Hearing the warmth in his words when he spoke about his son, she wondered how it was possible she had ever imagined he might have it in him to be like their father. Ed's voice never got that tone to it when he spoke about her, because he wasn't capable of love. Justin was so overwhelmed with his capacity for love that sometimes it threatened to undo him.

"You OK?" Justin asked, and she almost had to laugh at the absurdity of him being worried about her.

Hadn't she always been the strong one?

Hadn't she always made sure their sibling ship made it safely through stormy waters?

She thought about the drops of blood on his shoe, the insane way she'd been willing to believe the worst of him just because the worst happened to come true once before.

"Do you ever wonder what parts of us came from him?" she asked quietly.

Justin was quiet on the other end of the line, sucking in a breath through his teeth. She wondered if he was thinking about his answer, or just hoping she would move on to a different question.

"Do you remember the time Dad took me on that solo camping trip up in Desolation Wilderness?"

Margot hadn't thought about that in a long, long time, but Justin was now the second person to mention it to her in a week, after Ed had brought it up during their visit. She'd brushed it off then, but now the memory came rushing back to her and she let out a sharp laugh. "Yes. I was so mad that I couldn't go. I called Dad a sexist misogynist and slammed my bedroom door in his face."

Margot flashed briefly to the anger with which she could speak to Ed now, and realized he was no stranger to it. He'd had decades to learn about how her moods could crest like deadly waves and then settle again.

She didn't need to wonder which parent she'd gotten that from.

"I think he did that whole thing just because he knew that *I* knew you were his favorite. You were always his favorite."

Margot stared at the blank screens in front of her, her own reflection looking back.

"I wonder sometimes, when I see parts of myself I don't like, if that's Ed."

Justin laughed, but it wasn't an altogether warm sound. "I think that's probably normal. I wonder if maybe part of the reason I do some of the things I do is because I don't want to find out that I'm like him."

"You're nothing like him," Margot said quickly, especially now that she knew he wasn't.

"I think I need *him* to know that," Justin said finally. "Because when I was young, I wanted so desperately to be like him that it kept me up at night. I would have done anything to show him that I was good enough to love. I think that's probably the real reason I wanted to do that documentary so badly. Because I need him to know that he isn't going to have any legacy once he's gone. That it all ended with him."

Margot was quiet.

She'd never considered it that way. That by owning who she was she took all that power out of his hands.

That if she took Megan Finch away from Ed, she could let that part of her die in peace.

"Hey, do you know there was blood on your shoes?" she asked, trying to keep her tone light and friendly.

"Blood?" Justin was still bleary, like sleep was trying to draw him back down. She heard rustling, then footsteps. A small laugh. "Margot, that's not blood. I thought homicide detectives were supposed to know shit like this."

"What is it then?" she asked, a creeping mixture of relief and embarrassment filling her, making her cheeks turn red.

"It's paint. From a garage job I was doing a few weeks ago. We were trying to color-match old brick, so I guess I can see the confusion." He lapsed briefly into silence, like he might be looking at the shoes now, trying to see what she saw. Margot didn't dare ask him what he was thinking, and he didn't ask her what *she* had been thinking, for which she was grateful.

Finally he said, "You don't have to worry, you know?"

"What do you mean?"

"Whatever Dad has said to you, whatever he's made you think, you're nothing like him. You'll never be like him."

Margot found herself unable to breathe.

She wished she could believe him.

FORTY-SIX

Captain Gordon Tate stared at Margot across his desk and said nothing.

Margot met his gaze steadily, and said nothing in return.

At last, the man realized he was going to have to be the one to initiate this conversation or it would simply never happen.

"Detective, you and I have been in this position before." He paused. "And while I can appreciate that you don't invite the issues that arise around you, I think you can understand my concerns about sending you back out into the field following such a traumatic event."

"I can understand your concerns, yes, sir."

"And are you going to tell me I don't have a reason to be concerned?" he asked.

Margot mulled this over a moment. Was she still seeing Jimmy every time she closed her eyes, his skull plate opening, as e.e. cummings might say, *petal by petal*? Was she still standing longer than necessary under the shower, trying to scrub off blood that wasn't there?

Yes.

But she also still had a man's fingerprints on her throat. She still thought about watching a man get hit by a sniper's bullet for doing nothing more than getting out of his car to try and help someone else. She still saw her father jumping out of a moving car while teaching her how to drive, leaving her behind the wheel as he tried to outrun the FBI.

The thing about trauma was, it didn't leave just because you gave it time.

It was always there, a roommate who didn't pay rent, just waiting for you to have one really bad day before it came out to remind you of its presence.

Was Margot OK?

No.

Was she ever going to be?

The truth she'd come to realize after thirty-eight years of being alive, and twenty-three years after her whole world collapsed, was that *no* she probably *wasn't* ever going to be a normal person, living a normal carefree life. But the one thing she could do, could keep doing, was her job.

"Sir, while I can acknowledge the gravity of what happened to me earlier this week, I'd like to point out that there is no one in this building better at compartmentalizing than I am. What happened was horrific, I won't pretend it wasn't, but I do pay my therapist a very high premium to be able to help me work through the horrific on a weekly basis. I know you have to do whatever you think is right, but I have cases to solve, and that to me is more important than anything else. I think if you ask Detective Fox to keep you apprised of my behavior and let you know if he thinks I need a break, then I respect Wes's opinion on the matter more than my own."

"And if Detective Fox says you should be grounded?"

"Then you can ground me," she replied without missing a beat. And she was surprised to find she meant it. All of it. She *did* trust Wes to know what was right, to see if she was slipping. He would never let her go over the deep end without pulling her back from the edge.

If anyone could read her and know when it was time to stop, it would be him.

The captain nodded. "Normally, I'd stick you on desk duty awaiting a psych eval, but I'm going to be honest, Margot, I don't think you're a normal case."

At this, she couldn't help but smile. "No, sir."

"All right, get out of here before I change my mind."

Margot thanked him and returned to her own office, where Wes was waiting expectantly. She sat in her desk chair across from him, and looked at him thoughtfully, her fingers drumming on the arms of her chair.

"And?" he asked, when she didn't reply right away.

"You're my babysitter. You need to tell him if you think I need to be pulled off active duty."

Wes whistled. "You sure you trust me with that power?"

Margot smirked. "As Spider-Man's uncle would say: with great power comes great responsibility. Just don't let it go to your head."

"I can't make any promises. I can feel it feeding my massive ego already." He straightened his back, puffed out his chest. "You're going to have to be so nice to me."

"I'm already so nice to you," she countered.

"Eh, you could be nicer."

"I'm sure the capacity for *nicer* exists in the world, but I think you've seen the upper limits of what I'm able to achieve personally."

"I'm sorry to say, I think you might be right."

Margot snorted and looked at her computer; a file she'd requested on Roberto Riga was waiting for her, which she opened eagerly.

"Well, shit," she replied. "I had assumed Roberto Riga was going to be Emmanuel's brother."

Wes peered over his monitor. "And he's not?"

Margot shook her head. "It's his fucking *son*."

FORTY-SEVEN
1993

Petaluma, California

Justin sat next to Ed in the front seat of the family car, staring out the window, but not really seeing anything. He was focused on the middle distance, like he would rather just disconnect from the world instead of be present in it.

Ed angled the car into the parking lot of a grocery store—their mission, in theory, was to go collect some bits and bobs that Kim was missing to make dinner—but Ed had another reason for wanting to bring Justin along with him.

The boy's behavior since they'd returned from the trip was starting to make Ed uneasy. He didn't like how unreadable he had become, how he acted like he was sleepwalking through his days.

The change stemmed back to the night in the woods, and Ed wasn't stupid enough to think that the two things were unrelated.

He shifted the car into park, but as Justin undid his seat belt and went to open the door, Ed placed a hand on the back of his neck. "Hold on just a second, kid. I want to have a chat with you."

Justin stilled under his father's touch, then settled back into his seat, though there was an energy vibrating through him like a wild animal ready to bolt at the first sign of trouble.

"What's going on with you lately?" Ed asked, lacking the skills to take a more subtle approach with the boy.

"Nothin'." Justin stared down at his shoes, scuffed off-brand Converse, the white toes almost green from all his time outdoors.

"Now don't *nothin'* me, pal, I'm your dad and I know a thing or two, and you've got something on your mind. So spit it out, I'm sick of you dragging yourself around the house like a zombie."

Ed waited, an unfamiliar pinched feeling in his lungs making it hard to breathe. He was sure this would be the moment that his son confessed to following him that night, to forming some kind of conclusions about what that excursion had meant. Would he believe, like Kim did, that his father was interested in being unfaithful? Would he think Ed was a run-of-the-mill pervert just watching young women in the woods like a peeping Tom? Or would he have surmised the real danger in Ed's nighttime activity?

Ed wasn't sure which one of these options would be the easiest to deal with. He almost hoped it would be the latter, that something Justin saw that night had created an awakening in him. It wouldn't be ideal, but in terms of things Ed was equipped to handle, this was something he could manage.

He didn't *want* his son to be a killer, necessarily, but being a killer was engrained in Ed. He'd known who he was going to be since he was younger than Justin. Hell, he'd eliminated his own mother before his balls had even really dropped.

If Justin *was* like him, then it was better for Ed to know

now, because he'd have time to prepare, to guide the boy in all the lessons it had taken him a long time to learn for himself.

Maybe, Ed mused, it was something they could do together.

A real father–son bonding experience.

Justin finally lifted his head and looked back out the window. When he spoke, his voice was so quiet Ed needed to ask him to repeat himself.

"Why don't you like me?" Justin asked, his voice cracking as he spoke.

Of all the things Ed had been prepared for his son to say in that moment, this hadn't even been on his list.

He sat, stunned, and looked at the boy's thin, hunched shoulders. He was so taken aback he didn't have the ability to form a response right away, and this just made Justin slouch deeper into his seat, practically curling in on himself like a hedgehog.

"Why do you think I don't like you?" Ed asked.

Justin darted a glance over his shoulder, his expression hurt and a little petulant, as if Ed should be ashamed of himself for asking such a stupid question.

"No, seriously, why would you ever think a thing like that?" Ed wanted to know, largely so he could avoid continuing the behavior. The truth was he *didn't* like the boy. They were nothing alike—something even more evident now with this whiny revelation—and Ed had a hard time stomaching weak people. His son was weak.

"You love Megan more. You talk to her, you ask her questions, you spend time with her. She's your favorite."

Ed swallowed a knot in his throat and leaned back against the door of his car, giving Justin a good, long look. He needed to fix this, but he got the sense that if he lied and offered Justin coddling words, the boy would know he was full of shit.

"I'm sorry it feels that way to you," Ed said. "You and Megan are both very important to me, and if I made you feel like you weren't as important as her, then I'm very sorry for that. I'm glad you told me." None of this was a lie. He needed Justin. His children were a vital part of the facade he had very carefully created for himself. He also needed the people in his house not to be paying such close attention to the things he did and said.

One keen observation at the wrong time would be all it took to undo everything. And since it was clear that Justin wouldn't be joining the family business, Ed would need to be very intentional about how he handled the boy going forward.

"Let's plan more things we can do together, just you and me, OK?"

Justin stared at him for a long time, as if trying to decide if this was just lip service, or if Ed actually meant it.

"OK," he said finally. Then after a beat, he added, "Hey, Dad?"

"Yeah, pal?"

"Can it be something *other* than camping?"

Ed smiled as he opened up his car door. "Yeah, Justin. We can do whatever you want."

As they walked toward the store, Ed put a hand around his son's skinny shoulders and gave the boy a half-hug. He felt Justin lean against him, almost melting into his side in relief.

He might not be the son Ed wanted, but he was the son he had.

And he'd need to be more careful about keeping the boy on his side.

Otherwise, he might grow up to become a liability.

FORTY-EIGHT

Roberto Riga was a confident young man.

A little too confident, if Margot was being honest.

She and Wes had made their way to his home, a pretty Victorian that had been updated to give it a modern, almost cold look on the inside, with a lot of steel, leather, and precisely zero charm.

Roberto had been home. Alone. Perhaps it wasn't late enough in the evening for him to be partying. Or maybe he was too cool to go out on the weekends and did all his socializing mid-week.

He had let them in, even knowing who they were.

And now, Roberto Riga was sitting across from them in his living room, a bottle of beer in his hand, and an absurdly smug expression on his face. He looked from Margot to Wes, then back to Margot, where his gaze lingered, as unwelcome as a hand on her thigh, refusing to move away.

"Detectives, you mentioned there was something I might be able to help you with? Some kind of investigation, I assume?"

Roberto was in his mid-twenties. He was a good-looking kid, with dark, wavy hair pushed back from his forehead, a jawbone that could cut glass, and style that was expensive but practical. He was wearing gray trousers, paired with an eggplant purple cashmere sweater. His shoes were brown leather slip-ons that had been well-worn in and likely cost more than Margot's monthly rent.

His brown eyes twinkled as he spoke, and Margot expected that this was not a man who had a lot of trouble catching the interest of women. He had an easy charm to him that she found repulsive, but most people would be drawn in by. He was a bit too loud, too self-assured, too aware that he could own whatever room he was in.

The only piece of art in the room was a black-and-white portrait of a nude woman. The stark shadows and composition left Margot certain it was a Mapplethorpe, and probably an original if she was willing to make estimates on Riga's net worth.

A gift from dear old Dad, most likely.

"We appreciate you taking the time to talk to us," Margot said, forcing a smile onto her face. If he was going to keep looking at her like she was something he could have, she might as well take advantage of it.

"It's a pleasure," he replied, giving her a wink.

Margot's tongue tasted like ash in her mouth. She hated him, hated the coldness of this space, but she was here to do right by Angela, and by God she would get this man to talk to her if it was the last thing she did.

Still, being across from him, the drink so casual in his hand, she couldn't help but scan the room looking for anywhere he might have hidden a gun. Any opportunity for him to take the same exit approach as Jimmy.

She wasn't sure she'd ever be able to question anyone in their own home again without thinking about that, and she was aware that every shift Roberto made on his loveseat made her itch to reach for her weapon.

There was a good reason that people who had seen the

things she'd seen didn't get sent out into the field again right away.

But she also knew if they left here, Roberto would tell his daddy they'd visited, and they would never be able to get this close to him again without a team of Emmanuel Riga's lawyers standing between them.

If they were ever going to get something out of him directly, it would be now.

"Roberto, how well do you know this woman?" Margot had brought a picture of Angela with her, skin glowing, smile wide. No matter how often Margot looked at photos of the girl, she couldn't reconcile that lovely face with the one she'd seen that day in the park.

This was a version of Angela who would never come back again, even if she did defy all the odds and pull through.

She was still fighting now, days later, and Dr. Kaur said that every day she survived was another day closer to pulling through. She wasn't out of the woods yet, so to speak, but she had lived longer than any of her doctors thought she would. She was a fighter.

Margot handed the photo to Roberto, who took only a cursory glance at it before handing it back, but Margot saw the tension in his jaw. The bluster that had colored his features when they arrived was dulled.

"I meet a lot of girls, Detective."

"I think you know this one, Roberto," Margot answered, and she stared at him until she saw a flicker of understanding. She wasn't asking him *if* he knew Angela. She already knew he did. But Roberto couldn't know how much she knew, and that was where she had power over him.

He swallowed hard, shifted.

"Yeah, I knew her."

"Knew?" Margot asked, leaning heavily on the word. In that

moment, she realized something, just that one little slip of a word was enough for her to understand.

Roberto didn't know Angela had survived.

Margot smiled, and Roberto didn't like it this time. He took a long pull from his beer bottle, now looking at Wes as if the only other man in the room might help him. Wes, for his part, was playing the part of Bored Cop, and his expression remained unchanged, impassive.

"We used to go out," Roberto said. "But that was a while ago."

Margot nodded, lulling him into a false sense of security. "How long ago would you say it's been since you two were together?"

"Six months, maybe?" He shrugged, as if the timing of it hadn't been important enough for him to commit to memory. "She was a bit too clingy, y'know? Had to cut it off."

"Mmm." Margot reached into her jacket pocket and handed Roberto an evidence bag, this one containing the brochure for Bella Vista and the receipt for the couple's spa services. "I think your memory might be a little off."

Roberto held the bag, and now Margot could see his brain working overtime, trying to come up with a plausible lie, something that he could use to backpedal his way out of this. He glanced at Margot and his eyes weren't twinkling anymore.

He took another sip from his beer, then settled back in his chair. "Why don't you ask me what you want to ask me."

"What was your relationship with Angela Gromand?" Margot asked.

"She was someone I liked to spend time with. But I don't have a lot of room in my life for people to get emotionally attached, you know? Dating girls you meet at the club, or on apps, or whatever... that really doesn't work for me. So Angela... Well, I knew her as Whitney at first, but she and I had an arrangement."

"A professional arrangement?"

Roberto nodded. "I'd bring her to events, to things where I needed my date to act a certain way, to behave herself, to not let the temptations of high-end lifestyles get too appealing. I needed a girl who would be good."

"So, Angela was your regular girl for those events?"

He sipped his beer, then nodded. "I don't want you to get the wrong idea. I don't have any trouble getting women." Again, his gaze drifted over Margot's body, but this time she felt like it wasn't intentional, almost a habit whenever there was a woman in the room. "But the girls I meet aren't always suitable to spend time with the crowd I'm a part of. You can't go to a billionaire's cocktail hour and have some dumb bitch you met at the club acting all googly-eyed because everyone has a Louis Vuitton bag and lives in a penthouse, you know? I needed a girl who looked good on my arm but kept her cool, acted like she belonged."

A picture unfolded for Margot of the exact scenarios that Roberto was referring to. Parties among the ultra-rich, where a gawking bystander would stick out like a sore thumb. Angela wasn't rich. She and Fiona both had to work their asses off to pay for the little house they shared. But she was a pro, she was part of a very high-class agency that was able to cover their tracks well, and she would have known how to act in those situations.

"What happened at the resort?" Margot asked.

This question made Roberto quirk a brow. "What are you talking about?"

"Someone close to Angela said that when she got back from her trip with you she wasn't the same. More distant, not acting like herself."

"They tell you anything else?" His tone was crisp, a sharp edge to the words. Margot didn't often get a chill talking to suspects, but she felt one now.

"I'm not at liberty to say."

Roberto snorted. "Sure. OK, look. Angela was a pro, right? I'm not sure what she fucking expected, but she was there to do a job. Just because I bought her a few shiny toys, took her to some nice places, suddenly she forgot what her job was? And my boys just wanted to party. She acted like I was out of my mind saying she was a party favor, but a whore is a whore, no matter what pretty label or price tag she comes with."

Margot felt her mouth go dry.

Roberto had taken Angela to that resort, treated her like a girlfriend, taking her to a spa, giving her gifts, letting her dip a toe in the lap of luxury. Then he'd tossed her to his rich friends without a second thought, letting them do God only knew what to her, like it was just part of the deal.

Margot clenched and unclenched her jaw. She needed to stay focused, needed to get something she could use. She wasn't going to be able to do that if she said what she wanted to say in that moment.

"She didn't like that?"

Roberto shrugged. "She was acting like a pissy little bitch after. When I brought her back to the city she said she didn't want to see me anymore, but that only lasted about a week."

"But you stopped seeing her anyway, even after that?"

"Bitch stole something from me."

"What did she steal?"

He waved the hand with the bottle in it, the beer sloshing around inside. "It doesn't matter what she stole, I got it back. It's the principle of the thing. If you can't trust the people you hire, you gotta get rid of them. Clean break."

Margot could see the contents of Angela's purse strewn on the ground next to the car. The way someone had obviously gone through it looking for something. But she didn't think Roberto would go to the effort of such a violent murder for something as trivial as a stolen watch or other expensive tchotchke.

No, Angela had to have taken something that could really fuck up his life, and now Margot wanted to know what it was.

"Roberto, you ever have any relationships with other girls like Angela? Professional girls." Margot could see the way Wes looked at her, just once, quickly. She was veering into the territory of a different case now, but she couldn't resist the opportunity, and she would hate herself if she didn't try. Angela might not be a victim of the Redwood Killer, but there was always a chance, and Margot couldn't just say nothing. The coincidence of another Lark being attacked meant she *had* to treat these cases like they had the potential to be related. Ignoring that felt foolish.

"Sure. A couple."

"And did you have to get rid of them? Clean break?"

Roberto leaned forward in his seat, resting his forearms on his thighs and letting the beer bottle dangle between two fingers. "I'm not really sure what you're asking me, Detective."

Margot pulled out a photo of the Golden Gate crime scene, the charred rubble of the car, and held it out for him to see.

"I'm just wondering if that's how you solve all your problems, or if Angela was a special case."

Roberto dropped the picture on the floor like it was too hot to touch.

"I don't think I'm going to say anything else to you until I have a lawyer with me," he said coldly. Only he was about twenty minutes too late to make that decision.

Margot smiled at him, and he recoiled.

"I just want to know one thing, Roberto."

"What's that?" he asked, unable to take his eyes off her.

"Did you pay full price for your girlfriends, or did Daddy give you a discounted rate?"

FORTY-NINE

"Holy shit, Margot," Wes said as they got back into his car. "I thought you were going to make that kid piss his goddamn pants."

Margot snorted. "I think that would give me a full house in interrogation bingo."

They were about to pull out of their parking spot when Margot's phone began to vibrate in her pocket. When she pulled it out, the displayed number was one she didn't recognize.

"Detective Phalen," she answered.

"D-detective..." The voice wasn't one she immediately recognized, but it belonged to a young woman who was in clear distress. "I-it's F-Fiona."

Margot shot Wes a quick look. "Fiona, are you OK? What's going on?"

"I'm at the h-hospital. I th-think you should c-come."

Margot mouthed the word *hospital* to Wes, who didn't need any additional instruction. He pulled out into the thin night-time traffic and made his way along a familiar route to the hospital.

Margot tried to keep Fiona talking. "Is it Angela?"

"P-please hurry," was all the girl said, and then she hung up.

"What's going on?" Wes asked when Margot put her phone back in her pocket. She shook her head. "Fiona. She sounded like she was crying and just said we should hurry."

They both implicitly understood what that likely meant, and when they arrived at the hospital fifteen minutes later the bustle outside of Angela's room told them their worst-case scenarios were right. Nurses and doctors in a flurry of lab coats and scrubs were moving in and out of Angela's room, their pace frantic.

Shouted orders came from inside, but Margot couldn't make anything out among the medical jargon that wasn't meant for her to understand. It was a lot of calls for medication and machine settings.

On a chair, just across the hall from Angela's room, Fiona was sitting. Her expression was shell-shocked, her skin ashen. When she saw Margot and Wes arrive she scrambled out of the chair, and before Margot knew what was happening, the girl was holding her in a tight hug.

Margot froze, unsure of how to respond to the gesture, uncomfortable to be in it. She glanced at Wes for help and he just gave her a supportive nod, which was useless in terms of a rescue.

Margot put her hands gently on Fiona's back, giving her a light hug in return and offering a soothing *pat pat* that she thought might be part of what was required of her here. She wasn't a big *touch* person, and she liked it even less when she was unprepared for it. But she understood, as Fiona sobbed into her shoulder, that the girl had no one else in that moment.

And that was something Margot could relate to.

She let the girl hold her a few moments longer before putting some distance between them. She put her hands on

Fiona's shoulders and stooped so she was looking the girl in the eye. "What happened?"

"I went to get some coffee and ice. Angela likes the ice, I think it helps her. But when I came back all the machines were beeping. She'd been awake when I left, but she was just... she wasn't *there* when I got back. She looked..." Fiona let out a hiccup and a sob. "She looked dead. I think she's dead."

The three of them looked back to the room where it was very obvious that a number of medical professionals hadn't yet decided Angela was gone. Yet as the minutes passed, the shouting turned to murmuring, the pace of everyone's rushed footsteps became calmer, less hurried, and about ten minutes after Margot and Wes arrived, Dr. Kaur came out of the room.

Her face was damp with sweat, and Margot had never seen someone look so defeated before. Dr. Kaur, a woman who spent much of her day looking death in the face, was now the very definition of *crushed*. She let out a little sigh, her body trembling, then deposited her gloves and protective coverings in a nearby trash can.

That was when she spotted Fiona and the detectives. Margot actually saw the moment where Dr. Kaur adjusted from her honest display of feeling to her thick-skinned exterior. Her spine straightened, emotion drained from her face leaving behind only a calm, unflappable exterior.

Margot recognized the shift, because she'd made the same one walking into her own precinct that night.

There was no room for feeling in the world they inhabited.

"I'm very sorry," Dr. Kaur said as she came to stand before them. "We did everything we could, but it appears Angela suffered a cardiac arrest. I know she'd shown signs of improvement the last few days, but I'm afraid the damage done was just more than her body could take." She gave Fiona's arm a little squeeze. "Your sister was a brave woman. I'm very sorry for your loss."

She wasted no more time coddling them, and headed off in the opposite direction without looking back.

As the room emptied, Margot, Wes, and Fiona went back in. There was no need to don any protective clothing at this point, but Margot still felt like she should be wearing it, out of respect. She felt almost naked standing at the foot of Angela's bed in her street clothes.

"Just like that?" Fiona whispered, staring at her sister's body. It was clear she was in shock. The grief would come soon enough.

Angela was covered in bandages, the scant amount of skin visible on her body was charcoal black. Looking at her now, Margot didn't feel sad, she didn't feel heartbroken. She felt *furious*.

Not even an hour ago she had sat across from the man that she *knew* was responsible for this, and he had talked about Angela like she was little more than a blow-up doll. Like her life and who she was hadn't mattered. Margot gripped the end of the bed frame, riding out the red-hot rage that was burning through her.

She wanted to go back to Roberto's house and turn it to ashes the same way he had done to Angela's body.

She wanted him to suffer.

But the only recourse she had for that was shackled by the boundaries of the law, and she knew, deep down, that he was never going to see the justice he deserved.

Wes patted Fiona's back as the girl stared at her sister's body. "Is there anyone we can call for you? Anyone who can come pick you up? Or can we take you to someone?"

Fiona blinked, her lashes thick with tears, her curly hair a messy halo around her head.

"Can you take me home?"

. . .

They couldn't let her go in alone. Fiona had called a friend to be with her, but Margot wasn't willing to let the girl out of her sight until Fiona had someone who could stay the night. There was too much risk of the darkness closing in.

Fiona paced her living room, from one end of the couch and back again until Wes brought her a glass of water and made her sit down. He wrapped a blanket around her shoulders and sat beside her while Margot hovered near the kitchen island.

It was so peculiar to watch Wes don his white knight armor from the perspective of an outsider. His care and gentleness came so naturally to him she sometimes couldn't comprehend how he was the same person she had partnered up with almost three years earlier.

The man he'd been then was all bluster and flourish, wearing the tough-guy detective veneer he'd learned from watching Steve McQueen and Clint Eastwood. But the real Wes, the one she was looking at now, was a man of such powerful empathy she wondered how he managed to surround himself with all the pain that their job entailed without going mad.

Did Wes need saving as much as she did, and he had just never bothered to ask?

They locked eyes over Fiona's head, and just stayed in that gaze a long time as the girl cried.

Then, as if shocked, Fiona sat upright, knocking the blanket off of her. She bolted from the room, and Margot's heart shot into her throat as she tried to tamp down visions of Jimmy and his gun from the forefront of her mind.

"Fiona?" she called out nervously.

"I just remembered." The girl's voice was muffled, coming from a room down the hall. "I didn't know what she was talking about."

Wes and Margot exchanged confused looks, and then Fiona

returned, her expression bordering on manic, but Margot didn't think the girl was a danger to herself.

Fiona held out a phone to them. "It's hers."

Margot looked down at the cracked screen, the slightly dented case. She took the phone, not sure why it was being offered to her.

"When she got back from her trip, she said something happened to her phone, and she had to get a new one. But when I said she should just throw the old one out, she wouldn't let me. She said it was too important to get rid of. Yesterday, at the hospital, she said something to me. You know it was hard to make out what she was saying, it was *ome*. I thought she meant home. I wouldn't shut up about how she'd come home soon and I'd take care of her and it would be OK. I'd look after her for once." Fiona's voice hitched. She was moving steadily toward hysteria. "I think she meant *phone*. I think there's something on that phone." She pointed to the little rectangle in Margot's hand.

She stole something from me, Roberto had said.

He'd said he had gotten it back, but what if that had been a lie so they didn't press him about it?

Margot glanced down at the phone in her hand, and wondered if she'd just been gifted a golden goose or a ticking time bomb.

FIFTY

It was impossible not to notice the sleek black SUV parked in front of the precinct when Margot and Wes got out of his car. Her first thought was that the FBI had come, and her pulse was tripping even as she realized that the FBI weren't driving around in Cadillacs.

Margot and Wes approached the front steps of the precinct, and the front door of the car opened. A huge black man wearing sunglasses, even in the dead of night, stepped out and stood beside the vehicle. He didn't speak to them, and didn't move another inch, just stood there waiting.

The rear window of the car lowered, and the beefy guard at the side of the SUV gestured them forward.

Margot didn't like any of this, didn't like being beckoned by shadowy figures in the dead of night, didn't like that they'd obviously been waiting here for her and Wes to return.

But they were also standing in front of a police station, and Margot believed in her heart that no one would be stupid enough to commit a crime where they would be captured on no fewer than a dozen cameras.

As they got close enough to see into the interior of the car the occupant leaned forward so his face was at the window. His features were more weathered, hair more silver, but Margot recognized Roberto's features in their original incarnation.

Emmanuel Riga.

"Detectives," he said, his voice gravelly and deep.

"Mr. Riga," Margot replied.

He gave a thin smile. "I'm glad we can skip over introductions. It will save us a lot of time. I understand you had a conversation with my son this evening."

"We did. And I'd be more than happy to have one with you, too, if you want to come inside." Margot gestured toward the precinct.

Riga let out a little snort of derision. "No, this won't take long, it's not a professional visit. I just want you to understand that kind of chat won't be happening again. Not without a representative from my legal team there to manage things." He thrust his hand out of the window and Margot fought the urge to recoil. He wasn't holding a weapon, in his hand there was merely a business card.

When Margot made no sign that she was going to move, Wes took it from Riga's extended fingers.

"I'm going to assume tonight was just a little oversight on your part. That you didn't know better. Maybe he didn't know better. But now we're all a lot smarter, aren't we?" His voice was calm and professional, making this feel almost like a business deal rather than a discussion in front of a police station.

Nothing he said was a threat, but Margot felt threatened, nevertheless. She was beginning to understand why Leon and Wes were so adamant that she not make a push to speak to Riga.

Right now, though, Margot wasn't thinking like a smart woman.

She wasn't really thinking at all.

"Was Angela the first one, or did Roberto kill all the others, too?"

"Margot," Wes said through gritted teeth, grabbing her wrist to pull her away from the SUV. The big man standing beside her was no longer pretending to be scenery, he'd taken a step closer like he would physically move her if he needed to.

"I have no idea what you're talking about, Detective," Riga said, and he leaned forward enough that she could see his eyes, see the menace in them that told her now was the time to shut up. She'd seen that cool-as-ice look before, though, and from this man it didn't scare her. She just met his gaze with her own steady expression. "But if you feel the need to ask any more questions, then you can direct them to my lawyers."

"Maybe you did it yourself," she spat back.

He paused and cleared his throat, trying to maintain a cool demeanor. The bouncer beside the car stiffened.

His gaze on her was steady. "Ms. Phalen. Do I look like the kind of man who gets his hands dirty?"

Riga smiled then, and it took her a moment to realize why that smile looked so familiar. Just like his eyes had. It wasn't Roberto's smile. It was the same one she saw whenever she sat across from Ed at that prison table and she said something he found particularly amusing.

It was a predator's smile.

Riga didn't wait for an answer, just kept his eyes on her even as he rolled up the window. She could still feel the weight of his attention even through the tinted glass. The guard got back into the front seat, but through the open door, Margot caught one fleeting glance at a parking slip with the Saint Francis Hospital logo on it. The SUV peeled away into the night.

Her heart sank, but she wasn't surprised.

Wes was still holding her arm. "You are out of your mind, you know that?" He was shaking his head.

"Probably."

Inside, they made a beeline back to the media room, where

Margot was able to connect Angela's phone to a charger and then pull the data from the phone onto one of the room's many computers. It took the better part of twenty minutes, and in that time the shock of her own stupidity had begun to sink in.

Had she really implied to Emmanuel Riga's face that he might be a serial killer?

Now she was going to have a whole new reason to check her back seat every day. She might want to start peeking at her brake line in the morning as well. She certainly hadn't made a friend tonight.

The phone data finished loading, and if they were going to go through it all, through texts, through calls, it would take all night. But Margot felt certain that whatever Angela had wanted to protect on this phone was something more incriminating than a text, something that could cause a whole lot more trouble.

She opened the phone's photo storage, and the first thing she noticed was a video file over ten minutes long.

She selected it, and the video started to play on the monitor in front of them. The phone was situated in a hotel room, and based on the opulence of the space, Margot suspected they had to be looking at the Bella Vista. She would check their website later to compare, but it seemed the likeliest bet, given that Angela had replaced her phone after that trip.

Roberto Riga appeared from an unseen part of the room, wearing only boxers, and sat down on the bed beside a nightstand. He doled out a bit of white powder onto the marble surface, then stooped over to snort the line he'd just formed. He wrinkled his nose and shook his head, before running his finger over the counter to pick up the remaining dust, rubbing it over his teeth.

"Baby, come here, you want some of this?"

Angela, who must have been next to the camera until this point, came into view. It was startling to see her, looking so undamaged, so pretty and alive. She was wearing a dress, which looked out of place next to Roberto's near nakedness. "No, I'm OK."

"Come on, have a little."

A knock at the door interrupted them and Roberto waved a hand. "Go get that."

Angela obeyed, and when she returned there were three men behind her. She passed the phone, and for one heartbreaking second she looked right at it, knowing it was filming. Her expression was terrified.

She knew what was coming.

The video continued, and Margot watched with a sick pit in her stomach as the men shared more cocaine, lit cigars, and made passes at Angela, who stayed by Roberto's side the whole time, either trying to show loyalty, or hoping he would act as a buffer.

About five minutes into the video, Roberto got up and shoved Angela onto the bed. She tried to get up, but he slapped her hard across the face and pushed her down again. He held her face cupped in his hand, squeezing so hard her lips puckered and he pointed at her, so close his fingertip was almost in her eye.

"I pay for your time. When you're with me, you'll do whatever the fuck I want."

"Rob..." she said, her tone pleading, eyes wet with tears.

One of the men had come around the side of the bed and, unmoved by her obvious unwillingness, was undoing his belt.

Roberto pulled open the nightstand drawer and took out a gun. The movement triggered Margot's fight or flight, but Wes must have known it would. He reached out and squeezed her hand.

Roberto put the gun to Angela's head.

"Are you going to be a good girl for me?" he asked as one of the other men handed him a drink.

Angela nodded.

Margot wanted to stop watching, but then the man who was undoing his pants turned toward the camera, and Wes's hand tightened on hers at the same moment she let out a gasp.

She scrambled to pause the video, holding on a frame where they could see the man's face as clear as day.

"Jesus Christ," Wes whispered.

Margot had no words. But she understood now. She understood why Roberto had been willing to kill Angela to find this. Why Emmanuel Riga believed he was untouchable. And more importantly why there was now no one outside this room they could trust with this footage.

Because the man who was about to assault their murder victim was none other than Pressley Boyd.

The current chief of police.

FIFTY-ONE
ONE MONTH LATER

There were a lot of things in life Margot Phalen couldn't control. She couldn't control her past, she couldn't control her emotions, and lately, she felt like she couldn't control her job, the one area of her life where she had always felt the most like she had her shit together.

She and Wes hadn't shown the footage to anyone. Not yet. They had made a copy, so they each had one, and Margot had sent a third copy to her lawyer with the promise that if anything happened to her he would send it to Sebastian Klein at *The Sentinel*.

Margot just wasn't ready to expose what they knew. The moment it became public, or even released within the department, they would no longer be able to freely investigate anything. And Margot felt like they were getting achingly close to breaking the Redwood Killer case wide open.

She didn't know who they could trust, not with Boyd being so high up the chain. The top of the chain, in fact. There was a chance he was protected within every department. Could they tell Captain Tate? Could they turn the evidence over to

Internal Affairs? If they did that, would it just get swept under the rug?

Margot was sure she could trust Leon, but she also didn't want to put this on him.

So she and Wes agreed: first they find the Redwood Killer, then they bring everyone in Riga's web down with him.

Including Boyd.

Roberto Riga wasn't their killer. Not in the Redwood case. And despite the circumstantial evidence they had against him in Angela's death, the district attorney wasn't willing to prosecute unless they had something rock solid.

The tape wasn't even enough there, though it probably would have compelled a jury, and it certainly proved there was a violent history between the two. But they couldn't use it. Not yet.

The chief of police was involved, which meant they were walking on very thin ice with their investigation. Now they needed to be careful of every single step they took.

The tape was an insurance policy, precisely as Angela had hoped it would be.

It hadn't managed to keep her alive, but Margot and Wes were hoping it could protect them in the event that Pressley Boyd or the Rigas became too present of a threat.

So, every day she and Wes went to work like they were still in the dark, and every day they felt certain that they were being watched every step of the way, just to see if they stepped out of line.

They were getting very good at pretending.

But in other aspects of her life, Margot was tired of pretending. She had begun to understand that the shell she had built around herself to protect her from Ed's legacy was more of a cage than a shield. When she knew that Ed's wife Rhonda—now Toni—had figured out who she was, she figured it was only a matter of time before Toni or her son weaponized that knowledge. But all they did with it was tell Ed.

Even Ed knowing it had been the bombshell she had expected.

Knowledge was power, and this secret—the secret of who she was—was something that she no longer wanted to have power over her. It was just one more thing that could be used against her.

It was time for that to end.

Wes pulled up in front of an unassuming brick building, squinting at it in the bright afternoon light.

"Are you sure you don't want me to come in with you?" he asked.

She smiled at him.

They still hadn't talked, still hadn't come to terms with whatever they were or would be, but in the month since they'd watched that video, it felt like they had become more than just partners. They were a united front. Margot knew she could trust Wes implicitly. He wasn't going anywhere.

They could become whatever they were going to become when the time was right.

The time was not right with what they were presently dealing with hanging over their heads.

It didn't stop him from being there for her, and it didn't stop her from *wanting* him there for her.

"No, I've got to do this on my own."

"You don't *have* to do this," he said, for about the tenth time since he'd picked her up from her apartment.

She took his hand, squeezed it once. "I think I do."

She made her way into the building on her own, and she wasn't even two feet through the door when a pretty brunette in her twenties seemed to appear out of thin air holding a coffee and a clipboard.

"Ms. Phalen, thank you so much for coming, we really can't

tell you how much we appreciate it." She handed the coffee to Margot, then guided her through an open door into another room, where Margot was pressed gently into a chair and had all her makeup touched up until she looked about five years younger and like she had been born without pores. They wouldn't give her the coffee back once a mauve lip gloss had been applied.

Another young person came in when she was done, smiling, and thanking her again, then guided her out of the room and into another space, this one more open, with several bright lights all facing a brick wall. There was a view of the Golden Gate Bridge through the window that probably made rent on this space ten times higher than it would have been in any other building.

Someone dusted off Margot's blazer and straightened her necklace, then nudged her onward into the room, where yet another person—their faces all blurred together at this point—brought her to a straight-backed chair and had her sit down.

She faced the lights, blinking in surprise at how bright they were.

"Are you ready?" a voice asked. This one she recognized, because she'd spoken to its owner no fewer than a dozen times before she had been convinced to do this.

"If I say no, would I be in trouble?"

A few nervous laughs emanated from behind the lights. She couldn't see anyone's faces.

"I'm ready," she said finally, though she wasn't sure if she was telling them, or trying to convince herself.

There was a pause while some instructions were given behind the light, then that familiar voice came again.

"Can you introduce yourself?"

Margot cleared her throat, adjusting herself on the uncomfortable chair. "My name is Margot Phalen, I'm a homicide detective with the San Francisco Police Department."

"And what was your name before you were Margot Phalen? What is your relationship to Ed Finch?" the voice asked.

A pause, the words stuck in her throat. She stared right in the direction she knew the documentary camera was positioned.

"My name was Megan Finch. And Ed Finch is my father."

A LETTER FROM THE AUTHOR

Huge thanks for reading *In the Blood*. I hope you are continuing to enjoy Margot's journey. If you want to join other readers in hearing all about my Storm new releases and bonus content, you can sign up for my newsletter:

www.stormpublishing.co/kate-wiley

And if you want to keep up to date with all my other publications, you can sign up to my mailing list:

www.eepurl.com/ASoIz

Reviews mean the world to authors, as they can help new readers decide what to pick up next. If you've enjoyed Margot's books and want to read more, I would be so grateful if you would leave a review. Even a short review can make all the difference in encouraging a reader to discover my books for the first time. Thank you so much!

I can't believe we're already on book four! Only a few years ago, I wondered if this passion project would ever find the right home, and now here we are, four books in! This world I've created is meant to keep you up at night, and if I've made you put a book in the freezer, I've done my job right. Every new Margot book I'll be looking for ways to move her story forward and keep you on the edge of your seat.

Thanks again for being part of this amazing journey with me and I hope you'll stay in touch—I have a lot more planned, and if you keep reading, I'll keep writing!

Kate Wiley

www.katewiley.com

facebook.com/SierraDeanAuthor
x.com/sierradean
instagram.com/sierradeanauthor

ACKNOWLEDGMENTS

Writing a book is a very solitary experience. It involves a lot of exhaustion, frustration, euphoria, and generally a human body weight amount of junk food. But publishing a book is a team effort, and so I want to thank the people who made publishing this book (and all the Margot books) a reality. To Vicky Blunden first. You are such a tremendous champion for me and my work. I am grateful to you every single day for taking a chance on me and this series, and for making me believe it was good enough. To Oliver, Alexandra, Elke, Naomi, and to the wonderful, incredible copy editors I've worked with on this series—you are all so amazing, thank you.

To Lauryn Allman, my insanely talented audiobook narrator, thank you for bringing Margot to life. You are such a joy and I'm so thrilled to have you reading my books to others. (Audiobooks count as reading, I will die on this hill.)

This book was written in a fever-dream short time frame, and as such I would like to thank Zero Sugar California Dreamin' Shasta, Doritos, and mozzarella cheese strings for sustaining me through the duration. I would like to thank my cats for not accidentally deleting any passages, my Roomba for not pulling out my laptop's power cable, and my inconsistent rural power lines for not getting knocked over in a snowstorm before I was able to save my progress.

Thanks, forever and always, to my mother, who may never read these books but will always order a case of them. To my friends, who I listed last time and had to fill half a page with the name "Jessica," and to my incredible readers. Every time I release another one of these books I'm blown away by the growing support for Margot and her story. Thank you for continuing to come along with me.

And last, but never least, to my favorite bookstore on the planet, Whodunit Mystery Bookstore in Winnipeg, Canada. There are so few times in life that you can honestly say a *store* cares about you, but the amazing staff at Whodunit have been champions for my books since before they were ever published. I am forever grateful to them, and their ongoing support of all things mystery. (And if you're ever looking to find a signed copy of my books, they might be able to hook you up…)

Printed in Great Britain
by Amazon